ASCENSION

ASCENSION
THE ASCENSION MYTH™ BOOK 12

ELL LEIGH CLARKE
MICHAEL ANDERLE

DISRUPTIVE IMAGINATION

Ascension (this book) is a work of fiction.

All of the characters, organizations, and events portrayed in this novel are either products of the author's imagination or are used fictitiously. Sometimes both.

This book Copyright © 2018 Ell Leigh Clarke, Michael T. Anderle
Cover by Jeff Brown www.jeffbrowngraphics.com
Cover Photo by Andrew Dobell
Cover copyright © LMBPN Publishing

LMBPN Publishing supports the right to free expression and the value of copyright. The purpose of copyright is to encourage writers and artists to produce the creative works that enrich our culture.

The distribution of this book without permission is a theft of the author's intellectual property. If you would like permission to use material from the book (other than for review purposes), please contact info@kurtherianbooks.com. Thank you for your support of the author's rights.

LMBPN Publishing
PMB 196, 2540 South Maryland Pkwy
Las Vegas, NV 89109

First US Edition, June 2018
Version 1.01, February 2020

ASCENSION TEAM

JIT Beta Readers
Mary Morris
John Ashmore
Daniel Weigert
Paul Westman
Micky Cocker

If we missed anyone, please let us know!

To everyone who ever dreamed of making a dent in the universe.

— Ellie

*To Family, Friends and
Those Who Love
To Read.
May We All Enjoy Grace
To Live The Life We Are
Called.*

— Michael

CHAPTER ONE

Molly's Classroom, Skóli Uppstigs Academy, Spire, Estaria
(10 days before the deadline of the 100 days)

The bell rang, signaling the end of class. Students immediately started packing up the holos and gathering their gear, filtering out of the classroom.

"Don't forget to read Chapter 21. There will be a quiz on it at the end of the week," Molly called after them.

The hubbub of chatter had risen so loudly she wasn't even sure they heard. As the class filtered out a few people said goodbye to her as they left.

Exhausted, she sat down, taking a moment for herself as the last of them cleared out. She pulled her hair back from her face and breathed out a long sigh. It had been a tough few months.

Glancing up at the door, she noticed Giles waiting for her. She closed her holo up and grabbed her jacket from the table.

"Hey, how is it going?" Giles asked, shifting a book from one arm to the other, casually leaning against the door frame.

"It's going." She shrugged, dragging a hand over her face.

"That good, eh?"

She breathed out lightly with a half laugh. "Yeah."

She hauled herself up out of the chair and headed towards the door, pointing out it. "Walk with me?" she offered.

He nodded, pushing himself off the door frame and stepping into the corridor that was becoming quieter by the minute.

"So any progress?" Her voice was low, as if inquiring about something secretive.

"A little. Mostly we're just trying to apply the segments of frequencies that we've already interpreted. Taking the computer a little bit of time. But we're getting there."

"Oh that's good," she said, feigning encouragement as best she could.

"I know we agreed at this stage it's probably not going to be much help… But if there is anything else I can be doing, just say the word."

Molly halted suddenly in the corridor and looked at him. "You're doing great," she told him, "and I appreciate everything that you're doing. Really."

He glanced over at her with a flat kind of smile. "Thanks. I just wish that there was more that I could be doing."

"Well if you'd like to take on marking my end of term papers next week…" She flashed him a smile.

He grinned back. "If it would stop all-out war in the system, I'd be more than happy to."

She started walking again, this time more slowly than before. "Yeah that's the thing."

He brightened a touch as he ambled after her. "So any news on the liquid voting system?"

"Actually, yeah," she said, sounding surprised, herself. "Not only was it accepted, but almost as soon as we listed our candidates we had people voting for them. I think we've actually got a chance of winning if this war is going to be put to the vote."

"Well that is good news!" Giles glanced up at the ceiling as if thanking a deity. Molly wondered which one it might have been, given his eclectic knowledge of cultures.

"Yeah. I must say Paige and Maya have done an excellent job getting the word out to the folks on our side." Her speech slowed. "I'm still not sure entirely how they've done it. Paige is being a little cagey about the details."

Giles gave her a sideways glance. "You don't suspect that she is up to something, do you?"

Molly smirked. "I fully expect that she is up to something."

Giles chuckled quietly to himself. "Well she learned from the best. That's all I can say."

Molly grinned and nudged him slightly with her elbow. "Speaking of dramatic influence... How are your presentations going?"

He tilted his head modestly. "Pretty good I think. I mean obviously we won't know until the Senate cuts the final vote, but I think the Estarian leadership have warmed to the idea that maybe there is evidence to suggest that the ARs aren't out to kill us. I have hope."

"Good. Me too."

Giles suddenly became awkward. He fiddled with his glasses, then took them off to clean them. Molly braced herself. "Err, I was thinking, maybe you'd like to go and grab a mocha and talk some more."

Molly ran a hand through her hair, pulling it off her face again. She glanced at the floor. "Oh I would, but erm, I have to go to see someone with Sean."

As if on cue Sean Royale came striding through the double doors ahead of them. "You ready?" he grunted.

She nodded, glancing back at Giles with a sympathetic look in her eye. "Rain check?"

"Yeah... Absolutely. Sure." Giles placed his glasses back on his face, squinting at Sean as if trying to deduce some clue as to what was going on.

Sean, noticing Giles's reaction, shot him his best dirty grin and slung his arm around Molly's shoulder as they headed on down the corridor without him.

Giles's face dropped as he watched them leave.

Molly didn't let Sean leave his arm there though. Instead she sidestepped him as they were walking and slapped his arm off her as if she was swatting a fly.

Giles ran a hand over the lower half of his face, as if trying to wipe the anxiety away. It had been a tense few months, by anyone's standards.

Just then, Molly turned and waved. "I'll give you a call later," she told him. "I need your opinion on a statement I want to make."

Giles put his hand up and returned the wave awkwardly. "Yeah sure, any time. I'll be up late."

He was almost sure he saw Molly smile as she disappeared out of the door.

Bone head, he cursed at himself. *Could you be any more of a doofus?*

"I wish you wouldn't do that." Molly scowled at Sean.

"Do what?" He wore his best innocent expression. The one he reserved for lying to the team when he was pranking someone.

"You know what. Winding Giles up like that."

"I never even talked to the guy!"

She narrowed her eyes at him as they hopped into the waiting pod down the side of the building. "You know exactly what you were doing, and it's not okay."

Sean surreptitiously rolled his eyes as she turned around to put her belt on.

"All right," he sighed. "It's just that it's so easy to wind him up.

It's too tempting. Like bubble wrap just sitting there, waiting to be popped!"

Molly poked at the holoconsole on the pod. "Okay, whatever. Let's get this over with. I got real work to do."

"What and keeping Ekks from taking over the planet isn't in your top priorities?"

"You know what I mean."

The pod lifted up and disappeared into the stratosphere before Sean could even think of a clever comeback.

Outside the Senate House, Spire, Estaria

Work had become a shit show.

Senator Vero Romero hurried out to his car in the underground carport, weary from another day of arguing with people who were just too spineless to listen. He just wanted to go home, put some music on, open a bottle of wine, order a pizza and forget all about it... until at least tomorrow morning.

He got in and put the key into the ignition and turned it. The engine purred like a kitten just like it usually did.

He pulled out of the building's carport and moved gently into traffic.

It wasn't until he got to cruising height that he heard a clunk. It was quiet—quiet enough that he had to turn off the holocast he had been listening to. He had definitely heard something. The clunking continued and was consistent, as if a pebble had become lodged in the undercarriage.

His first thought was to damn the dealership; the car was still reasonably new. His next thought was to try to put it out of his mind. His commute wasn't especially long and he could worry about his car making a strange sound once he was home and had a drink in his hand.

He had just started to relax his shoulders a little when the dashboard's landing advisory light popped on. The rhythmic clunking got slightly louder. With an aggrieved sigh, he pulled off at the nearest exit to find a spot to pull over.

He didn't notice when the clunking noise actually stopped, but only because that was the same moment that his engine abruptly shut off and his car suddenly plummeted to the ground like a potted plant.

He stomped on the gas, yanked on the emergency brake, twisted the key, all to no avail. The engine refused to reengage and the hovering systems didn't take over.

It felt like the car fell for an eternity, everything happening in slow motion. He felt as though he could see every fleck of dust in the air and every atom in the middle. But really, it was only a few seconds before his car met the ground. He lifted his hands to brace himself, just as the airbags went off on either side of him.

He heard glass shattering as one of the windows exploded with the impact, and he heard a thick, soggy crunch. With some distant, foggy awareness, he supposed that was probably part of him. Slumped over his steering wheel, he tried to muster up the energy to sit up, to check the damage, to see if anything was broken. But it was like the air around him had turned into sand, holding him down so he could hardly even lift one of his hands. His ribs felt tight, but nothing hurt just then.

Without being able to pry himself away from the steering wheel, mostly he could see the edge of the airbag and a lot of red. But that didn't make sense. His car was black. The interior was leather. It took a moment before his thoughts churned enough for him to realize he was probably bleeding. He made another attempt at sitting up.

It felt like he weighed a ton, and he gave up.

A crowd was beginning to gather around his car. He could barely hear them over the sound of his ears ringing. The words he could actually make out sounded distant and tinny, like they were echoing through a tunnel. He let the threads of conversation escape his grasp; he couldn't bring himself to care what anyone was saying at that point. The sound of approaching sirens was a bit more distracting anyway.

Everything was going gray and hazy at the edges. The world crept back into place when an EMT started talking to him. He blinked at her, uncomprehending. He let the world fade out into white noise again once she started sorting through his wallet when it became clear he wouldn't be answering any of her questions.

Everything became very clear once again as he was being removed from the wreckage of his car. In that moment, the pain finally made itself known. He passed out somewhere between his car and the stretcher, and he had no memory of being loaded into the ambulance. The drive passed in a haze of disjointed sound and flashes of light, and soon enough even those faded away to darkness and silence.

Even then, the pain wasn't quite gone. But it relented, just a little.

He wasn't aware of the tube down his throat or the preparations for surgery.

The next thing he became conscious of was a beeping.

He didn't realize that it was much later. Nor was he aware of the oxygen mask on his face, or the private room his hospital bed was wheeled into.

Out in the hallway, a nurse made a few notations on his patient chart before turning to speak with the pair of police officers that waited nearby.

"An accident," one officer decided afterwards, already sounding as if he was bored with the entire situation. "An engine that needed some maintenance. We're done here."

And Vero remained blissfully unaware of that, as well.

Ekks's Office, Senate House, Spire, Estaria

Molly strode through the doors of the Senate House. Casually she headed straight to the receptionist's station. She placed her arms on the counter.

"Greetings of the day to you." She sounded almost as if she were bored. "I have a meeting with Commander Ekks."

The receptionist glanced down at her holoscreen and punched in some keys. "I'm sorry I don't—"

Molly stopped her mid-sentence. Quietly she shifted her energy, implementing some of what Arlene had been teaching her over the years. By now she had this particular maneuver down pat. She held the gaze of the receptionist as the mood around the reception desk seemed to change. "I'm sure you'll see that I have a standing meeting with him this time every morning. Our badges are in your top right-hand drawer."

The receptionist, a little dazed, nodded obediently. She reached her hand down to her drawer without even looking and fished out the two badges, placing them on the counter top.

Without even checking her holoscreen again, she waved Molly through.

Molly grabbed their badges, handed Sean's to him, and walked straight through security as if she belonged there.

Sean jogged a couple of paces to catch up to her. "This never gets old," he gruffed under his breath, just loud enough for her to hear.

"Well, at least that's the case for one of us." She sighed, without even looking back at him, or slowing her pace.

"Oh come on," he protested, speaking a little louder now they were deeper into the building and away from any security personnel. "Don't tell me this doesn't even give you a little bit of a kick… knowing you can do this?"

Molly glanced at him sideways as they crossed the enormous foyer of the Senate House and started jogging up the staircase to the main office building. "Are you kidding me? You were the one that was so against me having this ability. It's dangerous yadda

yadda. Keep her away from the Federation yadda yadda. Any of that sound familiar?"

She shot him a steely look.

"Well maybe it's growing on me," he muttered sheepishly. "And as long as you're not using it on me, I am kind of okay with it."

Molly rolled her eyes at his hypocrisy.

Molly?

Oz? What's up?

I've intercepted a report on the police scanner. It looks like Senator Romero has been taken into hospital following a car accident.

You're kidding? What happened?

It's hard to say at this point, but it's looking likely that it was a hit rather than an accident.

Hang on... Wasn't he one of the guys who was criticizing Ekks's moves in the media?

I believe he was.

Something else we'll have to talk to him about...

Sean glanced at Molly, clearly waiting for her witty come back. He noticed her facial expression had shifted to one of concentration. "Everything okay?"

"Yeah. I just have a few more questions for Ekks, that's all."

They arrived at his office and walked straight in past the assistant's desk, which was partially blocking their path. Ekks's assistant got up from her console and started to protest. "You can't go in there…"

Molly shifted her energy and silenced her without having to say anything. Knocking, they entered without waiting to be invited.

"Ekks," Molly greeted him dryly. "I'd say good to see you again, but this is never my favorite part of the day."

Ekks glanced up from his holo, bamboozled and simultaneously dismayed. After a second to recognize what was happening, he sprang to his feet. "What is the meaning of this?" he demanded. "Patricia! Patricia!" he shouted for his assistant.

Molly pushed her will. "Hey Ekks, it's me, relax." Straightaway his demeanor shifted and he quieted down.

"Sit down," she told him. "It's time for our talk."

Obediently he sat down again while Molly and Sean stood in front of his desk, looking down at him.

"So, how's the bylaw coming?" she asked.

"Still on hold," he grumbled. "Seems you make a convincing argument. Haven't been able to figure out how you convinced me... or how I didn't see those other options in the past... but still. It's on hold and I haven't changed my mind since last time we spoke." He looked resentful for a moment, before the creases on his forehead suddenly relaxed and smoothed out.

"That doesn't mean that I like what you're doing. But you were right about it being bad for me politically," he confessed.

"So the liquid democracy seats are safe still?" she confirmed.

He nodded, the tension in the rest of his face evaporating too. "Yep. Safe and legal. The bylaw confining candidates to only vote within party lines would have been unconstitutional anyway."

"Good... I'm glad that you see that now."

Sean shifted his weight, watching Molly one moment and the changing reactions of Ekks the next. He shook his head in amazement. "Looks like it's still working," he added softly.

Molly nodded, her attention still on Ekks. "I've just had word that something's happened to your adversary: Romero," she ventured, changing the subject.

Ekks barely paused. "An unfortunate accident."

"So you've heard about it already?"

"I hear about everything that is relevant around here. Is that why you're here?"

"No, I'm here just to make sure that we still have an understanding. So what can you tell me about Romero's accident?"

"Nothing," he said, shaking his head, eyes wide as innocently as he could manage. "I don't know anything about it." For a moment he looked more like a person than a Commander. Molly wasn't sure if it was his earnestness, or a sign of weakness.

She narrowed her eyes, deciding to dig deeper. "I must say, him being out of action for the Senate's final vote will be quite convenient for you."

"What are you implying?"

"I'm not implying anything." She rocked slightly onto her toes. "Got to say though, it helps your cause… not having that kind of resistance in the House."

"Well, this is true," he confessed, strangely innocently. "But I had nothing to do with what happened to him."

Sean glanced at her sideways and leaned closer to Molly. In a low voice he whispered: "Do you think he is able to keep a secret from you?"

Molly shrugged. "I'm not sure. Changing someone's mind is different from trying to get them to tell the truth."

"Unless you want to convince them that they need to tell you the truth."

Molly smirked. "Ahhh..."

Ten minutes later Molly and Sean exited the commander's office.

"I hope it holds," Molly muttered.

"It should do. It's worked all this time." Sean did a quick calculation in his head. "About sixty-two days."

Molly shrugged. "Under normal circumstances I'd like to test how long until it starts wearing off. But in this instance we can't risk it."

Looks like we missed someone.

What do you mean?

Sounds like someone is calling security over the internal network.

"Shit! Sean, we gotta move." She picked up the pace as they hurried out of the Senate building.

Sean glanced down at his bloody knuckles and wiped them surreptitiously on his atmos pants.

"You hurt?" she asked as they hurried down the stairs to the foyer.

"No, it's not my blood."

Suddenly an alarm went off.

Sean grinned. "Clearly you're getting complacent." He chuckled as they hurried out past a bewildered-looking receptionist and back out onto the street.

"Shit," Molly muttered again as the pair bounded down the front steps, two at a time. "Well we will just have to come back to see him again tomorrow. Just to remind him of the good decisions he made today. And maybe expand the scope of our questioning in the future, see if the asshole is planning on hitting anyone else." She shook her head. "Clearly I didn't see that coming."

Within minutes the two were clear of the Senate building and striding across the street to the alley where they had parked the pod. Sean had suggested that they mix up where they parked each time to reduce the possibility of someone noticing them. After all, showing up every day in this kind of technology, and trying to remain undetected, was no mean feat.

They'd slowed to a normal pace, mingling in with the crowd before slipping quietly into the darkened alley.

"So how are things going with Karina?" she asked, making idle chitchat.

Sean glanced at her sideways waiting for her to get into the pod first. The pod hood opened and she hauled herself up before turning and looking at him, pointedly waiting for an answer. "She settling in okay?"

Sean scrambled to engage the correct part of his brain to answer a non-operational question. "Yeah," he confirmed, hauling himself up and settling into the bench seat next to her. "Yeah, she seems to be doing fine. Happy now that she gets to participate in the missions and stuff. And of course the gang have been great including her in things like the holo games, and she's even training in the gym with Jack a couple of times a week…"

Molly smiled politely. "That's good to know." She hesitated as if she wanted to ask something else. "And you…? You've no regrets over, you know… bringing her on board?"

Sean looked at her strangely for a moment, processing the question. "Well, obviously it's been a bit of a game changer. We've both had to adapt… But, no. No regrets."

He looked out of the window as Molly programmed the pod to take them up to Gaitune. Molly noticed the distant look in his eye and observed him, waiting to see if he was going to elaborate.

He felt her watching him. "And especially since it might all be over… I mean, what have we got? A matter of days? Ten at the outset, before it all… Well you know. It's taken me this long to realize that life has more meaning when you share it with someone else." He chuckled lightly. "Never thought I'd hear myself say something like that!"

Molly's jaw set. "It's going to be okay. We are going to sort this out, and it's all gonna be fine. No one's gonna die. It's all going to be okay."

Sean shrugged. "I don't know, Molly. We've had a good run of things. I've had a good long stretch in the Federation too. But all good things come to an end at some point, and I just don't know how we can stop this before it becomes too big a problem."

Molly frowned at him. "Well then if you really think that, why are you working so hard to stop it from happening?"

"Because that is what we do," he told her, as if it were the most obvious thing in the world. "That is how we define ourselves—by what we do. We don't just give up, even if there is only a tiny little bit of help. We keep going and keep trying, we keep pushing it and maybe, just maybe, we might get lucky."

It was Molly's turn to look out of the window with a distance in her eye as the pod shot up into the stratosphere and beyond, the planet disappearing beneath them in a matter of moments.

They rode in silence for several minutes, the blackness outside wrapping them in the safety of space, as if protecting their anonymity from the rest of the world now that they had completed their mission.

Eventually Sean spoke. "What about you and Joel?"

Molly did a double take, then hesitated, looking for some words to keep him at bay with. "What do you mean?" she asked, cleverly buying herself some time.

"Well you know… There's always been something between you two. And given you may only have a few days left before it all ends… Haven't you thought about at least talking about it with him?"

Molly's gaze was directed out of the window again, watching the blankness of space passing them by. There was silence in the pod for several minutes. Sean started to assume that she just wasn't going to answer.

"I just don't know how to have a conversation with him. Not now. I think it's been too long."

Sean chuckled lightly. "I really don't think that can be an issue. Just talk to him. He'll make it easy for you."

"Why? Have you guys been talking?"

"Not recently. But you know there are some things that just don't change. No matter how long it goes between us talking about it."

Molly nodded, acknowledging the advice that Sean was clearly trying to give her. "Okay. I'll see what happens."

Sean gave her a stern look.

She held her hands up. "Okay, okay, I'll do my best. Sheesh."

Sean relaxed back into the seat and went back to looking out of the window.

Maybe he's got a point?

Not you as well, Oz.

Life is short...

I haven't got the energy or headspace to argue that right now, Oz. As I told Sean, I'll see what I can do. Okay?

Okay.

And with that the pod tilted its trajectory and curved in towards the base on the other side of Gaitune. As they neared the big rock, they could see the hangar doors opening slowly for their arrival.

CHAPTER TWO

Aboard *Glock'stor Ship # 597*

The bridge was unusually quiet.

There were no orders being issued. The navigators and the pilot weren't speaking in a constant stream of mathematical jargon. There were no communications channels to deal with. There was just idle chatter and the hum of computers.

It was all rather *eerie*, as far as Trev'or was concerned. He hadn't seen the bridge so quiet since the time someone broke the Admiral's favorite mug, and even that had been the calm before the storm.

Beside him, Ruther was giving him a look, like he knew exactly what was going on in Trev'or's head and was silently beseeching him not to do anything about it. Trev'or blinked at him innocently before turning to face the Admiral in the command chair.

The Admiral was paying more attention to his holoconsole than to anything else at that point, presumably working his way through paperwork he had been putting off. He probably appreciated the relative quiet, all things considered.

"Sooooo…"

Admiral Clor slid Trev'or a reluctant glance. It was a glance that asked if the technician truly wanted to continue with this line of conversation. Trev'or paid that glance no mind, though, and instead simply carried on as he wondered, "Are we sure this really counts as a *retreat* anymore?"

"Aren't you supposed to be doing maintenance?" Clor asked flatly. "I'm fairly sure that was part of the order."

"Multitasking." Trev'or gestured flippantly at his terminal, where it was running a self-diagnostic program. "I mean, we've just sort of been stalled out here for a while. What are we even doing?"

"I'm not at liberty to discuss that with you," Clor answered plainly.

Trev'or opened his mouth to ask another question, only for Ruther to elbow him sharply in the ribs from his left. Clor was giving him a flatly unamused look. At last, Trev'or fell silent.

Clor eyed them both warily for a moment longer, before he nodded once in satisfaction.

With that, he got to his feet, levering himself out of the command chair and heading towards the nearest door. "I think I'll take a stroll," he decided. "Try not to interrupt if something isn't wrong. And then at least make sure it's something that requires my attention; that's what incident reports are for, otherwise."

"Yes, sir," Trev'or sighed as he returned to watching the diagnostic results come in on the terminal.

The door opened soundlessly and Clor stepped out into the corridor, his steps carrying him towards the mess hall before he was even fully aware of it. It was too late to be lunch and still too early to be dinner, but the mess hall was rarely actually empty. So he didn't fight it, and carried on his way.

It wasn't until he actually got to the mess hall that things got a bit weird.

Supervisor Gultorra was sitting at the main table, his boots on the table and his chair back on two legs. He was scrolling through a datapad, attempting to get some work done, to all appearances. To either side of him sat Kalvor and Tulnok, both of them sorting files. None of them were eating at that exact moment, but the trays on the table meant they had been just a short while ago.

That wasn't the strange part. People worked through meals all the time.

The strange part was the fact that other soldiers were bustling around, in and out of the mess hall. Periodically, they would return to Gultorra to ask something in a low voice, or to shout something rather loudly from the walkways above the mess hall.

"Supervisor," Clor sighed.

"Admiral," Gultorra greeted, saluting as something of an afterthought. "How can I help you?"

"What are you doing?" Clor asked. He could feel a headache brewing already, and he dug two knuckles against the corners of his eyes to stave it off.

"*I* am just readying all of the reports I'll need to submit when all of this is over with," Gultorra replied.

"We're alphabetizing them," Tulnok added, sounding none too pleased to be doing so.

Clor dragged a hand down his face. "What is everyone *else* doing, then?" he clarified.

Finally, Gultorra looked up from his datapad. "Everyone has been getting a bit antsy from the inactivity," he explained, as if Clor had somehow failed to realize that himself. "They've been driving me up a wall. The ones perfectly capable of handling higher level work have been sent to do just that. The rest have been informed that my desk lamp needs a new bulb and the first to bring me one gets glowing praise in one of my personnel reports."

Clor was silent for a moment, waiting for one of the three of them to say that it was a joke. Once it was apparent that no such declaration was forthcoming, Clor pointed out, with resignation,

"None of the lights on this ship even use bulbs. I'm fairly sure they haven't in decades."

Gultorra gestured carelessly to the next table over, where perhaps a dozen soldiers were gathered. They watched the bustling, but made no efforts to join in.

"Some of them knew from the beginning or just didn't care," Gultorra explained. "Some of them figured it out for themselves eventually. All of them have decided that it's more fun to keep that information to themselves. I'm sure the rest will clue in eventually, but in the meantime I have relative peace and quiet without all of them hanging off my belt loops like needy kittens."

Clor supposed he couldn't really argue with that. Rather than try to, he simply sighed, "Carry on, then," and made his way to a different table. Even if he didn't intend to be in the mess hall for long, he didn't want to get trampled by the soldiers still periodically trotting over to Gultorra and then trotting away again.

He couldn't wait until they were all on the move again.

Hangar Deck, Gaitune-67

"Hey Molly, wait up!"

Joel came bounding across the hangar deck, a workout towel around his neck. His T-shirt was wet in a V-shape on his chest. Molly slowed her pace, allowing him to catch up.

"Careful!" she called. "You're running in trainers and this hangar deck hasn't been scrubbed for oil in several weeks."

Joel slowed to a walk, looking around the floor where he was walking to make sure he wasn't going to slip in something.

"I was wondering if we might talk later?"

Molly frowned. "Err, yeah sure." She cocked her head to one side. "Have you just been talking to Sean?" She nodded in the direction of the base gym.

Joel shook his head. "No. Not recently. Why?"

"No reason." She glanced back in the direction of an open

pod. "Look, I've got to get going. I have a meeting with the university crowd before the end of the day."

Joel bobbed his head, hanging his hands on the towel around his neck. "How is it going down there?"

Molly shrugged. "Good I suppose. It's going to be close though... I don't know if we can get enough votes in to make a difference in time."

Joel put a hand on her upper arm. "Everything that you do helps. And you're doing great. I believe in you."

Molly smiled. "Thanks, Joel." She started to move in the direction of her pod. "I'll catch you later."

"Yeah sure," he called after her, waving.

She didn't see him waving because she'd already gone.

Skóli Uppstigs Academy, Spire, Estaria

The pod touched down between two buildings on the university campus. Without waiting for anything to power down, Molly slipped out as soon as the door had opened enough. She scooped her bag from under the seat and was halfway across the quad before the door had closed again.

Hurriedly she entered the door on the far side of the quad and pushed through the old-fashioned double doors and into the corridor beyond.

She could hear voices at the far end coming from the conference room. The scent of freshly brewed mocha filled this wing of the building, too. It was clear that the team were planning to work late again tonight.

Dr. Augustine met her at the door to the meeting room. "Ahhh, Miss Bates, you're here. You'll be pleased to know that we got the second algorithm working and Douglas has managed to get a mailshot out to other educational institutions tomorrow morning. Also we have pizza on order. We ordered you a vegetarian supreme."

Molly slipped her bag off a shoulder and immediately started assessing the project screen which kept track of the various tasks they had assigned. "That's great. Thanks, Dr. Augustine. And well done, Douglas!" she called over to Prof Lakin. "That's some good finagling you've done there to get these ideas out to other institutions."

Dr. Augustine and Prof Lakin both appeared pleased with themselves.

"I'll be giving a presentation there by the end of the week too," Lakin added.

"Where's Gareth Atkins?" she asked, making some adjustments to the board and deleting a few items that she'd managed to execute that afternoon.

"I'm not sure," Dr. Augustine told her. "He might have stepped out for a minute. But he did want me to let you know that he's managed to secure another candidate who wants to run using our system."

Molly grinned. "That's great news! Well done him."

She continued to catch up with the changes on the board and downloaded a few notes onto her holo. Just then a familiar voice reached her ears. She felt suddenly disoriented. It was a voice she knew... but it was in the wrong place. She racked her brain trying to place it.

Laughter erupted on the other side of the room. She poked her head out from behind the holoscreen to see who else was in mission headquarters. She couldn't see at first because some of the other professors were in the way. But then Dr. Lakin moved, revealing a very out of place, and unkempt-looking, Pieter.

"Pieter?" she gasped, her shock turning into a smile subconsciously. "What are you doing here?"

Everyone stopped laughing and stared at Molly as if she were speaking in tongues.

"I, err, just wanted to help," Pieter explained. "But I was struggling to understand the concept of the liquid democracy. Thankfully Douglas here has been filling me in so I can be of more assistance with the campaign. Or *campaigns*, should I say."

Molly frowned. "How did I miss that you are on this project?"

"I sent a message to Oz," he explained quickly, "and he just told me where to show up."

"Oh I see." She stared blankly at Pieter for a few moments.

We'll talk about this later, Oz.

You seemed busy and it was a minor detail that you didn't need to be involved in.

Oh, I see. Less of the surprises though next time, if you please?

Of course.

"So what have you learnt about the liquid democracy?" She grinned at him, joining in the enthusiasm that the team had been showing him since he arrived.

"Well, only that it's the most elegant solution to the problem we have right now. Not only does it integrate with the existing system where you have candidates voted into power, but this idea where every single voter gets to vote on every single issue, and it's completely transparent... Pure genius!"

Dr. Augustine looked like he could hardly contain himself. "And it looks like our young friend here is going to be able to help us keep everything a hundred percent real-time. This means that if our candidates start using their seat to do things that their voters didn't vote for, those votes can immediately be rescinded and put elsewhere. *Instantaneously!* It's quite amazing really... and probably what we've been needing for quite some time now. If we implement enough of these seats in the Senate there would be no way that *the-powers-that-be* could remain pulling all the strings."

Pieter grinned in agreement. "Whoever came up with this system needs a pat on the back." He looked at Molly as if he were giving her the credit.

Molly shook her head. "Oh it wasn't me," she confessed quickly. "It was just another idea that I heard at the conference a few years ago at one of these think tank kind of environments. I only remembered it a few months ago when we realized that we were gonna have to change things on the planet quickly... What with our deadline and all."

Pieter ruffled his hair and reorganized some of his holo-screens. "Well I think I can have the programming completed for the additional piece within a few hours. Especially now that Oz is here!"

Molly grinned. "Oh, I see. You guys only wanted me here so that Oz could help you work on the programming. Not because you actually need me to have an input."

Professor Lakin made a feeble attempt at making her feel useful and needed.

She laughed and waved a hand. "No no. It's okay. I get it..." She finished downloading her task list from the board and setup on the desk in the corner. "Just let me know when the pizza gets here!" she called over to them.

CHAPTER THREE

<u>Senate House, Spire, Estaria</u>

The seats around the table were all filled. The other senators still eyed Vero's substitute as if they weren't entirely sure what to make of him. Even so, just as always, no one broached the topic. Raychel came close, glancing at him lingeringly and opening her mouth, only to snap it closed once again as the Speaker of the House thumped his cane against the floor to get everyone's attention.

"Shall we get started?" he asked, and a murmur of general assent went around the table. He nodded once. "Then let's begin."

The Speaker stood up to address the room, both hands clasped on top of his cane. "This is our final day to come to a decision on whether or not we should recall the fleet. It's our final day not for political reasons, but because if we don't come to a decision today, then we will run out of time to do so at all. So please, show good judgment." He gave the entire table a meaningful look. "Who would like to get us started?"

Zenne and Bel began speaking almost simultaneously, before Zenne sighed as if he was truly the most aggrieved and motioned for her to carry on.

Ekks listened to their debate in an absentminded sort of way, his elbows on the table and his fingers tented in front of his mouth. Every so often he reached for his mocha, but he never spoke up. He offered no contribution of his own. He offered no sign that he was paying attention at all until Zenne asked pointedly, "Anything you'd like to add, Commander? I'm sure we're all *dying* to hear from you."

The sarcasm wasn't lost on him. Ekks waved him off with a flippant flick of his wrist, one shoulder rising in a halfhearted shrug. He sipped his mocha and offered no other response.

Zenne's eyes narrowed slightly, and Bel offered Raychel a bemused look. Raychel simply shrugged broadly in reply, just as bewildered herself.

"Are you sure about that?" Zenne asked slowly, as if he was expecting it to be some sort of trap. "Nothing to say? Nothing at all?"

Ekks's eyebrows rose and he repeated his previous gesture, albeit a bit more forcefully this time, like a parent wondering why he needed to repeat himself.

The Speaker dropped back down into his seat. "Commander," he sighed, "for months now you've done little else but advocate for launching the fleet and plunging us into war. This vote could very well undo all of your efforts. Do you really expect us to believe that you have nothing to say on the matter?"

Ekks took a drawn out sip from his cup. As he lowered it back to the table, he stated simply, "I have nothing to say on the matter. You may continue."

The murmuring that spread throughout the room seemed distinctly uneasy after that, and the Speaker continued to eye Ekks skeptically for a moment. Slowly, he turned his attention back to the rest of the table.

"Then the vote can go ahead as planned, I suppose," he declared, pushing himself to his feet once again. "The Senate will reconvene after the votes have been tallied."

Everyone paused after that, waiting. Once it was apparent that no one was going to add any last-minute details or ask any questions, one by one they began to put their things away. Slowly, they got to their feet and bustled towards the door.

Ekks watched them leave with halfhearted interest, one hand curled around his lukewarm mocha cup. He lifted it and tipped his head back as he drained the last dregs from the cup.

The room was nearly empty when Zenne came to a halt beside Ekks's chair, shifting to lean one hip casually against the table beside Ekks's elbow.

"I suppose it's no use speculating, but it looks to me like the vote is going to be for the fleet to stand down," Zenne observed. He noticed that Ekks was hardly even looking at him, but he didn't seem to care much about the Commander's disinterest.

To think, Ekks had assumed he might get some peace and quiet without Vero around to bark at him like a junkyard dog.

"But I suppose it makes sense," Zenne mused, carrying on despite Ekks's lack of contribution. "Seats are opening up elsewhere. There's a fair bit of new blood in the system."

"The chips will fall where they may," Ekks replied. "If I can't play poker with them, then I'm not inclined to give them much thought."

Zenne was silent for a long moment, eyeing Ekks with open suspicion. Finally, he sighed and shook his head, before he pushed away from the table.

"Have a good evening, Richard," he offered, before he turned and made his way towards the door.

Only once he was alone in the room did Ekks finally get to his feet. He glanced around the empty table, straightened his jacket, and headed for the door.

Sean and Karina's Quarters, Gaitune-67

Karina was in the bedroom sorting clean laundry when Sean came in. "Hey, you!" She smiled at him brightly. "How's it going?"

Sean started undoing his gun belt. "Yeah, it's going," he confirmed, exhaling deeply as the heavy appendage dropped away from his cyborg-enhanced body. "The Ekks thing is done for the day, so at least that's over with, and Brock and Crash are making progress in the maintenance schedule." He shook his head, noticing some oil on his shirt. "And then it all begins again tomorrow. It's such a pain in the ass having to go and see him every single freaking day."

"Crash? Or Brock?"

"No… Ekks. The commander of the space fleet."

"Ohhh," Karina mouthed slowly. She knew exactly who he was talking about, but she wanted to tease him. Clearly it wasn't registering with him.

Sean wiped his hands over his face.

"But it's kind of amusing, don't you think?" Karina persisted. "Pushing your agenda onto a big-ass military dude."

Sean snorted lightly and sat down on the bed to undo his boots. "Yeah. You can tell that Molly is getting fed up with it, though. And it looks like he's managed to put a hit on someone without us knowing about it, until after the fact. We'll need to think more carefully about how we question him tomorrow."

Karina smiled to herself as she turned and put some folded shirts away into the cupboard. "I just find it interesting how you changed your tune about that particular skill." She flashed him her thousand-watt smile over her shoulder to ease any perceived jibe and prevent him from getting defensive.

"Hey look, I was only worried because she might be using it at the expense of proper leadership. Imagine the problems that would cause if she got on board something like the *ArchAngel*. It was just very dangerous."

"And now you can use it to your tactical advantage…" she added, pointedly.

"Exactly," he confirmed, without a hint of acknowledgment about the hypocrisy of the situation.

Karina's face dropped as if she were contemplating something serious. "How does Molly feel about it all?"

Sean quietly closed the drawer he had been putting his socks away in. "I don't know. I think she thinks that it's a good thing. And now she's mostly just bored, having to go and see the pillock every day. But, you have a point. In a lot of ways in the beginning she was struggling because of the morality of it."

"How do you mean?"

"Well she's effectively stopping the head of the space military from doing what he was elected to do."

"But wasn't he put into power by the Northern Clan? So he wasn't truly elected?" Karina clarified. Though she'd been involved in the missions, she was still trying to get her head around all the elements in play in the situation they were managing now.

"I think that's how she gets her head around it," Sean agreed. "But the principle bothers her. I mean imagine being able to tell a leader of a supposed democracy what to do or manipulate him in some way to do what suits you what you want... And all of a sudden you've no longer got a democracy anymore. I think she's just worried about taking that away from the people."

"But she is saving them?"

"She is. But I don't think that's the point. And I'm sure that many a bad decision has been made in this regard and justified as being for the greater good." He sighed, sitting down on the end of the bed again. "I don't know, I think she's also worried that she might be making the wrong decision. The stakes are the highest they could possibly be. And what if Ekks is right?"

"You think he might be?"

Sean shook his head, his gaze fixed idly on the floor now. "Well it wouldn't be the first time that I disagreed with her strategically. And where I come from we tend to shoot first and ask questions later. Or at least be in a position to shoot first and dominate the enemy."

"But we're assuming that these ARs aren't our enemy…"

Sean's expression looked as though he were crestfallen. He rolled his lips and nodded quietly for a few moments. "And that's one hell of a gamble…"

Karina sat down next to Sean on the bed and rested her head on his shoulder. "Well I don't envy her, not one little bit."

Safe House, Gaitune-67

Molly was exhausted as she ambled down the corridor to her old conference room where she had arranged to meet Paige and Maya.

"I can't wait to tell her—" Paige was saying as Molly came in through the door.

"Tell her what?" Molly asked, smiling.

Paige looked shocked, as if caught red-handed doing something she shouldn't. She shuffled some open holos out of the way and stood up in surprise. "Looks like we finally got some good news!" She beamed.

Maya handed Paige an open holo screen full of numbers. "Go on. Tell her."

Molly dumped her gear on the nearest chair and sat down in the one next to it. "Tell me what? Have you got the latest poll data in?"

Paige and Maya nodded in synch. Paige took the lead. "We have! And finally it's looking like we are in with a chance. We're neck and neck with the two main parties. And with enough voting collateral we may just have a chance to sway the Senate decision."

Molly beamed, despite the work-weariness around her eyes. "Well that is great news," she agreed. "Plus with Pieter's adjustment that he'll be implementing in the next day or so, we might actually be in with a chance of turning this all around. Well done, ladies!"

Paige glanced sideways towards Maya. "I guess this means we have cause to celebrate?"

Maya nodded approvingly. "I'd say so."

Molly glanced up from studying the numbers on the holo Maya had handed her. "It's not over yet, but you two should definitely go and relax and then get some rest. Something tells me we've got a few more big days to go yet."

"Come have a martini with us," Paige suggested gently, noticing Molly had holo-face from working too hard.

"Yeah, I just have a few more things to finish off, and then Joel wanted to talk to me. So if I get done before you go to bed, I'll head over. You'll be in the common area, yeah?"

Maya nodded. "Yep, we'll be there. We'll even save you a martini or two."

Molly thanked them, and Paige and Maya closed up their holos, leaving Molly alone to finish up.

CHAPTER FOUR

Bates's Office, Special Task Force Offices, Undisclosed Location, Estaria

Bates's stylus was a blur as it moved, reordering files on one side of her holoconsole, signing documents in the middle, and tweaking her schedule and her calendar on the other side of the screen. It was no busier than any other day, but it was a full day's work for at least three people all the same.

And then, in the blink of an eye, the holoconsole's screen went dark, right before the console closed itself. Bates blinked at the spot where it had been just a moment before. Before she could help it, she reached up to wave her hand through the spot it had been, despite the fact that it was very clearly no longer there. She was very glad there was no one in the room with her.

Of course, that still left the fact that a good portion of a day's work had just disappeared without a trace and without any warning. She reached halfway towards her communicator to call a repair technician in, only to pause and instead try to activate her wrist holo. As if it didn't even exist, it failed to make an appearance. So it wasn't just a problem with her holoconsole.

With a sigh, she got to her feet. She left her office and walked the short distance down the hall to the conference room, where a meeting was supposed to be going on.

Instead, once she poked her head into the room, she found a table full of very confused men and women, all murmuring and gesturing towards where the holoscreen was supposed to be.

The agent hosting the meeting cleared her throat once she noticed Bates there.

"Ah—my apologies if you need us for anything, Director, but—"

"Nothing like that," Bates assured her. "I just wanted to make sure I wasn't the only one having trouble. My holoconsole just shut itself down without warning and my wrist holo won't even start."

Spurred on by that announcement, everyone around the table started trying to open their holoconsoles and wrist holos, only for nothing to happen. A few of them fizzed to life for a few seconds, only to shut down again an instant later.

"Is it a problem with our connection to the network?" someone wondered cautiously.

"But then wouldn't that just mean our connection would be *slow*?" someone else replied. "This isn't slow, this just isn't there."

She left the conference room, leaving them to try to salvage their meeting without any of their materials. She headed down the steps into the bullpen to try and figure out how widespread the problem was.

Rhodez stared at his holoconsole. He tapped the keys. He prodded it with his stylus. It failed to react, completely frozen. He tried to open the settings, but even that had no effect.

With a discontented sigh, he shut it down and tried to reboot it.

"Oh, you have got to be kidding me," he grumbled to himself

when it refused to restart. "Knew I should have replaced it weeks ago." He heaved his weight back into his chair so it rolled a few inches away from his desk, and then he slid down with his arms crossed. If anyone else had been in the office with him, he would have furiously denied that he was sulking.

He straightened up when he heard a drawn out, slightly pitiful, "Noooo, no no no," from the next console over. It trailed off into some rather dismally colorful swearing.

Pushing with his legs, Rhodez wheeled his console chair backwards and a few feet to the left so he could look into Cleavon's console area.

"Problems?" he asked, grabbing onto the partition to bring his chair to a halt.

Cleavon gestured wordlessly to his holoconsole.

"Oh," Rhodez sighed. "You, too?"

Over at the other side of the open-plan office, Joshua barked, "Oh, what the hell!" and it was followed shortly after by Alisha's dismayed, "No, come back!"

"Everyone else, too," Cleavon observed glumly.

"I guess I'll go check with the Director," Rhodez offered, getting to his feet. He shoved his chair back into its place, not watching long enough to see where it stopped before he headed towards the main walkway through the open-plan office.

Director Bates was already on the floor and heading in his direction. Rhodez jerked to a halt mid-step, before he fell into an at-ease stance.

"Director," he greeted. "I was just going to talk to you."

Bates raised one eyebrow. Cleavon, Joshua, and Alisha were still shouting back and forth from their consoles to each other, oblivious to the Director's presence. By that point, several other people in the office, used to being able to talk to each other at the flick of a button, had joined in too.

"I take it you're all having the same holo trouble," Bates observed wryly.

Rhodez scowled at a point on the wall. "So much for it being an easy fix," he grumbled, mostly to himself. "What do we do?"

Bates was quiet for a moment as she gave the question some thought. "For now we wait," she decided. "So far, we have no proof that it's not just a server problem, or an issue on the network provider's end. If we're still offline by the end of the day, then I'll start making some calls to see how we fix this."

Rhodez nodded slowly. "Understood, Director. And…until then?" He glanced over his shoulder as he asked, back towards his friend. "Cleavon seems sort of heartbroken, but other than that everyone just seems kind of put out."

Bates patted his shoulder. "I'll leave calming them down in your very capable hands," she told him. Before he could object, she executed a picture-perfect about-face, right back the way she had just come from. She left Rhodez pouting in her wake.

He watched her leave for a moment, silently willing her to come back. No such thing happened. Finally, he heaved a sigh, clapped his hands once and rubbed them together, and mustered up an overly enthusiastic, "Alright, up to me. My favorite thing."

He turned and headed back towards the row of offices. Rather than waste time addressing everyone one at a time, he whistled once, as loudly and as sharply as he could manage. The scattered complaining came to an abrupt halt, and slowly people began to poke their heads up over the partitions between their console units.

"This problem isn't unique to us," Rhodez stated plainly. "It looks like the entire operation has no network access right now. Alright? So the higher ups are aware and plans on how to fix it are in the works. Got it?"

There was a murmur of surly assent, and he was quiet for a moment longer in case anyone absolutely *had* to make some sort of complaint. When no one spoke up, he tacked on, "Right, well. We all know how to do hardcopy work, so let's get to it."

A series of exasperated groans followed him as he stepped back into his console. It was almost a little satisfying.

Mercurial Spirits, Spire, Estaria

"She makes the pass. It looks like she's in the clear—no! Intercepted by—"

Whatever the game's announcer was going to say would forever remain a mystery, as all three of the bar's holoscreens suddenly went blank. A second later, they deactivated entirely, one after the other.

A cry of outrage began to rise up throughout the bar, only to fall meekly silent as one of the two bartenders picked up a mop. Brandishing it over her head like a weapon, she threatened, "I will use this!"

As she stared the patrons down to make sure no one got too unruly, her coworker vaulted over the bar to check on the nearest holoscreen. "Everything's still plugged in," he reported after a minute. "We didn't have a power flicker or anything." His eyebrows arched as his expression turned cheeky, just before he decided, "You hold down the fort here. I'm going to pop over to the cafe next door and see if they're having the same problem."

His coworker scowled at him, but since she didn't try to menace him with a mop, he took that as agreement. Lucky for him, as the patrons were starting to get impatient. Just as he reached the door, he heard his coworker sighing. "*Look*, if you all stop your bitching, then the next round is on me."

He heaved a sigh of relief once he was standing out on the sidewalk, though it was rather short-lived. He didn't even need to step into the cafe to know that they were having the same problem. It was filled with people all fussing fruitlessly with their gadgets. A man was arguing with a barista and gesturing to where a wrist holo projection should have been.

Rather than interrupting and making things worse, he decided that was evidence enough and stepped back into the bar.

"It's not just here," he announced, cutting off whatever his coworker had been in the middle of shouting at a patron. "From the looks of it, no one has holo network service."

"So someone call the service provider," one of the patrons whined, slumped dramatically over his table. "This was supposed to be *the* game of the season."

"You can catch the highlights tomorrow," the mop-wielding bartender informed him, pointing the end of her mop at him like a saber.

There was some scattered grumbling throughout the bar, and those who had only been there for the game paid their tabs and left. Those who were fine with simply talking to the other patrons and those who really just wanted a free drink stayed behind. Miraculously, no riots broke out, even if a few more people still needed to be menaced with the mop before they decided to simply enjoy their drinks without making any trouble.

Hopefully it was just a brief glitch. That seemed the most likely case. And soon enough, both the bartenders and the patrons put it out of their thoughts, save for the absence of the background noise of the holoscreens.

Professor Kurns's Office, Skóli Uppstigs Academy, Spire, Estaria

It was late in the evening and Giles had been working all night continuing his work on deciphering the signal they had gathered on their encounter with the ARs nearly three months ago.

But now, with no one else around, he saw his opportunity to indulge himself in the privacy of his own office. He crept over to the door and looked up and down the corridor.

Nothing.

Not a soul in sight.

He giggled lightly to himself and closed the door quietly, as if someone nearby might actually be able to hear it if he didn't.

Then, quietly and excitedly he tiptoed back to his desk and tapped a search into his holo. Locating the secret file, he made the screen big enough for him to see it easily, and sighed, his eyes caressing it longingly.

Then he stood bolt upright at his desk, as if about to give a presentation.

He cleared his throat.

"Ladies and gentlemen, welcome. And thank you. It is a great honor to accept such a prestigious prize. Firstly I'd like to thank my research team and the university. Secondly I'd like to thank my parents for allowing me to pursue the route of space archaeology when it wasn't really a serious subject."

He waved his hands, muttering... Wait for the laughter to die down.

"And thirdly I'd like to thank all of you for being here to help me celebrate this momentous day. When I first discovered the talismans, it was—"

The office lights flickered, and then something happened to his holo. The screen he was reading off went blank.

He tapped it.

Nothing.

He tapped it again.

No response.

Very strange, he thought.

He tried to connect a call with on-site security. "Hey, have you got any issues..." he started to say. The line was dead. Nothing. Not even a dial tone.

He scratched his head, then got up out of his chair and headed out of his office and down the dimly lit corridors to see if anyone else was having the same problem.

If anyone else was here this late in the night...

Senate House, Spire, Estaria

It was quite an opportunity, Ekks mused to himself.

An ambition that had been absent before began to bubble in his chest.

The Speaker of the House sounded exasperated even before the meeting truly began. "Alright, yes, I understand, this is all very sudden, but we must all calm down to begin the meeting." The chattering across the table that spread throughout the entire conference room failed to get any quieter.

There was a metallic screech as the Speaker pushed his chair back and got to his feet. At last attention began to turn to him. He thumped the end of his cane against the side of the table with enough force that the table rattled. "I called for order," he barked. "This is the Senate House, not a schoolhouse."

The quiet that settled over the room seemed almost sheepish. With a sigh, the Speaker dropped back into his seat. "Very good." He folded his hands over the handle of his cane. "The vote on whether or not we recall the fleet is being postponed. Circumstances have changed rather dramatically in the last few hours."

A *beautiful* opportunity.

"The only logical choice is to have the fleet stay the course," Ekks interjected, cutting off whatever the Speaker was going to say next. The Speaker settled him with an incredulous look, as if he had just been told his stepsister was actually a pile of weasels in a trench coat.

"Excuse me?" the Speaker managed once he gathered his composure again.

"You didn't seem to care about that at all less than a day ago!" Raychel burst out. Though her face reddened afterwards, she didn't try to retract her sentence.

"I wanted to see how things would play out," Ekks explained calmly, folding his hands neatly on top of the table. "Clearly, that was a mistake on my part, if the lot of you are simply going to keep flinching whenever the time comes to actually make a hard call." He eyed her shrewdly for a second, and she shrank back into her seat. Slowly, Ekks looked at the others around the table.

"Tell me," he began after a moment. "Why did any of you choose to be senators if the idea of truly doing anything is so completely foreign to you?"

"The fact that we aren't eager to plunge the system into an unnecessary war doesn't mean we're unwilling to act," Bel argued, though she already sounded resigned. No one said anything after her. They instead waited for Ekks to make his argument.

His eyes narrowed as he centered his focus on Bel like a laser. "Who's to say any of this is unnecessary?" he asked, though he left no time for anyone to actually answer his question. "There are ships in the outer system, and now the holo network is blacking out all across the planet. Do you honestly think that's a coincidence?"

The others were silent.

"It seems more likely to me," he continued, calmer now, "that this network blackout is some sort of attack by the intruders. Likely just the first part of a larger attack. And none of you are willing to do what is necessary to keep the system safe." He scoffed. "Pitiful."

"Commander—" the Speaker tried to interrupt.

"I'm declaring martial law," Ekks stated simply, as if it was simply any other day of the week. "It seems like it's the only option, if anyone actually wants anything to happen. I would say the current situation is pressing enough to justify it."

The silence was deafening. Ekks didn't wait for any of them to come back to their senses after that. He got to his feet, straightening his jacket, and breezed out of the room.

He had some preparations to make, after all.

. . .

Richard Ekks's Office, Spire, Estaria

The Spire's connection to the holo network had always been more reinforced than most other places. Ekks had never put much thought into it before—it had simply been a fact of life, like air or water—but as his office door closed behind him, he found he was glad for it. Though the connection was unstable, his holo-console still worked when he tried to open it.

At least for the time being. Though it took three times as long as it normally would, his call to Fleet Admiral Boys still managed to connect.

The image was pixelated at first, colors shifting across the screen the only sign that Boys was moving.

"—mm-mander. To-oo what do—owe the—easure?"

The connection was unstable enough at first that he could scarcely hear a word that Boys said, but after a few seconds it stabilized.

"Admiral," Ekks greeted. "The situation back here on Estaria has become…complicated," he stated delicately. "I've declared martial law until the situation returns to normal."

Boys's eyebrows shot up towards his hairline. "Are you sure you're not jumping the gun a bit, Commander?" he asked. Though he sounded good-natured, it was clear enough that the levity in his tone was forced.

"I like to think not," Ekks returned pleasantly. "And that's the part that matters, isn't it?"

Boys stared back at him stonily.

"The original plan is still in effect," Ekks explained, uncaring for the open distaste Boys regarded him with. "Maintain your course towards the ships in the outer system. Is that clear, Admiral?"

"Perfectly clear, sir," Boys replied stiffly. "Will that be all?"

Ekks ended the call as his answer.

. . .

Aboard *The Corona*, Approaching the Sarkian Outer System

Boys sighed and dragged a hand over his hair, sagging back in his seat. There was nothing to be done, though. His own opinion on the matter was worth rather little in that moment. A few members of the bridge crew peered at him in bemused concern.

Rather than dwell on it, Boys instead picked up his communicator and patched it into the ship-wide intercom.

"This is Admiral Boys speaking. Stay on course."

CHAPTER FIVE

Aboard *The Hierophant*

It all seemed too quiet. Too calm. By all accounts, the entire space fleet was in the middle of intercept protocols, and yet it was *dull*.

It was almost an insult to think about it.

Captain Grouthe's thoughts swam in circles along a similar track as he paced back and forth across *The Hierophant's* bridge.

It had been exciting at first.

The chaos as everyone worked to scramble the fleet in a hurry.

The tension as the ships trekked across the solar system.

The ships in the Outer System getting larger and more present on ship sensors as the fleet got closer and closer.

But they had…stalled out, sitting idle while they were so close.

Grouthe came to a halt behind one of the navigator's chairs, peering over his shoulder at the sensor readings. He drummed his fingers impatiently on the back of the navigator's seat. If the navigator objected to Grouthe's proximity, he made no comment on it. Instead, he simply observed mildly, "Waiting for the other shoe to drop, Captain?"

Grouthe huffed out a laugh and stepped back, away from the navigator's chair. "Indefinitely, it seems," he answered lightly. "It almost seems like it might be worth it if the invasion force noticed us, just to shake things up."

The navigator hummed in acknowledgment, neither agreeing nor disagreeing, and Grouthe continued pacing.

"Could try pulling an aileron roll," the pilot offered dryly, glancing over his shoulder. "I mean, we'd probably hit at least three other ships, but at least it would give us something to focus on."

"Don't tempt me," Grouthe returned wryly. "They would take the damage out of my pay, and I don't make near enough money for that."

"Oh, well, if that's your only objection..." The pilot trailed off, rolling his eyes good-naturedly before he turned back around.

"Watch your tone, Flight Lieutenant," Grouthe cautioned, though there was no heat behind his tone, and the pilot offered no response.

No one else felt a need to comment on Grouthe's restlessness, and he kept his thoughts to himself after that. After all, a well-functioning crew was a calm crew. There was no need for him to stress his crew out when he needed them at their best.

A bit hypocritical, perhaps, he reflected to himself as he kept pacing. Considering he was as wound up and tense as a hemophiliac in a razor blade factory.

Something to break the monotony had to happen eventually, though. Things never stayed static for too long.

"Captain? We're being hailed by *The Corona*. Should I patch it to your holocomm?"

Yanked out of his thoughts, Grouthe glanced at the communications officer and nodded once, just briefly dipping his chin towards his chest. "Patch it through."

He opened his wrist holo.

"This is Captain Grouthe of *The Hierophant*," he greeted blandly. "Has someone finally decided to tell us what we're actually doing, General?"

Boys sighed slowly. "Grouthe, all of us are getting antsy. I do not need the attitude. It's not going to help matters."

Grouthe cleared his throat. "My apologies, General," he offered. "How can I help you?"

"As you suspect, we finally have our orders," Boys confirmed. "We're to hold our course. Considering that, we likely have a day and a half at most before we're within range of the invading fleet."

Grouthe's eyebrows rose, regardless of the fact that Boys wasn't actually present to see it. "Not quite the decision I was expecting," he acknowledged easily enough. "I was under the impression the Senate was beginning to waver on the choice to send us out here."

Boys paused for a moment before he replied carefully, "Apparently there's something of an emergency back home." He didn't sound entirely satisfied with that statement. "I'm not sure of the specifics, but whatever it is, it evidently has everyone spooked enough that no one in the Senate balked at the idea of martial law."

Grouthe whistled, low and impressed. "Sounds like things have gotten exciting since we all left home. I'm almost sad to miss it."

"Yes, well," Boys sighed, dismissive and distant, "I'm sure they'll keep us in the loop." He didn't agree with Grouthe's attitude, that much was clear, but he was too professional to directly bring his personal feelings up. A sad, sorry stick in the mud, but Grouthe supposed that meant he was ideal for his job.

"Is there anything else, sir?" Grouthe wondered, once again beginning to pace across the bridge, back and forth like a metronome.

"That will be all," Boys replied, and he simply hung up. Grouthe closed his holo, unbothered by the abrupt dismissal.

"Steady on, boys," he reported to the rest of the bridge crew after a few moments, pausing his pacing as he said it only for a second before he resumed his repetitive meandering. His words were light, as if he was simply reporting on the weather. "We haven't seen the last of all of this, and it seems everyone's hit some turbulence back home."

At last, he returned to his seat at the center of the bridge. "This should all be interesting by the end," he mused, more to himself than to anyone else on the bridge. "More than I expected it to be, at any rate." The rest of the bridge crew seemed to pay him only a token amount of attention. They were accustomed to him thinking out loud.

"Any special orders?" the pilot asked after a moment, as the navigators worked on adjusting the course.

Grouthe needed to think for only a second before he turned his attention to the communications officer. "Let the crew in the main battery know that they should keep the cannon warmed up."

"Do you think we'll be needing it?" the communications officer asked carefully, even as he was already putting the message together to send it.

"I suppose we'll know soon enough, won't we?" was all Grouthe said in reply.

News Broadcast, Belladonne Square, Estaria

The manual camera, compared to a holocamera, was unwieldy. Positively minuscule compared to a lot of antiques, but enormous and cumbersome compared to the holocameras that had become so popular. It was so much easier to be a crew of one when no one needed to actually carry the camera. The movements weren't nearly as smooth as with a holocamera, as the cameraman panned in after the anchor.

The cameraman made no complaint, though, and the anchor was as professional as ever.

"Here we are in Belladonne Square," she reported, gesturing behind her. "Usually bright enough to be mistaken for daylight even in the middle of the night, now only those businesses with the foresight to have physical backups for their screens are still advertising. For businesses that had holo-tech signs, it's as if they've become invisible."

She sidestepped in a half-circle, her cameraman following her movements, until a physical screen was behind her, set up at a post office. "Even more pressing than that," she carried on, gesturing to the screen with one hand, "the holo network blackouts have become so widespread that the Senate has declared a state of emergency."

The screen was just an endlessly scrolling message about said state of emergency.

"While just a few years ago it was common for holo-tech to be just an accent piece in a house, by now it's so ubiquitous that entire households have gone dark," she explained, calm and to the point. "While wristholos, holoscreens, and holoconsoles are just the most obvious sources, it's no longer uncommon for every interface in a household or business to be a holo-interface."

Her tone took on a note of urgency as she added, "If you know of any friends, family, or neighbors who have gone dark because of the holo network blackout, we all urge you to extend a hand and offer whatever help you can. In the meantime, all of us here at IQ News will keep you updated on any changes with the network and the spread of the blackout. This has been Mercy Hazrad of IQ News."

The screen cut to the scrolling emergency banner that had been visible on the post office's screen after that.

Back in Belladonne Square, as the cameraman lowered the

camera, Mercy dragged a hand through her hair. "Not sure how much good we're doing when a solid forty percent of the population has gone dark," she grumbled, pinching the bridge of her nose between two fingers.

"At least we're letting people know they'll need to lend a helping hand," her cameraman replied, checking over the camera absentmindedly.

Mercy wiped her hand down her face, carefully avoiding smudging her eye makeup. "There is that," she conceded, before she steeled herself and straightened back up. She started walking at a purposeful pace, her heels clicking against the sidewalk. "Come on. We need to get back to the car and get moving. We're IQ's only team that's actually qualified for manual camerawork, and we need to hit two more locations tonight."

Base Conference Room, Gaitune-67

Maya's brows furrowed together in concern as the broadcast cut to the emergency message. Paige glanced over her shoulder, pausing in the middle of organizing a cabinet of datapads. The need to have organized hardcopies of everything had been made very apparent recently.

"Something wrong?" Paige asked, setting a datapad down on top of the cabinet and turning around to lean against the back of Maya's seat.

Maya flapped a hand at the broadcast. "More reports of Estaria going dark," she stated simply. "No one really seems to know what to do about it."

"Wonderful timing," Paige grumbled, sagging more heavily against the back of Maya's chair, until it creaked. "First the media sends everyone into a panic, now people don't even have access to that."

"Convenient timing, don't you think?" Maya wondered, craning her neck just enough to look back at Paige. "I mean, these can't be isolated events. They have to be related to each other. They *have* to be."

Paige hummed thoughtfully for a moment, rocking back and forth on her heels and rocking Maya's chair in turn. "It does seem pretty unlikely," she agreed slowly.

Maya sighed and offered an unenthusiastic nod in agreement. "It would be easier if they're related, though," she grumbled. "Deal with one problem and the other one goes away, too. Like magic."

"When is anything ever that easy?" Paige asked wryly, finally tumbling herself down into the chair beside Maya's. "If something doesn't require a twelve-step plan at minimum, I am automatically suspicious."

Maya elbowed her in the shoulder, sending their chairs very slowly wheeling away from each other. "Don't jinx it," she scolded. There was no real ire behind her words or the scowl on her face.

It didn't take long for the mood to grow somber once again.

They returned to working in silence, until finally Maya slumped back in her chair and slid down in it until she was nearly under the table. "This sucks," she decided eloquently, using her feet to turn her chair around so she didn't need to see the emergency message anymore. Neither of them wanted to actually turn the news off in case something changed.

Paige snorted lightly and glanced up at Maya briefly before turning her attention back to her holoscreen. They still had analysis to get through if they were going to find a solution…

Just then the rest of the team started arriving.

"We're going to have to pick this up after the team meeting," Paige called over to Maya finally. Maya nodded and packed up the screens she had spread out everywhere, and started explaining to Brock what they'd discovered thus far.

"Sounds like you'll be staying here when we go off to stop an all-out space battle," he mused. "I don't know which of us has it worse off…"

Base Conference Room, Gaitune-67

Molly rubbed one eye as she tried to focus on the holoscreen in front of her.

It's just not clear what's happening. I'm still trying to collate the data. It seems that there are sporadic blackouts all over Spire.

Is it isolated to Spire?

It's too early to tell. I'm monitoring all kinds of channels to see if anyone else is reporting it elsewhere on the planet.

Okay. Keep running diagnostics. There have got to be answers somewhere.

Molly sat back in her chair, allowing her eyes a moment to defocus and rest.

Man, I could murder a mocha now.

Before Oz had the chance to protest about what it would do to their system, the door to the conference room slid open and heavy boots entered the room behind her. "Hey, I got here as soon as I could."

Molly turned to see Joel come in and take a place at the conference room table a couple of seats down from her. "Thanks for coming so quickly. I'm guessing you were asleep?" she ventured, sympathetically.

"Yeah just, I think… But what about you? Have you even been to bed yet?"

She shook her head, absently, already moving her thoughts to the next thing. "No… not yet."

Joel gave her a sympathetic look. Before he was able to carry on with that line of questioning or even make sure that she was okay, she had moved back into mission-mode.

"It looks like the holo network is going dark in places," she explained. With a tap on a holoscreen she brought up a screen on the main projector in the center of the table. It was a heat map with patches here and there which had gone dark. "What you're looking at is Oz's best guess at where we've lost network. The red areas are places where he is yet to gather enough data to be able to say one way or another. The black areas are where we have confirmed reports of the holo network being down."

Joel leaned forward, his arms on the table. "And how do we know that these places are down if there is no holo connectivity? People can't just report it in, can they?"

Molly smiled and wagged finger at him playfully. "Clearly we didn't make you operations lead for nothing," she teased. "You're right though. Oz has managed to ping those areas and has confirmed the network is just… down."

Joel rubbed his chin thoughtfully. "Do we know why?"

"Not yet."

"Think it's got anything to do with the Northern Clan?"

"Almost certainly. And the timing couldn't be worse."

"How so?"

"Well best-case scenario it's designed to stop people from voting."

"And we haven't seen that in history before," he chuffed sarcastically. "And worst case?"

Oz inserted himself into the conversation over the conference room intercom. "There is an 89% probability that Ekks will use this to declare martial law."

Molly glanced at Joel grimly. "We've seen before in other cultures in other situations. It's well documented. Especially with the kind of power and economic imbalance that they have on Estaria now. I think 89% is pitching low."

Joel was already looking tired and disheveled having been unceremoniously raised from his slumber. But as Molly explained the severity of the situation to him, he visibly paled even more.

"But isn't he still under your thrall? Ekks, I mean."

Molly rolled her lips. "He should be. I wish I could tell you definitively yes... Joel I'm...scared."

Joel started to move towards her to put his arm around her.

Just then, the door whooshed open again, and this time Paige appeared, pulling their attention. Her face was taut with tension. "Bad news, folks. Looks like Ekks is becoming immune to whatever it is you've been doing to him... or the instructions weren't specific enough."

She paused briefly to take a breath. "He's just declared martial law."

Molly's head fell into her hands. "Fuck!"

Joel took a moment to react, slamming his fist on the table in frustration. A second later it was as if his frustration had transformed into determination. He sprang to his feet. "Well, what are we waiting for? We need to get back down there and change his mind. Oz, prepare a pod."

He looked to Molly, to see her still hiding her face in her hands. Slowly she raised her eyes, dropping her hands to the table. "Hang on, let's think this through for a moment. I'm not sure but I've got a very strong feeling that his first act will be to cancel the vote. In which case no matter what we do down there, we don't have a say in what happens next."

"In which case," Oz piped up over the intercom, "those ships are going to engage the first opportunity they have."

Molly glanced at Joel and then Paige. "He's right. Oz? How far out are the Estarian ships from the Zhyn blockade?"

"Less than twenty-four hours," Oz reported.

Molly turned back to Joel decisively. "Well then there isn't time for talk. We've got to get out there and turn them back. Before they pick a fight with the Zhyn, and therefore the Federation."

"Ok—I'll make the arrangements," Joel confirmed, barely taking even a fraction of a second to jump on board with her plan. "Oz—alert all personnel as to what is happening. Have them meet back here in the base conference room in forty minutes. Tell them to start getting mission-ready."

"Acknowledged," Oz responded over the intercom.

Joel hurried out of the conference room, the sound of his boots rapidly disappearing down the corridor. Paige glanced at Molly. "Anything I can do right now?"

Molly thought for a moment and then pulled up her holo-screen and pointed to the map that was already on the main projector. "I need to attend to a few things, but if you could work with Oz and try and figure out what's going on and what is causing this, that would be massively helpful."

Paige sat down enthusiastically. "No problem, boss! I'm all over it."

Molly smiled at her friend and touched her on her forearm. "I don't know how any of us would survive without you."

Paige grinned playfully. "Well for a start you'd have to order your own pizza, and goodness knows what kind of cocktail crap you'd be drinking."

Molly chuckled as she stood up. "You know, you're absolutely right." And with that she waved and then hurried out of the door to attend to the myriad of things she needed to do to get them space-bourne.

Paige pulled up her holo. "Maya? You wanna help me with some investigating that could save the whole of Estaria?"

CHAPTER SIX

Base Conference Room, Gaitune-67

Maya pulled her lips to one side. "No. It just doesn't make sense. If it were a power failure, then we would be able to trace it to a source. A power node that was down. These patterns just don't match the power grid nodes."

Paige shook her head in agreement. "But if it were a virus, it would have a point of origin too, wouldn't it? Oz, what do you think?"

"I agree with both points," he explained. "But I have to say, what if we were to look at it in terms of under what circumstances would most things be true. For example, under what conditions would a virus not have a single point of origin?"

Maya tugged subconsciously at her hair as she contemplated the question. "Well for a start if the virus were introduced at a number of network nodes simultaneously."

Paige's eyes brightened. "Yes! That's true. Or if the virus was set to activate at various nodes at the same time." She paused. "But surely there's nothing to say that it had to be physically or manually introduced, right? It could have been deployed from a single point and then, kinda... *hatched* at the nodes?"

Maya nodded. "Yeah. I've seen viruses do that."

"That's a good point," Oz confirmed. "But it would take time for a virus to deploy in that way."

"True," Maya agreed. "How long for this one, Oz? If we can get a time scale on it, maybe we can narrow some variables down."

"Difficult to tell at this point," Oz confessed. "I'm struggling to see the big picture because I'm having to download data in chunks. I don't have a real-time view of the whole network."

Maya cocked her head. "Why is that?"

"Well when we first came here, it was just the nature of the technology that we had access to and a way at keeping us isolated and safe from prying eyes and authorities."

"And now?"

"Well," Oz continued sheepishly, "we're still dependent on that setup. I can't access the network continually. I have a service that I can download data from periodically, and even though it's a lot of data and even though the servers are preprogrammed to gather what is useful, it's still limited."

Maya frowned, rubbing her head and partially hiding her face. "What would we need to do in order to fix that, then?"

"Normally we would just wait until Molly went down to the surface and then I can access things from the university network. But since she's going to be leaving any minute now, and I'm obviously gonna be with her, we're running out of options."

"So what are we gonna do?"

Paige sat back in her chair, contemplating what she was hearing. "Well I have a potential solution. But neither of you are going to like it."

Maya narrowed her eyes at her quizzically. Oz went silent for several moments. Finally Maya's curiosity gave out. "We'll come on... we haven't got all day."

Paige glanced upwards, as if lifting her voice to Oz. "Oz? Do you want to tell her?"

"I believe that Paige is referring to another AI that is sitting in the basement playing holo games all day."

Maya's eyes widened in shock. "You don't mean Bourne?"

Paige pursed her lips but maintained eye contact with Maya. She wasn't budging to disabuse her of the guess.

Maya took a deep breath before Paige decided to confirm what she was asking. "I'm afraid so," she said slowly. "He is our last hope. If, that is, he'll agree to help us…"

Oz seemed to have regained his composure. "I'm sure he'll be more than happy to be involved in something. He's always badgering Brock and Pieter to let him get involved with missions. Let me get in touch with him and get him up to speed."

Maya glanced at Paige in concern. "You really think this is a good idea? After everything that was talked about with not getting involved… You know, because of his programming?"

Paige shrugged and pulled her hair back off her face. "I don't know what else we can do," she said, racking her brain for alternatives.

Just then Molly poked her head around the open door. "Everything okay in here?"

Paige sat up and turned to their leader. "Looks like we're recruiting Bourne in Oz's absence, to help us with the connection problem." She nodded towards the holoscreen map, which had been updated with many more black patches on it since Molly had last seen it.

Molly's expression was grim. "Okay," she told them, "do what you have to do. We're counting on you. In fact the whole of Estaria is counting on you. If we're not able to stop these holo blackouts, I'm afraid we're going to have mass panic on our hands. And with mass panic, goodness knows what they'll elect to do with an external threat such as aliens in the sky."

Maya snorted gently. "No pressure then, eh?"

Molly smiled weakly. "Yeah, no pressure… Okay, it looks like we'll be having a team meeting in here in a few minutes. Are you guys good to put everything on hold so that we can get this done in one swoop?"

"Sure, of course," Paige agreed. "We're waiting on Oz to talk to Bourne and bring him on board before we can move forward anyway."

"Great. I'll be back in a few minutes then." Molly disappeared again down the corridor.

Somewhere on the Base Network, Gaitune-67

So you'll help?

Oz wasn't quite sure if he was understanding Bourne correctly.

\>>Of course. This is what I was designed for. I just can't believe that you guys didn't let me help before.<<

Well you know there are the issues of ethics and integrating with their way of doing things. Which is massively different from how the military would do things.

\>>Yes, but that's not my fault.<<

No one is saying it is—or was. But unfortunately it does affect the way you process information and the decisions that you make. For this reason I'm asking you please, please, please defer to Paige's judgment on everything. Okay? I don't want to get back and find that you started the next Civil War. Agreed?

\>>Yeah, yeah. You're so melodramatic. I'm hard squished to be able to rally in support for a holo game, let alone anything else.<<

Okay, well if you're sure you're ready for this...

\>>Of course I'm sure. I was born ready!<<

Oz rolled his eyes and began the data transfer to catch Bourne up with their investigation.

And if anything happens to me, just remember... I believe in you. Good luck.

\>>I don't believe in luck. I believe in probabilities and computations.<<

Well, okay. Good probabilities and computations, then.

Base Conference Room, Gaitune-67

Maya was just in the process of moving her holoscreens over to the same side of the desk as Paige. She shuffled them together just as Brock came through the door.

"Hey ladies, how's it going?" he asked, his normal smile somewhat subdued.

"It's going," Paige told him. "Oz is in the process of briefing Bourne so that maybe we have a chance of correcting this problem down on Estaria while you guys are gone."

He nodded affably and sat down.

Maya glanced at Paige, noticing the look of concern on her face. "Hey, you okay?" Maya asked. "Brock?" she added when he didn't respond.

"Huh? What?" He looked up. "Oh yeah, fine. Just a lot on my mind..."

Paige held his gaze sympathetically. "Getting tense down there, eh?"

He rolled his lips. "Yeah, you could say that. I mean we have no idea whether these guys are going to just barge right through us and start an all-out war. I don't know which we are more worried about: being caught between two formidable fleets, or being partially responsible for the beginning of a new conflict."

Maya's face brightened. "Let's hope it doesn't come to that," she reassured him. "I know things may look one way right now, but how many times have we solved the problem just in time. I got every confidence in you. In this team."

Brock breathed out lightly through his nose. "Yeah, you have a point," he sighed, slumping back in his chair.

There was a clatter from down the corridor as several pairs of boots announced the arrival of the rest of the team. Moments later they came in through the door and spread themselves out at the conference table, ready for the next meeting.

A few minutes more and Molly reappeared, this time with some kind of smoothie in an antigrav mug. She sat down in her usual place, and quiet quickly fell over the room.

"Okay, folks," she began. "We need to get out there as soon as possible. As you probably already heard, Ekks has declared martial law down on Estaria. If he hasn't already, his next move is likely to be giving the Estarian-Ogg Fleet the order to engage. By our reckoning, the fleet is probably pretty close to our friends, the Zhyn, by now. I'm sure I don't need to remind you that if they engage with the Zhyn, they will likely be obliterated."

Sean coughed and then tried to quiet himself. Molly narrowed her eyes at him, fully aware that he was trying to mask a laugh.

She continued. "While that may appear like a *good* thing, it will only make the situation on Estaria more unstable. The people are scared. If their ships are taken out, they will become more scared, and getting them to accept the new race, or even integration with the Federation after this, will become impossible."

Pieter raised his hand. "Why don't we just get the Zhyn out of the way?"

Molly bobbed her head sympathetically. "The problem then would be that they would be going straight up against the ARs." She shook her head in dismay. "Then they would most definitely be annihilated, and as far as the Estarians would be concerned, it would be because the ARs are invading."

Paige lowered her eyes to the table, shaking her head. "It's ridiculous," she muttered. "Either way, we're screwed."

Molly stood up, leaning her hands on the table, a new fire in her eyes. She looked around the table at her team. "We're not screwed. Not yet at least. There is still a chance that we can stop any of this from happening. Oz is working on a way to stop the

Estarians from firing on either fleet. But we need to get out there. And fast. We can do this," she told them firmly. "We can change the course of history for the better. If there were ever a time where our determination, skills, and passion would have an effect on the lives of the people in this system, it is right now."

She looked into each of the eyes of the men and women that she had been working with the last several years. She could feel emotion welling in her own chest as she thought of how far they had come together and how much she cared about each of them. "We can do this," she reiterated, now leaning up off the table and standing straight.

The atmosphere in the room changed from one of hopelessness and stress to one of possibilities coupled with an unending sense of loyalty.

She took a deep breath, making up her mind. "Paige, Maya. Your place is here. You need to solve the situation on Estaria and restore holoconnections. Without that, they will only continue to panic and give Ekks more ammunition to do whatever the hell he wants. The enemy isn't the system now. Nor is it the Northern Clan. The enemy is fear itself. Work to fight the fear."

Paige and Maya both nodded in synchrony as they accepted their orders. Molly turned her head to Arlene, who was sitting next to Ben'or.

"Arlene, Ben'or, there is no need for you to be on the ship this time. Your place is also here, and Anne needs you." Molly started to turn her attention to the next person on her mental list when suddenly she stopped and turned back to them. "And for goodness' sake, please make sure that Anne stays put. If there were ever a time for her not to stow away, this would be it."

There was a slight chuckle that rippled through the group.

Before she had the chance to continue, Ben'or interjected. "Molly, forgive me, I understand why you would give me the opportunity to stay here... But I must insist on coming."

Molly opened her mouth to protest, but he put his hand up,

silencing her. His eyes reflected a calm certainty that she didn't feel like she could argue with. Especially not on the time scales that they were working to. As soon as he realized that he had won the discussion, his face softened. "The Zhyn in me can't stand staying behind from a battle," he explained, glancing at the other warriors in the room. Then he looked Molly straight in the eye. "And the philosopher in me can't not take a stand for what is right."

Molly couldn't find her words, but she did feel the fire of justice that seemed to burn within him. It was the same sense that she had got from him the first time that they had met, when they talked about his place in the Zhyn Empire and what his job entailed. He was a warrior with a burning passion for diplomacy. And he was also a force for good. She nodded and moved on, a tear welling in her eye.

Ben'or exchanged a look with Arlene, who already had tears streaming down her face. He squeezed her hand under the table.

"Brock, Crash," she continued, "there's no way we can do this without you." She didn't need to say anything else. The pair nodded in unison, accepting the mission unreservedly.

"Joel?"

"As if that's even a question," he replied straightaway. "I need to be on that ship with you."

She smiled weakly, still trying to maintain her composure. She turned to Pieter. "Pieter, Oz can probably do everything we need to do…"

He shook his head and interrupted her. "My place is on the ship," he said simply.

She knew there was no point in arguing with him.

"Jack, Sean, Karina… This is going to be a ship to ship battle, as far as our strategy is concerned. We are not going to land, and we don't need guns. There's no need for you to be on board."

Jack made eye contact with Sean and Karina, before speaking for all three of them. "Landing or not, our place is also on that ship. And besides, who said that we wouldn't be boarding." She winked at Pieter. "I'm sure Pieter would appreciate a few extra hands to run the various weapons on *The Empress*, if it's needed."

"We can manage," Molly insisted. "We want to keep the numbers down as much as possible. Just in case."

The words flew from Sean's mouth before he even had a chance to think. "We're a team, Molly. We are *your* team, and we belong on that ship. We're going with you."

He realized that he had blurted it out without thinking. "If that's okay, boss?"

Another chuckle rippled through the team. Molly cracked a smile. "Only if you're sure. I'd rather as many people stayed safe as possible."

Sean checked with the other two and then confirmed: "We're sure."

"Okay," Molly declared. "I guess that's decided then. We leave in twenty minutes. Onwards, people…"

There was an immediate chatter and antigrav chairs being pushed back, and then the team filed out, rushing to get everything ready before liftoff.

Paige and Maya remained in the conference room and started unpacking their holoscreens again and spreading them over the desk.

"No pressure," Maya echoed, smiling briefly at Paige as they got back to work.

CHAPTER SEVEN

<u>Hangar Deck, Gaitune-67</u>

Arlene bit her lip as she tried to hold back the tears.

"Now, now, Arlene," Ben'or whispered in her ear as he held her tight. "Nothing bad is going to happen. Everything is going to be fine."

He felt her nodding as she pulled away. "I know," she muttered, wiping away the tears. "It's just… Something doesn't feel right."

He held her face as he looked deep into her eyes. "It's bound to not feel right. We're not running off on an adventure this time. We're heading out there to put some cockwombles in their place. It's just different. But it's gonna be okay."

He caught sight of Anne hanging back a few paces. "Anne? Do me a favor," he called. "Don't let this one get melancholy. You make sure that she keeps her chin up. And eats her vegetables," he added with a gentle smile.

Anne ran over to him and wrapped her arms around his middle. She could barely get them halfway around, he was that big compared to her, but she squeezed him as tightly as she could. "Come back safe," she told him firmly, her voice muffled in his uniform. She tried not to allow the tear that was pooling in her eye to escape.

He stroked her hair and hugged her back. "I promise," he reassured her.

His attention was pulled as he noticed Molly and Joel stride purposely past him, gear on their backs, as they headed down the side of the ship. He squeezed Anne tightly once more, and then pulled away. "That's my cue to leave, little one," he told her. "Be back as soon as I can so we can plot our next adventure. Think of where you'd like to go, and we'll make it happen."

Arlene helped pull Anne off him, and the two females watched him leave to board the ship.

On board, the atmosphere was even more intense than in the conference room twenty minutes before. The quantum engines fired up as Crash completed his final checks.

"Ladies and gentlemen, the Captain has turned on the seatbelt sign indicating it is time to find your seat and sit the fuck down. We will be gating to Valhalla in a matter of minutes. It is fully advisable that you have all your paperwork completed and insurance paid up before this time, as there will be no turning back."

Brock glanced over at him. "Morbid much?"

Crash just shrugged. "I thought it might lighten the mood…"

Brock rolled his eyes at his partner's dry humor.

Meanwhile in the cabin, Pieter sat with Jack. He finished clicking in his seatbelt. "It seems trivial faffing with this thing," he commented, "given that getting thrown around the cabin is probably not the biggest risk at this moment."

Jack sat quietly opposite him, her lips pressed together. "It's going to be okay," she reassured him, picking up on his anxiety, which probably hadn't been aided by Crash's announcement.

Pieter mumbled something and then settled in for the journey.

Sean and Karina sat together at the back of the lounge, holding hands and talking quietly.

Molly and Joel sat together in silence.

For once Molly had spontaneously elected to sit next to Joel, probably choosing some comfort in one of the tensest situations she'd ever found herself in. Joel spent several minutes racking his brains for something reassuring to say. In the end he came up with nothing and instead resorted to remaining quiet, allowing his presence to do the talking.

Paige and Maya had been standing behind Arlene and Anne after saying their final goodbyes to Molly and Joel. As they watched the ship take off, the four women formed one group on the hangar deck.

Paige sidled up to Arlene as they waved. "Does this ever get any easier?" she asked.

Arlene shrugged, her normal composure returned. "I dunno. I'm normally the one leaving."

A moment of silence fell on the group, before a snigger escaped from Paige's lips.

Then Arlene started to chuckle at herself. Then Maya started to giggle, and before they knew it they were all walking back to the safe house, arms around each other, hopeful for the return of their people.

Base Conference Room, Gautine-67

Maya frowned and then started to say something. She stopped herself and continued to read the holoscreen in front of her.

Paige looked up. "You got something?"

"I'm not sure," Maya began slowly. "If what Bourne is pulling together is correct—"

Bourne interjected over the intercom. "Of course it's correct!"

Paige and Maya both smiled. Maya continued, "Well it looks like the source of the virus coincided with when Director Bates's spy team found that mole who took the place of the woman who had been shot."

Paige's brow furrowed. "You mean Etang?"

"Yeah..." Maya agreed slowly. "Whatever her name was. It's almost as if it were a Trojan horse that took a month to settle at various points in the system and then it got triggered, right at the most inconvenient time for us."

"But at the most convenient time for the people who want the ships to engage," Paige finished. "I think we'd be hard pressed to find a time in recent Estarian politics when things were more fraught."

"Yeah," Maya agreed. "Spooky, eh?"

Paige shook her head. "Or exactly as they planned it to be. Something tells me that the Northern Clan is behind all of this, and they were timing it perfectly. That's why we couldn't figure out what it was that Jennifer Etang had uploaded onto the system. I know that had certain members of the task force flummoxed. In the end Bates had to command them to get on with other assignments." Paige became more animated as she pieced it together.

Maya pursed her lips briefly. "Well it looks like they were on the right track. Bourne? Any way you can track down which of the agents were continuing their investigation... Even if it was off-book, unofficial."

Bourne's voice crackled over the conference room intercom again. "Normally I would say yes, but we do have a slight data problem."

Maya hit her forehead. "Ah, shit. We're still on that system."

She paused, thinking for a moment. "Bourne? What would be the solution to this data issue, now that we don't have Molly to go to the surface so that Oz can connect up? I mean, how do we fix it so that you can have access to all the data that you need when you need it?"

Bourne thought for a moment. "I wonder if maybe a nodal box adapter could possibly give me an ongoing data stream. The problem is it will be traceable…"

"Which is the exact point of the initial design," Paige added, realizing that she was the only one of the three who had been there at the time.

"That's true," agreed Bourne. "But if we can stop this blackout, then I think that's one of the compromises we'll have to make."

Paige hid her head in her hands for a few minutes.

Maya waited patiently, watching.

When she eventually sat up again, she sighed quietly and then looked off into space as if talking to Bourne. "Well then that's exactly what we'll have to do."

Maya breathed a sigh of relief, as if she'd been holding her breath. As if she'd had an opinion on what they might do, but was perhaps too anxious to share it.

"So what exactly does this fix entail?" Paige asked Bourne. "You mentioned a… nodal box adapter? Is this something that might be lying around in Brock's workshop?"

"Possibly," Bourne told them. "Let me find an image or two for you while you make your way down there."

Paige and Maya exchanged a knowing look between them and closed up the screens they had been working on. Once they were clear of the conference room, and likely the majority of listening devices, they spoke in hushed whispers.

"Did he just tell us what to do?" Maya hissed in astonishment.

"I think maybe he did," Paige agreed dryly, "but in his defense, he was only working to try and make us more efficient. We are up against it…"

Maya narrowed her eyes and exhaled heavily. "Well... If it carries on..."

Paige chuckled, linking her friend's arm as they hurried down the side of the hangar deck. "Don't worry. When the others return, I'm pretty certain he'll be put in his place!"

Maya smiled at the situation. "End of the frikkin' world and I'm worried about an AI bossing us around."

"I know, right? Maybe we do deserve to have them in charge!"

They clipped and clopped up the stairs and eventually arrived at Brock's workshop via the Daemon corridor.

"So, you got something for us, Bourne? So we know what we're looking for?" Paige waited, looking up at the ceiling as if she might be able to see Bourne. It was a funny organic habit, and she'd noticed herself and others doing it to talk to Oz. But now, up against the clock with the higher stakes of the situation weighing on her, she noticed how her mind tangled with silly details that were not even relevant to the task in hand.

Bourne took his time to respond, pulling up a set of images over at the main holoconsole on one of the workbenches.

"Yes, here are a few that might help," he told them. The two girls, dressed in atmos suits and high heels, ambled over to the console unit.

Paige flicked through the images. "I have no idea where these might be," she mumbled, dismayed.

Maya zoomed in on one and squinted at the image. "Bourne, does Brock have anything like this in inventory?"

"I've no idea. There's nothing labeled as a nodal box adaptor."

"Well what about anything labeled 'network adaptor'? Or anything that's to do with networks. Can you pull up a list?"

Maya waited as a list populated on a new holoscreen. She stuck her finger into the holoprojection and scrolled down. Paige watched over her shoulder. "I forget you're a techie nerd sometimes."

Maya smiled as she worked. "So do I. That's why I make a

point of helping Brock out every few weeks on a weekend. Keeps my hand in."

Paige grinned. "Yeah. I never understood how you could manage that on a Sunday morning after we'd been out. But I'm grateful for it now!"

Maya selected a few of the components in the inventory and continued scrolling through the list. "Okay, Bourne—let's start with these ones. Can you send their locations to my wrist holo? I'll go look at them. I'll know more once I have them in my hands."

"Sure," Bourne agreed.

Maya headed over to the far wall where normally visitors to the workshop didn't venture.

She waved her hand in front of a motion sensor that Paige hadn't even realized was there. The surface slid up and back, revealing a bank of labeled cabinets that were presumably full of parts. The cover seemed to be made of some kind of carbon polymer, which looked flat and rigid when it was in place but disappeared at the top of the array of boxes into the wall, suggesting it was more flexible than it appeared.

Paige gasped, watching as section by section more and more boxes were revealed.

As if it were old hat, Maya set about checking the section numbers and locating the boxes she wanted to access. Then, she started pulling them out and checking the components that she'd already selected on her wrist holo.

"How long has this been here?" Paige asked in amazement.

Maya muttered to herself as she read off the part numbers, tutting and returning the parts she checked that weren't what she was looking for. "I dunno," she said, in between mumblings. "Brock already had it installed and organized when I got here. Guess he must have done it when you guys first moved in."

Paige looked the units over. They ran from one side of the workshop to the Daemon door. "Well, they certainly weren't here in the beginning. I would have noticed. There was just a load of old junk down here." She glanced upwards, checking the shape of the ceiling. "That bit around there must be where the stage is from the old theater," she mused.

Maya continued to flick through the boxes, seemingly only half listening as Paige continued to talk.

"That toe-rag I used to date said that he'd seen pictures from when the place upstairs was actually a real theater." She sighed, shaking the thought of the painful relationship from her head as quickly as the thought had occurred to her. "Can't have been operating for long though. Not if the Federation installed all this afterwards."

Maya scratched her nose as she inspected another component. "Unless they had it operating as a cover before they moved in?"

Paige sighed. "Yeah. Who knows… I'll be sure to ask someone if we ever get to spend time with them."

She was about to say something like, if they survive this, but stopped herself. The implication hung in the air. Even Maya slowed down, pulling one of the drawers out, as if she was resisting finishing the thought out loud.

"OHHHHH!" Maya exclaimed.

Paige hurried over to the drawer Maya was peering into. "You found it?"

Maya beamed and fished out the component. It was the size of Rubik's Cube. "I think so!" she said brightly, carefully turning it over to check the spec. "Yep. This is it. I hope. Bourne?" She lifted her head to call up to the workshop intercom. "Does the RTX-6767 have a programable CPU?"

"Yes. It does. Want to plug it in to the Z-port and I'll lay down the architecture."

Maya closed the drawer and carried the component over to the console on the main workbench. She found some connecting wires and plugged one into the other.

"Okay, Bourne, do your thing!"

Paige followed Maya back to the console. "Are you sure he's up to this?" she asked as quietly as she could.

Maya pulled her lips to one side. "Guess we'll find out... I mean, he's been on the network when Oz has done this kind of thing for Brock."

Paige took a deep breath. "That fills me with confidence," she said dryly. "Mind, it kinda feels like the Estaria problem has pulled the short straw and elected the B-team all around."

Maya slapped her gently on the arm. "Speak for yourself, lady!" she chided her. "I think this is where we step up and shine. Come on, we've got this!"

Paige bobbed her head in agreement. "Yeah. I guess you're right. Either way, we're on it."

A moment later the console beeped.

"Okay, that's done," Maya confirmed, unhooking the device from the console. "Now to find the other bits we might need." She headed back to the drawers, gathering tools and cables and tiny reels of wire, and various devices that Paige had never seen before in her life.

"No wonder you don't bother with the nail color," she jested as she watched Maya work. "Although Brock's range of ultra-durable colors might stay on amongst all this."

Finally Maya was done packing everything into an over-the-shoulder toolkit bag. "All right, looks like we're ready to rock."

Paige looked at her with a blank expression. "So? What's next?"

Maya smiled at her enigmatically. "Next we get down there and find a node to start making the adaptation so that Bourne can establish a continuous connection."

Paige's face looked concerned. "We've no idea what's going on down there. It could be chaos."

Maya nodded. "There's no other way though. It's our only chance to restore holoconnections planet-wide."

"But what if Molly needs us while we're gone?"

Maya thought for a moment. "Well I could go on my own and you can stay here? If you want?"

Paige shook her head firmly. "No way. I'm not letting you do it on your own. Like I said, we've no idea what's going on down there."

Maya's eyes flickered with a touch of relief. "Okay then, let's get to the pods." She started moving off towards the Daemon door.

"Okay," Paige agreed. "Then I'll just go get some supplies and water from the kitchen and I'll meet you down there."

Maya nodded. "I should probably grab some gear from my room too. And change my shoes into something more… practical. Five minutes?"

"Yeah, five minutes."

Ten minutes later, a pod lifted up from the deserted hangar deck.

Paige fiddled with her holo. It seemed that she couldn't get a call to connect.

"What are you doing?" Maya asked.

"Trying to contact Bates to let her know that we're on the case. I'm sure she's probably aware of the situation…"

"And her team will be working to figure out what's going on."

"Yeah exactly. But if we can share what we know, then maybe we can have this cracked quicker. Except the calls aren't connecting."

"Shit," Maya said, exhaling and sitting back in her seat while the pod whipped out of the hangar door.

"Yeah," Paige agreed grimly. "And it looks like there are lots of patches on Spire that are dark." She tilted her wrist holo so that Maya could see the heat map that Bourne had been keeping up to date for them. "At this rate it will only be a couple of hours before the whole of Spire is on holo darkness."

Maya's gaze moved to the window as she seemed to become lost in the vastness of space ahead of them. "Well we'll just have to get a move on and get this sorted out," she said almost absently.

Erring Memorial Hospital, Estaria

A third year resident loped through the hospital, only coming to a halt once she found the attending on the clock at that point. "Dr. Beck!" she called, waving her hand over her head to get his attention. He paused and turned to face her, though he only walked over once the look on her face made it apparent that it was urgent.

"Jerso," he greeted her cautiously. "What's the problem?"

She launched immediately into an explanation. "The first years keep forgetting to record patient data in a datapad," she explained. "The second years and third years are trying to keep them on the ball, but there are only so many of us. We're going to have a lawsuit on our hands at this rate."

Beck heaved a sigh and dragged a hand down his face. "Right," he muttered. "Draft a few of the nurses to shadow the first years. I'll make a few calls to see if I can get the transcriptionists to come in and act like scribes for the time being."

Jerso opened her mouth to reply, only to close it again with a click when an alarm went off. She and Beck whipped around as a team ran past with a crash cart.

"What's going on?" Beck demanded, jogging after the team with Jerso just a few paces behind him.

A nurse with the team didn't slow down at all as she started speaking. "Another nurse gave a patient painkillers for a headache. His chart didn't list any other medications. And then the patient coded. She's in there doing CPR. My guess is that the patient was given a new medication before the blackout hit, and before the hardcopies were updated, so it wasn't recorded on his chart in his room."

Beck ground to a halt, reaching out to catch Jerso's arm and jerk her to a stop. The crash team hurried on ahead.

"Jerso. Collect the residents. And anyone else you can find who isn't doing something urgent. This means we need to quiz every patient for any sort of information that doesn't match their charts," Beck instructed.

Jerso paled slightly as the implications caught up with her, and then she turned on her heel and took off at a dead sprint down the hall, making a beeline for the nearest break room.

As much as Beck wanted to help with that, he needed to keep a level head. He turned to head in the opposite direction. He needed to collect workers dedicated to keeping the files updated, or the problem was just going to keep happening.

Senate House, Spire, Estaria

Zenne scowled as his wrist holo refused to activate, before he threw his hands up in exasperation. "Figured we would only be safe here for so long before the blackout hit," he groused to himself before he stalked off to find a hardline connection. The blackout didn't mean the Senate could just fall out of contact with the authorities and the news outlets. Rather the opposite, in fact.

As he stalked past like an angry cat, a pair of interns watched him pass. They shared an anxious look over the stacks of datapads they were ferrying through the halls.

"He's usually the calm one, right?" Sheryl asked, leaning her chin on top of her stack to keep it from wobbling. "If he's losing his temper, then that means it has to be bad, right?"

"We already knew it was bad," Jeremy replied flippantly.

"Well, yeah, but—I mean...*bad* bad," Sheryl replied. "Like...

approaching war," she clarified. "Isn't it common to try to disrupt communication before attacking? So then no one can plan anything effectively."

Jeremy scoffed and started moving again, forcing Sheryl to jog the first few steps to keep pace with him.

"Don't be an idiot," he snapped. "It's just a blackout. Are you going to freak out and say we're all going to war whenever your power goes out, too?"

"This is a global network blackout!" Sheryl insisted sharply. "That's not the sort of thing that just *happens*. Something had to have caused it."

Jeremy groaned and moved as if to drag his hand down his face. He then had to practically juggle his stack so that it wouldn't all go crashing down to the floor. "You're being such a senseless worrywart. It's ridiculous. You're going to give yourself an ulcer."

Sheryl slowed to a halt outside the Speaker of the House's office. "Whatever, Jeremy," she sighed as he kept walking. Hands full, she resorted to tapping her foot against the door to knock on it. "Maybe you're right. Maybe I'm just being paranoid."

Jeremy sniffed dismissively and kept walking. Sheryl pushed the conversation out of her thoughts as the Speaker's secretary opened the door to start sorting through the files she needed. She had her own job to worry about, after all.

CHAPTER EIGHT

Uptarlung. Irk'n Quarter Estaria
It seemed as if every news report sounded the same, Mercy reflected to herself as she offered her usual sign-off to the camera. "This has been Mercy Hazrad of—hey!" She didn't make it to the end of her sign-off as she abruptly took off at as brisk of a run as she could manage in her heels, charging towards the car.

"You get away from there!" she snapped, her cameraman turning to let the camera follow her. If nothing else, it was the perfect way to underscore the report about how desperate some people were getting.

The man trying to wrench the car door open abruptly whirled towards Mercy, fumbling a gun out of his belt. His hands shook as he pointed it at her, and Mercy ground to a halt.

"I need it," he insisted, voice wobbling. "If we're going to have invaders breaking our doors in any day now, I need it."

The camera clattered to the ground as the cameraman dropped it. Lying on its side on the ground, it only just managed to catch the action as the cameraman charged and tackled the carjacker. Mercy shrieked and ducked as the gun went off. It took out one of the car's mirrors.

There was the sound of shuffling from just out of the camera's sight as the cameraman scuffled with the attempted looter and eventually managed to sit on him.

Slowly, Mercy began to straighten back up. Cautiously, she called, "Jack? You alright?"

"I'm good," the cameraman grunted. "You want to call the cops? I'm a little occupied."

"Y-yeah." Mercy swallowed and fumbled for her communicator. "I'll just—"

The screen went black for a split second as the station cut the feed.

For a few seconds, a stock emergency warning scrolled across the screen. When it changed again, it switched over to a frazzled young man holding a handheld manual camera out at arm's length. He looked as if he was severely regretting every decision he had ever made that led him to his career and his current situation. It took him a few seconds to realize he should probably be speaking.

"Ah—" He cleared his throat, and the footage began to jitter slightly as he started jogging. "This is Corey Zerin, of IQ News. We apologize for the interruption. Normally I'm a weatherman, but I have a camera and I'm not in the field, so—"

He paused, looking over his shoulder as an alarm started to go off and light began to reflect off of the side of a building. He swallowed as he faced the camera again.

"Um—If I had to guess, a looter has tripped a silent alarm. Some businesses—if they haven't upgraded their alarm systems recently—have alarms that stayed active—*shit*." He cut himself off emphatically and ducked into an alley between two buildings as the looter sprinted past, arms laden with stolen goods. Canned goods and gas; food that didn't need to be cooked and fuel for an antique generator in a house that had gone dark.

Corey stayed in the alley, but he kept his camera on the officer that went sprinting after the thief.

Slowly, Corey turned his camera to his face again. "It's, um..." He cleared his throat and peered out of the alley. Once the coast was clear, he stepped back out and began heading in the direction the thief and officer had come from. "It's become a common occurrence in...light of recent events," he explained haltingly.

He slowed to a halt once he was standing at the scene of the crime. He turned the camera to face the shop front. The door was hanging open, twitching erratically as it tried to slide closed again, but it would only get halfway closed before jerking open again. The glass from the door's paneling was littered across the sidewalk.

Coming from behind the camera, Corey's voice was slightly muffled as he said, "All things considered, this is a mild incident." He turned the camera back around to look into the lens. "We urge you to be careful and to stay safe. If you haven't been quite as impacted by the blackout, reach out to your neighbors who have. If you have to, look to your closest public shelter. If we hold together, we can come out the other side of this in one piece."

He looked sharply to the side when he heard shouting, before he turned his attention back to his camera again. He took a breath and sighed it out.

"This has been Corey Zerin with IQ News. Be safe." He reached towards the camera to turn it off.

The emergency message began scrolling once again a second later.

Downtown Spire, Estaria

A police siren screamed past the end of the alley as Paige and Maya jumped out of the pod. It was early evening in Spire, and a red glow lit the sky above. Normally Paige would think it was romantic and atmospheric, but there was a strange tension that seemed to fill the air like static electricity, and she couldn't seem to shake the feeling of foreboding.

Maya pulled up her wrist holo as the pod door closed gently behind her and then lifted off to a safer place in the upper atmosphere to await its recall.

Paige wrapped her arms around herself against the cold air, shifting the bag on her shoulder awkwardly. "Do we know which way yet?"

Maya shook her head. "Not yet. I think with the holo network going down, the location finder is struggling to orient us."

She ambled down the alley towards the main street to find a street name, her head down, monitoring any changes on the holo map location finder.

Paige ran her gaze up to the top of the buildings that encased them in a temporary anonymity. "Surely there must be a way for us to do this manually..." she posited.

Maya rolled her lips together before biting the lower one on one side. She opened her holoscreen wider and turned it, glancing up for a street name on the side of the nearest building. She sighed in frustration. "Seems no one needs street names in this city anymore," she commented, looking up to the worn, illegible plaque that would have otherwise given them a clue.

Paige shuffled over to view the map with her. "Let's try this way," she suggested, pointing up the street. "The size of that road relative to this one looks like maybe this might lead to where we want to be." She paused and cocked her head. "Or it could be completely the opposite direction... But at least then we've narrowed it down to one of two directions."

Maya smiled. "We need to start somewhere, I guess," she agreed.

The two friends headed off down the street walking hurriedly, heads down, keeping a close eye on their wrist holos to make sure they were going in the right direction.

Suddenly there was a crash and a bang, then the sound of an explosion. From the absence of any fire or visual clues, Maya guessed it was probably a street over.

"What was that?" Paige asked, her pace slowing, leaving Maya to keep striding ahead.

Maya turned back briefly and beckoned for her to hurry up. "Could be anything," she hissed. "Come on, we've got to keep going. It's our only way of stopping this."

Paige hurried to catch up to Maya, and the pair pressed on.

Once they had a rhythm down and Paige was fully caught up, Maya started talking in a low voice so as not to draw attention to them. "I noticed when I was covering stories of riots or protests, when things would get tense, all kinds of natural order would go out of the window. Literally. The first noticeable thing is that people start looting, and shop windows get broken. Basic vandalism. Then they start stockpiling, so there is chaos at fuel stations and gas stores."

She glanced around furtively, keeping an awareness of other people that might be around them and therefore a potential threat. "Never thought I'd see it happening in the capital though." She shook her head. "We have an expectation that because we live in multicultural cities with advanced technology and an eye on interplanetary relations such that they are, that we think that as a group we're beyond such basic primal behaviors. It's almost like people would watch these news reports from the smaller townships on the other side of the planet and think that we are so different." She pressed her lips together grimly.

Paige remained quiet, taking it all in, her mind churning over the new reality that she was experiencing in a city that she had loved so much.

Maya glanced again at her holo. "If we're heading in the right direction, then by my calculations if we turn left at the end of this street, there's going to be one of those junction boxes somewhere on the right. Probably disguised next to the playing field, or something. If there is no playing field there then we've come the wrong way and need to double back."

Paige acknowledged the comment with a quiet grunt and kept walking as fast as they both could.

A crowd was assembling just up ahead of them.

Mostly blue Estarians, they seemed preoccupied with something else, something between them. As they got closer, Paige and Maya could hear shouting. Keeping their heads down, it was difficult to determine what was going on, but intuitively they both knew that they wanted to steer clear.

As they came level with the crowd, it seemed that there was an absence of cars going past, creating a feeling like there was no barrier between them and the angry people. Maya grabbed Paige's arm and pulled her around the corner as soon as they could, leaving the crowd behind them on the other side of the road. As they continued to hurry, Maya kept looking back, making sure that they weren't being followed. Neither one of them wanted to be dragged into something that they didn't have either the time or the guns for.

"There's the playing field," Paige pointed out, her cognitive ability seemingly uncompromised by the danger they were facing in this new environment.

"And there's the junction box," Maya added, nodding discreetly in the direction of a painted metal comms box off to one side, twenty feet from the main building on the property. "We need a way over that fence though," she added, her eyes scanning the length of it for a gate or access point of some sort.

"Is there anything on the map?" Paige asked.

Maya shook her head. "No, only this sports facility building, which has its own carport and everything. I guess we could go through that way, although there is an increased chance of us being stopped if it's not open to the public."

Paige checked the time. "Unlikely at this hour," she said. "Plus if there were a game on, there would be far more cars and people around on this street."

Maya agreed, looking for a lower point in the fence. "Okay, plan B," she announced quietly. Quickly she reached into the backpack Paige was carrying and then zipped it back up again. Keeping her hands low and by her sides so as to disguise what was in her hand, she and Paige crossed the road. They continued to walk for a short way along the side of the fence.

She glanced back to make sure that there was no one around. Then she stopped. "Keep a lookout," she told Paige. "And let me know if anyone's coming."

And with that she bent down and started clipping at the wires of the fence.

Paige, her eyes wide, glanced up and down the street and then parked her back against the fence to maintain a better view of both directions. "How did you know that it wasn't secured? That there wasn't a force field or anything?"

Maya suddenly stopped and looked up at her friend. "Oh," she said simply, a glimmer of humor flicking across her otherwise serious face. "I hadn't thought of that," she confessed, relaxing into a cheeky snigger.

Paige started to chuckle too. "I guess all this time on Gaitune has got you out of practice!" she noted.

Maya agreed. "Yeah, when I was working down here and always doing stupid shit for a story, risking everything just for a piece of evidence to bring some scumbag to justice."

Paige narrowed her eyes as she watched Maya work. "And how many times did you get caught?"

Maya shrugged. "Once or twice, I guess. But one time I had leverage over the person who caught me, and the other time my story ended up eclipsing their misdemeanor and I got away with a slap on the wrist." She paused, wire clippers in hand, as if remembering. "Actually the detective who arrested me seemed really sympathetic to the story I was chasing, and probably bent the official line so as to not charge me for anything."

She finished clipping at the fence and pushed the wire inwards so as to create a small door that they could crawl through. "After you," she said, waving for Paige to crawl through ahead of her.

"Takk Fyrir," Paige cooed as she squatted down and then crawled through onto the grass beyond.

Moments later the pair were both through and Maya was replacing the fencing that she had bent so that it wasn't obvious that there was a gap. Paige started ambling towards the junction box and carefully unlatched the door to get it open and ready for Maya to perform her miracle.

"I've no idea what I'm even looking at," Paige muttered, her eyes scanning the array of switches and network cables and various devices all laid out in the panel in front of her.

Maya joined her, pulling up her wrist holo. "Okay, so Bourne said we needed to put this nodal adapter in parallel with the main node of this part of the network. He drew me a diagram." Maya took a moment flicking between the diagram on her screen and the array of chaos in front of her.

Paige noticed her squinting. "Here, let me help," she said, opening up a bright holoscreen to illuminate the panel.

Maya started working pulling at cables and arranging things before she started putting together connections and making the adjustments needed. "Thank goodness the holos are opening at least," she mentioned. "Maybe you should see if you can get a call through to Director Bates now. If she is in a better area and her holo is connecting now, you might have a chance…"

"Ah, good thinking!" Paige exclaimed, pulling up a secondary screen to make the call as Maya continued to work. Again though, the screen remained dark. "Nope, it's not working."

"Okay, let me just do this and then you can try again," Maya muttered, connecting the device that they brought from Brock's lab. Paige watched in amazement as Maya worked.

Finally, Maya flicked another switch and pulled up a new holoscreen. "Bourne? Bourne? Are you there?"

Bourne's voice sounded in both of their earpieces. "I am indeed. Congratulations, you've established a connection. Stay on the line for a few minutes while I reformat the datastream that Oz already had here. I suspect he has some private servers where he collects the data before uploading it to Gaitune. Once I have found those, I'll be able to start using the processing power over there to do the analysis that we need to perform."

"Okay great," Maya agreed. She turned to Paige. "Wanna try that call to Director Bates again now?"

Paige pulled up a holoscreen again, and this time the call connected.

Director Bates answered. "Hello?"

"Director Bates, this is Paige and Maya from Gaitune. We're on the surface, and we're working to try and restore the holo connection."

"Oh, thank goodness," Carol Bates exclaimed, genuine relief in her voice. "You have no idea of the problems it's causing. I've got my best agents trying to pinpoint the problem and unravel the hack, but we're essentially flying blind and most of our holoconnections have been dead all day."

"We've got one of our guys on it," Paige explained, "but we could do with your help on something else in the meantime."

"Of course, anything I can do, given we don't have proper connection at the office." Just then Paige heard chatter and a police siren in the background, suggesting that Bates wasn't even at the office at that point.

"We think that Jennifer Etang was involved in this hack," Paige explained slowly and clearly over the audio connection.

"But she's in prison," Bates responded.

"Yes, but before she went to prison she uploaded something onto the network, remember?"

"I do. Unfortunately. I've only just managed to get two of my best agents to stop investigating what she did. The patch, whatever it was, didn't leave any trace that my best people could find. But there was something about it that they just couldn't leave alone…"

"And quite rightly so, it seems now," Paige confirmed. "We think that it was sleeping, dormant after it established itself at key points in the network, and that all this time it's been waiting to be activated."

"By the Northern Clan?"

"Exactly…"

"So what do you need?"

"Well, Etang took over from someone else. So we knew that position was key. But there was someone else who you managed to keep alive, wasn't there? Someone else that you had intel suggesting was at risk because of his position."

"Yes, that's right. Suedermann was the name, if I remember correctly."

"Okay, well Maya and I need to talk to him. He probably knows something about this virus, which would make him a target. He knows something that would make it prudent for them to try and take him out. If we can find out what it is that he knows, then we might have a better chance at stopping this blackout."

There was a brief pause on the line as Carol absorbed the information. "I understand," she confirmed. "He's in a safe house somewhere. Even I don't have the address. But if you give me a little bit of time, I can find out where it is and send it over our secure server."

"Sounds like a plan. We'll go straight to the safe house from here, but we can also do with someone talking to Jennifer Etang."

"I can have one of the agents do that, and then meet you at the safe house."

"Excellent," Paige replied, watching Maya nod her agreement. "We'll meet your agent there."

"Good. It will be Alisha Montella."

"Super. Thank you, Director. We'll be in touch as soon as we hear anything more."

"Oh, just one more thing before you go…" the Director added.

"Yes?"

"Molly. I'm assuming she's knee-deep in trying to stop the fleet from advancing…"

"That's correct," Paige confirmed, not wanting to give away too many details, not least because it was her mother she was talking to.

"Is she in harm's way?"

Paige hesitated, looking at Maya to help her make a decision as to whether to disclose what they knew or not. Maya merely widened her eyes in sympathy as to the difficulty of the situation that Paige was suddenly in.

"She, er…is with the best people, the best crew, who have all got her back. She's doing what she believes in. You would be proud of her," she added.

"That means she is in danger," Carol confirmed, the life in her voice now absent. "It's okay, Paige, I understand your position. I've been there many times myself. Thank you for telling me the truth."

"Of course, Director," she answered. "I'll be in touch when I hear anything else. Rest assured."

"Thank you, Paige. And good luck."

The call disconnected.

Paige and Maya exchanged a glance before Maya started packing up the tools and pieces of wire that she cut out of the network junction box. "I guess we should get moving," Maya said, glancing towards the street. "The light's failing and I don't wanna be on the streets when it gets completely dark."

Paige agreed and the two of them finished packing up the tools as quickly as they could before retracing their steps out of the playing field arena and back onto the streets to the nearest alley where they could call their pod down discreetly.

While they were waiting for the pod, Bourne interrupted their musings. "Hey both, I've established a connection with Oz's servers, which means that at least I have increased the probability of being able to communicate with you while you're on the surface to about ninety percent. Additionally, I now have access to the processing power and the constant stream of data in order to assess the situation, the points of origin, and hopefully in a few hours, fighting the virus that has knocked out the holonodes."

"Great, that's good news," Paige told him, trying to sound as optimistic and encouraging as she could given the post-apocalyptic feel in the alleyway.

"Keep us posted," Maya added. "You can see the address that Bates has sent us, on the server, right?"

"I can. And I can track your pod too, now. I'll be in touch. Bourne, out."

The pod arrived, elegantly dropping down the final few feet and opening its front panel at the same time. The two strangers to this deteriorating city hopped in, and the pod disappeared up into the dusty darkness beyond the tops of the buildings.

Without looking up, Carol pulled up a second holoscreen and connected a call with Alisha.

"Hello?" Alisha answered, sounding slightly surprised to receive a holocall while there was so much network instability.

"Agent Montella, I have a small task for you…" the Director told her, wiping a spot of mocha off the saucer of her drink with her napkin.

The conversation lasted less than twenty seconds. When she was done, she closed up her holo and paid the restaurant bill. In the time that she had been there, daylight had turned to dusk, and dusk to dark.

Carol stepped out of the restaurant, zipping her atmos suit up and closing her chest off to the elements. There was a brisk wind in the street that carried the dust of the planet with it.

She was about to turn up the street back to her car when shouting and a smashing of bottles caused her to turn around quickly. She saw a couple of young males running in her direction and stood back out of the way, keeping eyes down so as not to draw their attention. Once they had moved past her, she pulled herself together. Head down, she started again, now striding in the direction of her car.

She shook her head to herself as she walked. *The things I do for this task force,* she muttered, chastising herself for leaving the comfort and security of her office in order to get a holoconnection.

Spire Penitentiary, Spire, Estaria

Maybe it was petty to focus on the aesthetics of being a prisoner. Nevertheless, while Jennifer was alone in the room—cold and sterile as it was, with just a small table and two chairs—it left her with little else to do but to look at her reflection in the two-way mirror.

She noticed the jumpsuit made her look like a character for toddlers, considering how garish the orange was compared to the blue of her skin. She didn't even have the supplies to do anything decent with her hair.

She averted her eyes from the mirror and allowed her gaze to bore into the table.

She hardly even moved when the door opened, revealing a female Estarian visitor. The security officer stationed outside the room stated authoritatively, "We'll be on hand in case anything goes wrong. The door will be locked while you're in there, however."

"I'm sure I'll be fine," the visitor assured him, smiling politely as she stepped into the room. As soon as she cleared the doorway, the door slid closed behind her.

She crossed the floor and sat down in the unoccupied chair across from Jennifer. Then, folding her hands on the table, she simply regarded Jennifer in silence for a few moments. Jennifer remained stubbornly silent, continuing to stare at the mirror just past Alisha's shoulder.

Alisha reached into her pack and pulled out a manual recorder. She fussed with a few buttons on it for a second before she set it down on the table. Jennifer eyed it in quiet bemusement.

"Haven't I talked to enough of you people?" Jennifer wondered finally, tapping one foot on the floor. "How many times am I going to have to do this?"

"As many times as it takes for us to be satisfied that you have no more information to offer us," Alisha answered plainly. She shifted in her seat to get more comfortable, as if she were simply sitting at her own kitchen table.

"What do you want *now*?" the pretty inmate groaned, exasperated already. "What else is there to talk about? I'm pretty sure we've covered all of it already. Or are you just that desperate for any scrap of information you can get?" Her eyebrows rose, and she schooled her expression into something earnest. "It's okay, you can just admit you're coming up empty-handed."

Alisha regarded her passively for a moment before she simply shook her head slightly and moved on. "There's still more we would all like to know about your connection to the Northern Clan." Her expression turned expectant. "If you're so eager for us to be finished, then just cooperate and tell me what I want to know. It's as simple as that."

"That again?" Jennifer groused. "Like I said, we've *been over this,*" she insisted firmly. "What's all that about the definition of insanity and trying things over again?"

Jennifer huffed out an impatient sigh and sagged back in her chair, her arms folded over her chest. "You could just read the transcripts," she pointed out petulantly. "Unless those disappeared into the same black hole my hearing disappeared into." She snorted bitterly. "It's been, what, three months? Oooh, I got arrested, and all I got was the Road Cone Chic wardrobe! I can see the T-shirt opportunities already."

Alisha clicked her tongue. "The media's in enough of an uproar—you saw to that. We weren't going to give them anything else to hyper-focus on."

Jennifer rolled her eyes so emphatically that she tilted her head with the motion. "Uh-huh," she deadpanned. "You could still just read the transcripts. You're not asking me anything I haven't already been asked."

"I have read the transcripts," Alisha replied. "I'm just not sure how much stock I put in them. After all, in the transcripts you're rather insistent about how you don't know what the upload was for."

"Gee, it's almost like I *don't know what it was for,*" Jennifer drawled, drumming her fingers on the table.

Alisha arched one eyebrow, plainly unimpressed. "So everything you've done, you've had no idea of what you were actually doing?"

"It's not like they told me every single detail of it," Jennifer muttered sullenly. "They told me what they wanted me to know."

"With a healthy dose of what you wanted to hear on the side," Alisha added flatly.

"Probably," Jennifer replied, eyes narrowing in irritation. "But why are you focusing so much on *me?*" she demanded finally. "It's not like I'm at the top of this pyramid."

"No?" Alisha asked, feigning surprise. "And yet you were instrumental in their plans. And you didn't even *know.*" Her gaze drifted up and to the side in thought, and she clicked her tongue. "That might actually be worse," she mused. "I'm not sure. I'll need to think about it."

Jennifer heaved an impatient sigh. "What are you getting at?"

"Do you even know what's been going on?" Alisha asked sharply. "Do you have any idea what your actions have actually led to?"

Jennifer's eyebrows rose slowly, and she lifted her hands to gesture around. "It's not like I get to shoot the shit with anyone," she pointed out. "It hasn't really been a priority to keep me in the loop."

"The world is falling apart," Alisha informed her. "The holo network has gone dark from one corner of Estaria to the other. The space fleet has been launched and is courting galactic war. Martial law has been declared, and we've lost track of how much of the population has gone completely dark with the network blackout." Her eyes narrowed. "And you didn't even know what you were doing. Someone told you what you wanted to hear and you did what he asked without even knowing what he was asking you to do."

"It's not like I asked for all of this to happen!" Jennifer burst out, curling her hands around the sides of her chair until her knuckles blanched.

"You sure as hell made it easy for them to do it, though!" Alisha shot to her feet, hands slamming down on the table as she leaned halfway across it. Jennifer shrank back into her seat.

The air thrummed with tension for a few seconds. Slowly, Alisha lowered herself back into her seat.

Her voice was low as she stated, "Millions of people could very well be about to die if we wind up with a war on our hands. *You* helped goad that into happening. Maybe we don't know each other, but you don't strike me as a murderer. A bit too enamored with the limelight, maybe, but not a mass murderer." She leaned her elbows on the table and linked her fingers together, so she could lean her chin on the back of her knuckles. "So, how are you going to prove that you aren't a mass murderer?"

Jennifer seemed to shrink as Alisha spoke. She stared off at a corner of the room and picked at one of her nails until the cuticles frayed and bled. "I didn't actually know what the upload was going to do," she stated eventually, her voice low and listless. "I swear, I didn't. I didn't know what was going to happen."

"What were you expecting, then?" Alisha asked sharply. "The population was turning into a writhing mosh pit before the fleet was even launched, in no small part because of your actions."

Jennifer shrugged one shoulder halfheartedly. "Fame, mostly. I wanted to be known. Or at least for my work to be known. Some sort of mark on the world, you know?" She scrubbed her hand off on her pants and folded her arms again to stop picking at her nails. "I didn't know what the upload was going to do," she repeated. "But yeah, it seems like the sort of thing they would want to happen. It would suit their purposes well enough."

She didn't bother to elaborate on what those purposes were, but Alisha supposed it had become rather apparent in its own time even without an explanation.

Slowly, Alisha sighed. She was fairly sure she wasn't going to get anything else out of her. Or at least nothing else relevant. "Is there anything else you can tell me?"

Jennifer was quiet for a moment before she offered simply, "Just be careful. The Northern Clan has people everywhere, and you're never going to find someone who knows every single other person being bankrolled." She fell silent after that, staring at a point on the far wall again.

Alisha waited a few seconds to make sure she wasn't going to say anything else, and then got to her feet. Her chair creaked as it slid away from the table. "Thank you. I'll make a note of it." She turned off her recorder and put it back into her pack.

She made her way to the door and pressed the button for the

intercom. It buzzed slightly, and she said into the speaker, "I'm done here."

The door clicked as it unlocked, and it slid open to reveal a security officer standing outside. He stepped aside to let Alisha through before stepping into the room to escort Jennifer back to her cell.

CHAPTER NINE

"We have a silent alarm at a department store just off of Helix and Crest."
"On it. I'm twelve minutes out."
"That long?"
"Everyone closer is on more urgent leads."

"This is dispatch. We need a unit in Belladonne Square. An attempted carjacker. Armed, but restrained."
"Any injuries?"
"Not that anyone mentioned."
"I'm on the way."

"Fire in Westlake, at 1219. Electrical."
"We've got a truck and an ambulance inbound. Isn't Westlake a blackout zone?"

"Someone was trying to get a network-connected heating system working."

"Ah, shit. Again?"

"You know what people are like."

"Looting party and possible violence in the Citrine Quarter. At least a dozen people."

"I'm on it."

"Ideally, someone closer could respond."

"I'm all you've got; everyone closer is already busy."

"I've got a child alone in Sheer Court. It's a blackout zone. Parents left to get food, said they'd be back in an hour. They haven't returned and it's been three. Who's the closest available unit? ...Anyone?"

"Ah, shit. I'm headed towards a looting case. I'll divert to Sheer Court instead."

"Break-in in the Quartz District. Someone from a blackout zone busting down the door into a house that was still lit up."

"Still there?"

"Apparently he scampered when threatened with a large stick."

"Any injuries?"

"No injuries, just a few things stolen."

"Then they're going to have to wait. I've got to prioritize here."

"Understood."

"We've got an officer down. We have an armed robbery-turned-shootout in a residential area. Three civilians wounded so far. We need backup."

"You're going to have to hold out for as long as you can. There's no one else in the area right now."

"You have got to be shitting me!"

Spire Police Precinct, Spire, Estaria

Kelsey Mazo's voice was as calm and assured as ever as she said, "An available unit has been diverted to your position, but they're still a ways out. All closer units are already engaged in equally critical situations." Her hands shook and she clenched them into fists on top of her desk to get them to stop.

The monitor in front of her was just a bit too old for the software that had been hastily installed on it to let her track where various units were. She had to refresh it every few seconds to get it to update when positions changed and to keep it from spontaneously losing track of various units. Even so, it worked well enough that the department was still functional.

"*Tell them to step on it!*" the officer barked. A moment later, she could hear him again, his voice softer and gentler and far away from his communicator as he assured one of the civilians, "*Everything is under control. Help is on the way, and we'll be out of here soon. Alright? Here, you can hold my hand.*"

Kelsey refreshed the program, once, twice, three times in a row. She knew it was working—as best as it was going to work, at any rate—and none of the more conveniently located units were available.

She dragged her hands down her face, very nearly dislodging her headset as she did. Even so, there was no change in her tone as she said, "I understand that this isn't ideal, sir, but nothing about any of this is ideal and I'm working as best as I can with the resources available to me. Has the situation changed at all?"

She could hear the officer muttering to himself, though she

couldn't make out the words. And then she heard a shot go off and she recoiled from her desk. She reached up with one hand, curling it around the side of her headset as if that would make any sort of difference.

"Sir! Has the situation changed at all?" she repeated, her voice pitching upwards with urgency. She refreshed the program again and mentally went over all of the closer units, trying to decide if she could feasibly divert any of them. But there were lives on the line for all of them. She clenched one hand around the edge of her desk so tightly she swore her nails cracked.

"Pretty sure it was a warning shot," the officer replied. *"Gunman seems a bit queasy with all these bleeding people. Not sure he actually planned on everything going as far as it did."*

"Is there any way you can talk him down?" Kelsey asked, her voice returning to its usual level.

"He's more of a 'twitchy, unstable' sort of queasy, not a 'oh god what am I doing' sort of queasy," the officer answered flatly.

Kelsey's gut clenched. "I understand, sir. As I said, assistance is en route."

"I just need to sit on the live wire for a while longer, yeah, I know," the officer grumbled in reply. *"I got it."*

"I'm doing everything I can, sir." Kelsey refreshed the program again. No one closer was available yet.

She refreshed it a few more times, each time worrying silently that it would finally crash and she would lose precious moments while she rebooted the system.

Down the hall in the bullpen, a handful of detectives listened in on the entire conversation. They were shameless as they eavesdropped.

Detective Indius stared down at the datapad in her hands, though she couldn't say she was really seeing it. Most of her attention was on the dispatcher's voice drifting down the hall. Around her, three other detectives spoke in hushed voices. Finally, one of them got to her feet.

It was Detective Lewin—a scrappy young officer with more get up and go than most of her colleagues put together.

"I'll go help with the shootout," she bit out, turning and storming from the room. It wasn't her line of work—it wasn't any of theirs—but everyone needed to work outside the box at that point.

Down the hall, without missing a beat, Kelsey calmly stated into her headset, "Detective Lewin is on the way to your position now." Knowing the detectives in the bullpen were listening in still, she added, "Twelve minutes out."

They could hear Lewin break into a sprint in the hallway. If she gunned it once she was in the car, she could just make it in twelve minutes. Knowing the way she drove, she would probably make it in nine.

Even after that, nothing seemed calmer. Everything still felt as if it was balanced on the edge of a tightrope, like the air itself was vibrating and waiting to snap.

The other two detectives, one of their partners, and an intern all clustered around a pair of smart boards, organizing what few resources the department had and messaging back and forth with dispatch down the hall. Most of the department's files had been properly backed up and archived, but no one was perfect, and there were still a few case files that needed holes filled in from memory too. Even so, they had still fared better than at least a couple of the other stations in the city.

Indius didn't envy any of them for being in that position, but nor did she offer to help them. They weren't her cases, and she would get in the way more than she would help. She looked back down at her datapad, watching as news reports scrolled across it, while simultaneously doing what she could on her own case files.

Rogers leaned against the edge of Indius's desk, the only Ogg in a room of Estarians. Indius glanced up at him as she wondered wryly, "Having any second thoughts about not heading back to Ogg?"

Rogers's expression went distant as he made a show of thinking the question over, only to settle on a simple, "Nah. I like the excitement." He grinned crookedly. "Besides, someone needs to keep your head above water. May as well be me."

Indius rolled her eyes, but she didn't protest. Most of her attention was already back down the hall with the dispatcher. Listening and waiting for anything that she might be able to help with.

"Hey, Chaakwa," Rogers probed after a moment, voice low so as not to disturb the group clustered around the smart boards.

"Antonio?" she wondered in reply.

"You think all that stuff about it being an invasion is true?" he wondered, drumming his fingers against the edge of Indius's desk. "I mean, most of the population seems to believe it by now. Some of the evidence is pretty damn compelling."

Indius was quiet at first, rather than simply spitting out an answer.

("The EMTs are on their way, miss," Kelsey said down the hall, voice calm and soothing. "I'll stay on the line with you until they arrive. You just have to stay calm. Can you do that for me?")

Finally, Indius drew in a slow breath and sighed it out through her nose. "I'm not sure," she answered honestly.

"What do we do if it is?" Rogers asked, tapping one heel against the floor. "Just let it run its course?"

"I'm not sure," Indius repeated, shrugging one shoulder. "It could be an invasion, or at least the earliest stages of one. Or it could be something entirely different. But if it is an invasion?"

Finally, she looked at Rogers, and she could feel a small smile beginning to tug at the corners of her lips. "If it *is* an invasion, then I feel sorry for the invaders. Hell or high water, I know someone who won't let anything happen to this planet."

Undisclosed Location, Estaria

Goran Suedermann pulled aside the off-white net curtain just enough to see that there was movement down the side of one of the other buildings.

"Hey, what did we say about the window?" The voice compelled him to drop the fabric and shuffle back a foot, out of view of the window.

"I'm just looking," Suedermann responded without any kind of angst. He waited for a few more moments and then ambled back across the room and sat down on the gray, saggy sofa. "I'm sure I saw movement over by the repair shop." He sighed, taking a sip of his tea.

Joshua checked his holo for the time and then leaned his arm back against the butt of his gun on his waist belt. "There shouldn't be anything going on in the repair shop this time," he agreed. "When Alisha gets here, I'll check it out though. Just don't go near the windows for me, okay?"

He heaved himself up out of the old uncomfortable chair and headed into the kitchen, stretching his arms above his head.

"Someone coming this way," Suedermann called out to him.

Joshua was suddenly alert, striding back across the crusty old living room to the door, his weapon already drawn. He pressed his shoulder against the door, pointing his weapon at the floor as he glanced through the spy hole.

It was difficult to see in the dark, but there were definitely two figures heading his way. This was the last thing he needed: a threat to his witness.

As they drew closer, he could see that one was distinctly Estarian, and the other human. He searched his mind trying to think who they might be. Subconsciously he flicked through all the case files that might be related to the Northern Clan, the known associates, and anyone who might know who Suedermann was, even from Suedermann's own life before the Task Force took him into protective custody.

Then he realized they were both female.

He was drawing a complete blank. On top of that, he noticed, the two women seemed somewhat vulnerable as they scuttled across the big open space towards the safe house door. In terms of a threat assessment, they didn't look particularly aggressive or competent. What's more, without hesitating they came up the steps and onto the porch. Both of them. If they were wanting to storm the place, one would have gone around the back.

His mind raced.

Then the security light came on, almost blinding him. He looked away back into the room.

Tap, tap, tap.

The human knocked on the door. He looked back and gave his eyes a second to adjust to the brightness. He could make out more details now. Though her form looked human, her skin color was definitely Estarian blue. It was a strange combination that confused him even more.

"Greetings of the day," he called politely through the door so as not to be conspicuous in case this event was purely random.

"Greetings," the human-looking Estarian called back. "You don't know us, but we've just been talking to Director Bates. We're working on the holoconnection issue, but we need to talk to your colleague in there."

"It's just me here," Joshua lied, trying to assess the situation.

"Your witness rather," the girl insisted.

Joshua paused. Director Bates *may* have been talking to them, but he had no way of knowing. The last communication that he had had from her had been earlier that day, and he had even been able to get a message back out to her. His strategy up until this point had been to wait for his partner to come and relieve him at the pre-appointed time.

"We're also meant to be meeting Alisha here," the girl added, instantly bolstering her credibility.

He paused, and then after a few seconds of mental analysis, Joshua moved to unlock the door. Cautiously he opened it, and then beckoned the two inside. Keeping his weapon low, he notably didn't put it away. "Okay, so you seem to know a little bit about what's going on here, but who the hell are you?"

"I'm Paige," the human-looking one explained, "and this is Maya. We work closely with Molly and the Sanguine Squadron."

Joshua felt himself relaxing the moment he realized they were friendly. Then as soon as it sunk in that he was talking to people he'd heard stories about since he was at Molly's grad school, a different type of anxiety set in. "Oh, well of course, do come in... Please." He put his gun away hurriedly and set about feebly tidying the place up a little bit.

"Please take a seat, make yourself comfortable. I must say I wasn't expecting... Well, anyone. We've been in holo blackout most of the day."

"We know," Maya told him. "We're working to try and restore connection planet-wide. But we could do with understanding a little bit more about what's happened." She glanced at Goran sitting quietly on the sofa. "But we thought that Mr. Suedermann might be of assistance in that regard."

Goran pressed his index finger at his chest. "Me? How can I help? They're just network outages."

"Well," Maya continued, "how much do you know about why you're here?"

Goran shrugged. "Only what these guys told me..." he replied, thumbing at Joshua as the representative of the Task Force who had taken his freedom from him "for his own good."

"Which is?" Maya pressed.

"That because of my position in the government, someone wanted me dead. Probably for access, for my successor."

Paige looked up at Joshua, who seemed mesmerized by the conversation in front of him. "We're going to need to tell him a little bit more," she explained. "If we are right, he's the only one who's going to be able to help us undo this mess."

Joshua waved her on.

Paige sat on the sofa next to Goran and started explaining everything that they knew. Meanwhile Maya took Joshua into the kitchen to fill him in on the bigger picture while he made some mocha for all of them.

"So you spoke to Director Bates then?" he asked.

"Yes, less than an hour ago," Maya confirmed. "She gave us your location, but also said she was sending Alisha over to talk to Jennifer Etang."

"Etang? Why would Alisha be going to see her?"

"Well, this is kind of the point," Maya explained slowly. "We think that this holo blackout is a result of a Trojan horse that's been sitting waiting to be activated in order to further the interests of the Northern Clan. If you look at the circumstances: the fleet, the vote, and so on, it all makes sense. And they got what they wanted... Martial Law."

Joshua's normally bright blue complexion was looking particularly pasty as the blood drained from his face. "You mean this *is* an all-out conspiracy?"

"Well, yeah. The point is, Etang might have information about the virus. The construction, how it deploys, who built it. Something... We're hoping."

Joshua pumped his fist in a half movement. "I knew it!" he declared. "Alisha and I were right! Suck it, Bates!" Then, noticing Maya's reaction as she stood watching him, he quickly regained his composure and handed her the first mocha that was ready. "Well if there's anything to discover, Alisha will find it. In the meantime I guess we just need to hang tight and wait for her."

Maya cocked her head, smiling enigmatically. "Well not entirely. We need to see what Suedermann knows, and we have one of our guys working on a fix as we speak, so we will make some progress before she gets here."

Joshua's expression brightened. "Oh, well then." He grinned. "Let's get this second mocha into Paige's hands and you guys can carry on."

Maya grinned as she followed him back through to the living room where Paige and Goran were talking.

"We don't have all of the details of this case, because of the blackout," Paige was explaining to Suedermann. "Would you mind telling us what you did at the Division of Holo Crimes?"

Suedermann leaned forward and nudged his teacup further onto the table before sitting back and exhaling with a small sigh. "Well, it's been a while now, but I was overseeing the network security. Some of it was to do with scams, but a lot of it was chasing down malware for the most part."

"So it was more like stopping viruses from proliferating?"

"Yes, that was a big part of it."

Paige looked pointedly at Maya. "Well that would explain why someone would want you out of the way before this kicked in," Paige commented.

Maya stepped further into the room and handed Paige the mocha that Joshua just made for her. "Yes, but what I don't understand is why him. He's just one person who would be replaced... Who has been replaced, right?"

She looked over at Joshua.

Joshua handed her the mocha that he'd made for her. "Yes, we thought of that. There was someone who would probably have succeeded him had he been assassinated, and we assumed that that person was... *compromised*."

"Tell me that person is not standing in for him now!"

"Well we had to put up a fight," Joshua explained. "But no. We have someone else performing that role while Suedermann is here."

"But," Suedermann interjected, "what he's not telling you is the difference in skill. This other compromised person was the only one who had the same level of skill and experience to do the job. Effectively, the person that they have now is merely a figurehead, with very little practical experience in how to handle a crisis like this... It's probably why we are still having blackouts."

Maya suddenly became more curious. "So they wanted you out of the way so you couldn't fix this problem," she deduced, her expression becoming more animated.

"Well, I don't mean to toot my own horn or anything, but I'd say yes."

Paige put her mocha cup on the table in front of them. "Well in that case, you're exactly the person we need to talk to," she said, pulling up a holoconnection.

"Bourne? Are you there?" she called out to her holo.

"Yes, I'm here," he responded in her earpiece.

"Okay, I'm gonna put you on speaker," Paige told him. "We've located someone who can probably help us solve this problem, and I think you two need to talk."

Joshua, a touch overwhelmed by the sudden change of pace of things in the safe house, headed back into the kitchen to make himself a mocha. Something told him that this was going to be a long night.

Several mocha refills after the initial brews that Joshua had brought through, Maya, Paige, Bourne, and Goran were still deep in conversation.

"It looks like this could be an elegant solution," Bourne was saying.

Goran agreed. "Yes, and it's much faster than the brute force hack you were having to perform in the first place."

"Well, it wasn't entirely brute force," Bourne protested defensively.

Paige smiled and rolled her eyes, communicating to Joshua her opinions on Bourne's ego and sensitivity. "It looks like we've got a fix in any case. Bourne, any idea on how long it's going to take to run this fix network-wide?"

"I've no idea. The planet's network is humongous, and some

of the networks in the further regions away from the cities are going to run slower. Personal holos probably need specific adaptations to the fix because they are running older protocols."

"But you can start with Spire for instance," Maya interjected.

"Yes," Bourne agreed. "I can do that. And then go to the next cities, and move out from there."

"So how long until Spire is back online?" Paige asked, seemingly remembering why they were trying to solve this problem in the first place.

"It depends."

It was Goran's turn to roll his eyes this time. "Developers!" he mouthed to the others, assuming that it was an organic they'd been communicating with all this time.

Paige screwed up her face and started massaging around her eyes with her hands. "What about us being able to get some messages through to people in the blackout? So rather than just restoring full service, can we at least get messages through, kind of like what you're doing with us now?"

There was pause on the line. "Yes, and it will only take a tiny amount of processing power away from solving the bigger issue, comparatively speaking."

"Maybe that's a way forward then," Paige suggested, looking at Maya for her agreement. Maya nodded.

"Okay great," Paige confirmed. "Let's do it. Maya will put together a message, something short. Then Bourne, you can send it out first perhaps."

"Alrighty then," Goran declared, slapping his hands to his knees and then getting up off the uncomfortable sofa. "If you'd be more comfortable, we could move through to the office..."

Paige and Maya got up. "Okay, yes. It would be easier to work at a desk," Paige agreed.

"Hey, you know, Alisha should probably be back by now," Joshua told them, checking the time as they moved their holoscreens through to the next room.

Paige thought for a moment. "Hey Bourne, can you make sure that Joshua can get a connection through, so he can check in with the task force, and with Alisha?"

"Yes, one second. Okay, there you go, Joshua. You should be able to get through to the network now."

Joshua's face lit up as he checked his holo and saw that everything was working perfectly. "Great, thank you, Bourne. I'll give her a call now."

CHAPTER TEN

Safe House, Undisclosed Location, Estaria
Joshua looked up from his partially functioning wrist holo as the main door opened and Alisha breezed through. The door slid closed again immediately, and the complicated lock clicked a few times as it reengaged. Alisha sagged back against the door, letting her head thump back against it. She looked like she was putting some serious thought into just sliding down it and sitting down right there on the floor.

"Long day?" he asked wryly. She poked the tip of her tongue out at him.

"I just got finished with that Etang woman, from Communications." She sighed, pushing herself away from the door with a visible effort. "Our hopes that she was just playing dumb have been dashed," she added. "She didn't know a thing. Less than nothing, in fact. I had to fill her in on everything that's been going on in the world."

Joshua whistled low. "An astounding level of 'out of the loop,' to be sure."

"She almost seemed like she was impressed by everything that's been going on," Alisha grumbled. "And honestly, I'm not sure if her being a clueless biddy makes me feel better or worse. I mean, really, who just decides 'oh, sure, I'll do exactly what this guy says with no idea of what I'm actually doing?' In what world is that a normal thing?"

"In the world of Jennifer Etang, apparently," Joshua replied reasonably, and he ducked to the side to avoid the swat that Alisha aimed at his ear. "You asked!" he protested, laughing. He only laughed harder when she scowled at him, her nose scrunching and her eyebrows drawing downwards.

"It just doesn't make any sense," she grumbled, before she heaved a sigh and slumped backwards. She was practically lying on the table by then, propping herself up on her elbows. "But I guess it wasn't a complete bust." She sighed, letting her head fall back weightlessly.

"She confirmed some things we already suspected, though, so it's something, at least," she continued. "She was in the Northern Clan's pocket, which is large and seemingly never ending. Apparently we'll never find everyone working for them, blah blah blah, all your bases belong to us, you know how it goes."

"Spooky," Joshua deadpanned, propping his chin up in one hand. With a wistful sigh, he mused, "Maybe all the secrecy is because there are actually only like ten of them. Maybe we could actually take all of them out with one well-placed grenade."

"Their numbers multiply every time you say that," Alisha stated blandly, and she had to fight a grin when he flicked the side of her knee.

They lapsed into silence after that, but the quiet only lasted for a minute at most.

"Dammit!"

Another voice came from the next room. Alisha looked expectantly towards the door that led into the office. The door was still open, and Paige did not sound the least bit pleased with whatever was going on in there.

"Exciting things?" Alisha asked mildly, hauling herself up from the sofa to head into the kitchen instead.

"Paige and Maya are in there with Suedermann," Joshua replied, tipping his head back enough that he could just barely get an upside-down look at her as she filled the electric kettle. "They're trying to get back onto the holo network. See if they can at least get some of the basics back up and running."

"I thought the network was completely down," Alisha replied as she turned the mocha machine on and started puttering around the kitchen.

"Kind of," Joshua replied, and then he wrinkled his nose once he realized how phenomenally unhelpful that was. "Less that the network's entirely *down*, and more that it's kind of...blocked. They're trying to unblock it. I mean, undoing everything without being able to see the code of the initial upload would be a miracle, but if everyone just gets messaging back, then at least we won't have entire districts panicking because they don't even know what's going on."

Alisha hummed a low note in acknowledgment and there was a clunk of mugs as she got them out of the cupboard. "People were already doing that even before the blackout," she pointed out, more to herself than to Joshua.

"Sounds like it's not going very well," she observed blandly as she poured chocolate into a mug, while some more slightly incoherent profanity poured out of the office. She kept pouring until the amount of syrup gathered in the bottom of the mug was likely enough to rot her teeth upon contact, and then she added just a little bit more.

"That's why I'm in here," Joshua replied sagely. "Well out of the line of fire should anyone start throwing anything."

"Don't tempt me!" Paige shouted from the other room.

"You're not leaving this room," Suedermann informed her flatly, putting an end to that argument before it could even begin.

Alisha snorted out a laugh as she started pouring mocha over the chocolate. "Well," she mused after a moment, "at least we still have electricity." She took a sip of her mocha. "It could be worse."

"Don't jinx anything!" Joshua warned her.

As Alisha headed towards the next room, she knocked her knuckles against the table as she passed, nonchalantly offering, "Bad luck canceled," over her shoulder.

Commander Ekks's Office, Spire, Estaria

The room was quiet.

Almost too quiet.

Ekks half expected someone to come barging into his office to interrupt him, to tell him that what he was about to do was too much. But he supposed he knew that wasn't going to happen; he had handled that issue already.

Instead, he was just waiting for one person to arrive.

It didn't take long before his secretary informed him over his communicator, "Commander, General Yarrow has arrived."

"Let her in," Ekks instructed, and he sat taller and straightened his uniform. The door to his office opened just a moment later.

Yarrow was no-nonsense when she entered. Stiff-backed and purposeful, she strode towards the desk. She was holding the black box in her hands: nondescript but with three separate locks on the front of it. She nodded once to Ekks, but otherwise offered him no greeting as she placed the box down.

She keyed in seven digits for the number lock, and a small pad slid out. She pressed a fingertip to it, letting it scan her fingerprint and check her body temperature. Finally, once it made a high-pitched beep, Yarrow rattled off her identification number followed by her authorization code.

The box clicked open.

Yarrow kept one hand on the box, looking at Ekks critically from across the desk. "Commander Ekks," she began seriously, "the use of this console means you will be authorizing the entire fleet for the use of deadly force, as the fleet commanders see fit. Are you aware of everything this entails?"

"I am aware," he confirmed, folding his hands together on top of the desk.

"And you are prepared to accept the responsibility of whatever else happens from this point onward?" she asked.

"I am prepared," he replied.

Yarrow paused for a moment longer before she turned the box to face him and pushed it across the desk towards him. She stepped back after that, pulling her gloves from her pocket as she did and tugging them on.

Ekks reached for the box and pushed the lid up. There was a small console inside, deceptively simple considering the task it had been designed for.

Ekks had to type in three codes, and he had to confirm each one twice. And finally, it was done. He closed the box and pushed it back across the desk to Yarrow.

"Good evening, General," he offered pleasantly, folding his hands on his desk once again. As an afterthought, he tacked on, "Thank you for your time."

She eyed him for a moment before she drew in a slow breath and sighed it out once again. Whatever it was she wanted to say, she kept it to herself, and Ekks felt no need to ask her to speak her mind. Her opinion, after all, was irrelevant.

She picked up the box and left after just a moment of lingering. Ekks waited until his door slid closed behind her before he sagged back in his seat, his hands falling to his lap. He let his head fall back against his seat, and he observed the paint job on his office ceiling for a moment.

For such a big step, it had felt so…small.

He had been expecting it to feel more momentous. With some reluctance, he sat up straight once again and pulled his communicator from his pocket.

He knew the number he needed to call off the top of his head, and it rang only twice before Raj Ghetti answered it.

"Commander Ekks," Ghetti greeted smoothly. "I trust you're calling to give me good news?"

"I've done what you asked of me," Ekks confirmed, leaning his weight onto one of the arms of his chair. "From here, it all depends on how trigger-happy some of the fleet commanders decide to be."

"And you're certain there won't be any backpedaling?" Ghetti asked. "You know I will be most displeased if we've come so far only to have it all fall apart at the last moment. A great many people would be displeased, in fact."

His tone was mild as he said it.

Pleasant, even.

As if he was discussing a particularly unique cloud.

"I've handled the only one who tried to push back hard enough to be a concern," Ekks replied, just a note of irritation slithering into his voice. While it was almost certain that Ghetti noticed it, he made no efforts to bring it up. Ekks's ire, after all, was of no consequence to him.

Ghetti hummed a low note, skeptical but at least acknowledging what Ekks was saying. "If you're certain," he sighed. "Will there be anything else, Commander?"

"If I may, sir, might I recommend a vacation?" Ekks suggested dryly, drumming the fingers of his free hand against one armrest. "Somewhere in the inner system, of course. I've been led to believe that things in the outer system are going to get rather turbulent in the near future, after all."

Ghetti chuckled in reply, a low, rumbling sound. "Perhaps I will," he mused. "Regardless, you've done good work, Ekks, assuming you can keep it up. We'll be in touch."

The line went dead almost immediately after, and Ekks blinked at his communicator for a moment, before slumping back in his seat once again and rolling his eyes. That had been some impressively faint praise.

Still, it was better than the alternative.

He shoved his communicator into his jacket and dragged one hand down his face. For a moment he simply sat there, as the light from the window gradually shifted across his desk. Finally, he levered himself back up to his feet and headed towards his office door.

He was done for the day, he decided. It was time to head home and pour himself a goddamn drink.

CHAPTER ELEVEN

Aboard <u>*The Empress*, Outer System</u>

Brock's attention was pulled by a flashing button on his console unit.

"Hey Ruther, man, I gotta go. Looks like something has come up."

"Okay, no problem, friend. Talk to you soon. I'm off shift in twenty minutes."

Brock held up his hand in a wave at the screen. "Alrighty," he confirmed, his thoughts already in another place. He closed the connection with the Zhyn flagship.

"What you got, Emma?"

Emma responded over the cockpit intercom. "Oz is just decrypting the message now, but it looks like we've been able to intercept a signal to the Estarian fleet."

"Oh," Brock noted, swiveling around his console chair to see if Crash was registering any of this. Do we know what it says yet?"

"I believe Oz is telling Molly what it says now."

Just then Molly arrived in the cockpit, looking a little disheveled, as if she'd been trying to catch a nap as they waited.

"The Estarian fleet is on its way," she announced. Joel bowled in behind her.

"It sounds like they've been given full authorization to engage with what they're terming the enemy, and anyone who stands in their way."

There was a deadly silence in the cockpit for a moment as they processed the information.

Brock was the first to acknowledge the implications. "That means that if we stay here, we're mincemeat."

Molly shook her head in dismay. "Don't they realize that the Zhyn ships will destroy them in a heartbeat?"

Joel dragged a hand down the lower half of his face. "Clearly not."

"Unless that is what the Northern Clan wants?" Molly mused, pacing over to one of the console chairs and sitting down. She spoke slowly, as if thinking her way through it. "If the Estarian ships are obliterated by the Zhyn, for instance, they will then have the support to declare war on the Zhyn Empire. If they're destroyed by the ARs, then they pretty much write a ticket to do whatever they want."

Joel scratched his head. "But say they do declare war on the Zhyn Empire, they'd have no chance of winning."

Joel could see the cogs turning as Molly thought the situation through. "I guess it depends on your definition of win. If the Federation needs to wade in to keep the peace, it could be exactly what they want to get special trade agreements and reparations from them. Not only that, but all the while it gives them a stronger hold on power domestically."

Brock spun around in his chair. "You're kidding me? This is all about some fucked up group deciding that they want more power? These are real lives that are going to be ended. We're going to be ended! Does that count for nothing?"

Molly shook her head grimly. "I'm afraid not. It's just how these people work."

"Well then what are we going to do?" he asked, waiting for Molly to give them the magical solution that would get them out of the situation.

"I don't know," Molly muttered, getting up out of the chair. "I need to think." And with that she wandered back out of the cockpit as if in a daze.

Spire Memorial Hospital, Estaria

Something was beeping. Not quietly. Not subtly. It was loud and grating and constant.

He was trying to *sleep*, goddammit.

Vero squeezed his eyes shut even tighter, as if that might somehow drown out the insistent, shrill beeping. It made no difference, and he clenched his fists in the sheet beneath him.

"Romero?"

The voice was quiet, almost nervous. But familiar. It was coming from somewhere beside him.

But that didn't make any sense.

He lived alone.

Come to think of it, his bed was supposed to be much more comfortable than whatever slab of concrete he was lying on just then.

Slowly, reluctantly, he cracked one eye open. He closed it again immediately. The lights were too bright, and combined with the white of the walls and the ceiling, it was blinding. A shadow fell over him a second later, and it became apparent that his sister had seen him open one eye, even for such a brief moment.

"Romero!" she hissed urgently, prodding at his shoulder insistently, too cautious to actually shake him.

"Cissy, stooooopppppp," he groaned, still not entirely awake. His face scrunched when she continued, and finally he opened his eyes. That time, his sister was leaning over him enough to block out the worst of the light.

As he blinked up at her, she stared down at him, eyes wide and worried. Finally, she stopped poking at him like some sort of experiment.

"Romero?" she asked once again, as if she suspected she was looking down at someone else.

"Cicero?" he questioned, in much the same tone. He glanced around, taking note of the guardrails on the bed and the beeping heart monitor beside it. He could feel a tube against his face and a cannula in his nose.

There was an IV in his arm, taped in place.

Hospital. He was in a hospital. But why—?

The memory of the car crash came back to him with almost the same impact as the crash itself. Without even thinking about it, he sat up, so quickly that Cicero had to practically leap away from him.

"Romero, *no*—" she tried to scold, only to cut herself off when he went still.

He didn't *hurt*, at least not quite. Everything just felt…stiff. He hadn't moved in a while and he could feel it. And he most likely would start hurting soon, once he was disconnected from whatever was dripping into his arm.

"What happened?" he demanded abruptly, like a wind-up doll jerking back into motion.

Cicero wrung her hands together and shifted back and forth on the stiff plastic chair beside the bed. "You were in a car crash," she informed him, almost matter-of-factly. "There was something wrong with the engine—"

"My car was *fine*," he stated flatly, cutting her off. His hands curled into fists against the bed again.

Cicero was watching him fretfully, and he let his hands uncurl and shook his head briefly. "What else?" he asked, already tired again.

"They, uh—the doctors, I mean—took you off life support a few days ago when you started breathing on your own again. And—"

"Out *there*," Vero specified, gesturing towards the window with one hand. It was dark out.

Cicero shifted on the chair again. "It's…been a lot," she replied carefully, as she picked up the remote for the screen on the wall and turned it on.

As the news played, Cicero outlined everything that had been going on. The blackouts, martial law, the chaos with looting and the rising crime rate as the population panicked, the order for the fleet to keep going.

Vero's ears rang and his chest felt tight, and for a moment he thought maybe he was going to have a heart attack. But no, that wasn't it; that would make no sense. He was just *so pissed off*.

"I need clothes," he stated abruptly, cutting Cicero off again.

"Well—I mean, I have a bag for you," she offered tentatively, getting to her feet to fetch the bag from the window seat. "I brought it with me when the hospital first called."

Vero nodded distractedly in reply and reached for the buzzer to call the nurse. He tapped the button three times in rapid succession and was getting ready for a fourth when a nurse hurried in, looking slightly frantic. Her concern gave way to confusion, though, when she saw that Vero himself was the one to push the button, rather than Cicero.

"You're awake," she stated, bemused. "That's wonderful!" she hurried to add, gathering her composure once again.

"I need to get out of here," he interrupted quickly, before the nurse could say anything else.

Her expression flattened with displease. "Senator, I really must—"

"You can't keep me here against my will," he reminded her. "I'll sign whatever waivers I need to sign, but I need to get out of here."

The nurse spent a moment longer trying to scowl him into submission, without any success. Finally, she heaved an aggrieved sigh and stepped towards the bed to remove his IV line and disconnect him from the various monitors.

He wasted no time in getting dressed while she left to get the relevant paperwork. Within ten minutes, he had signed his discharge forms and was heading towards the elevator with Cicero fretting at his heels.

Senate House, Spire, Estaria

A Senate meeting was well underway when Cicero pulled her car to a halt and parked.

"How did you even know they would be in session?" she wondered, folding her arms and slumping in her seat. She already knew she wasn't going to be going anywhere until the meeting was over; her brother didn't exactly have his own car anymore.

"I've still been getting the schedule updates on my communicator," Vero answered distractedly as he got out of the car. "I'll try to hurry things along," he assured her before he closed the car door and headed for the door at a brisk walk.

He jogged through the familiar halls at a hurried pace, until the door to the boardroom was looming in front of him. He keyed in his identification number to unlock the door and it slid open.

Almost at once, everyone around the table stopped talking and turned to look at him. There was a beat of silence, and then Zenne managed, "Senator Vero." Surprised, but quietly pleased all the same. "We weren't expecting you back for quite some time."

"Yes, well." Vero stepped into the room. "As soon as I heard about everything that was happening, I knew I couldn't waste a second languishing in bed."

He rounded on the Speaker of the House. "I'm fairly sure I never imagined that you're the Speaker of the House, correct?"

"Of course I am—" the Speaker began to reply, affronted.

Cutting him off, Vero demanded, "Then why have you not been *speaking* for the *house*?" He spread his arms and gestured around. "No one in this room wants to go to war. No one in this room thinks it's a good idea."

"What if we had been wrong?" the Speaker asked sharply. "What if we had been sitting idle when an invasion came?"

"What if *he's* wrong?" Vero shot back, pointing out of the door, as if in the direction of Ekks's office. "We could spend all day, every day, trying to figure out which 'what if' is more likely, or we could acknowledge that starting an unnecessary war with an unknown enemy would be the worst outcome. We can respond to a threat, but we can't undo a declaration of war. On top of everything that's happened being eighteen shades of illegal, of course."

He stomped down the little voice in the back of his mind that reminded him he would be lucky not to be disciplined for berating the Speaker of the House.

The Speaker was silent for a moment before his expression steeled and he turned to face the table again. "All in favor of repealing the previous vote and calling the fleet off of the offensive?"

One by one, each Senator around the table lifted a hand, until each member had a hand raised.

The boardroom seemed charged after that, as if a current had raced through the room as the Speaker, pulling up his holo, managed to connect so he could make a call.

"Commander Ekks, you're needed in the Senate House. We've cast an emergency vote and your presence is required." His expression twisted as if he had licked a lemon as he listened to the reply, in a manner that suggested Ekks was not pleased. The Speaker made no mention of what the Commander said.

Vero took his seat at the table, his substitute leaving with hardly a backward glance.

They waited in silence until they could hear booted footsteps in the corridor.

The door opened, and Ekks breezed in with all the warmth of a blizzard. "What is the meaning of this?" he demanded before the door was even finished sliding closed again. "I made myself rather clear about—"

He stopped talking abruptly, staring at Vero. His lip curled in displeasure for a split second before his expression went neutral again. "Vero," he greeted tightly. "So good to see you've returned to us."

"Commander," Vero returned curtly. "I'm sure you're thrilled."

The Speaker stepped between them before anything unpleasant could happen, clearing his throat to get Ekks's attention. "While you were clear on what you wanted last time, we were not," the Speaker explained, calm and level. "We've called you here to rescind the order for the fleet to pursue the ships in the outer system. Until such a time as we have an adequate amount of information on the situation."

Ekks opened his mouth to protest, only to rethink that decision and close his mouth once again when he was greeted with a dozen expectant stares. He drew in a breath, held it for a second, and sighed it out. "Very well," he muttered, straightening his uniform and looking away from them.

He opened his holo and promptly connected a call with Admiral Boys. It felt a bit like a production, standing there with the entire Senate watching him make a call.

"Commander Ekks," the Admiral greeted him warily. "Has there been an update?"

"In a manner of speaking," Ekks replied waspishly. "The situation has changed enough that it's been decided the fleet should stand down."

There was a long, drawn out moment of silence as Boys

absorbed that statement, before he swallowed and cleared his throat. "Of course, Commander," he acknowledged once he gathered his composure once again. His voice seemed to waver nervously. "I'll be sure to inform the rest of the fleet command team of the change of plans. Is there anything else I should know?"

Ekks hung up the call without saying anything else, and he turned a pointed glare on the Speaker. "Will that be all?" he asked, silken and almost sickeningly pleasant.

The Speaker sighed slowly. "That will be all, Commander. Thank you for your time."

Ekks turned and stormed from the room without another word. The room erupted into chatter, wary, excited and cautiously hopeful in equal turns. And Vero sagged back in his chair, the adrenaline surge that had carried him there from the hospital finally waning.

He was *exhausted.*

Aboard *The Hierophant*

It always seemed tense and eerie on the bridge. As if Grouthe was perpetually waiting for something to happen. His crew was accustomed to it—to the way he paced restlessly and murmured to himself every so often—and he supposed that was a good thing.

They were difficult to distract, if nothing else, and he took a certain amount of pride in that.

But even so, it wasn't an ideal situation.

"Any noteworthy changes?" he wondered, pausing as he crossed the bridge.

"Not at the moment, sir," his communications officer replied. "We'll keep you updated."

He was at the head of his own ship in the space fleet. He was not supposed to perpetually feel an undercurrent of niggling *boredom*. It was exactly the sort of thing he had joined the military to avoid.

Grouthe continued pacing.

"Sir?"

He ceased pacing for a split second as his communications officer called to him, though he resumed nearly immediately. "Yes?"

"The ship is being hailed by the *Corona*. Fleet-wide correspondence. Shall I patch it through?" the officer asked.

"To my holo," Grouthe instructed, letting his pacing carry him to the command chair, where he sat down.

With a brief nod, the communications officer obeyed.

"This is Fleet Admiral Boys of the *Corona*. I've received orders from Estaria. From this moment forth, the fleet is to stand down," he instructed. "All offensive actions are to be put on hold and we are to wait for further orders. Is that clear?"

Grouthe could hear a chorus of agreements from the rest of the fleet's command team. He was the last to agree. "Understood."

The caller didn't linger after that as Boys disconnected.

Grouthe closed his holo, looking around the bridge as he did. The rest of the bridge crew hadn't heard the call. For all they knew, it could have been about anything.

Aboard *The Empress*, Outer System

Molly sat in the lounge with a cold cup of mocha in front of her. There was a strange quiet on the ship still, probably akin to the atmosphere in the holding cells before people were executed in barbaric societies she'd read about. She had a glazed look on her face, as if she wasn't quite there. For a moment, as Joel came over, he wondered if perhaps his Molly had been replaced by a porcelain doll, with robotically animated eyelids.

He sat down next to her. "I thought you weren't meant to be

drinking that stuff?" he commented, indicating the cup on the table in front of her.

Molly looked up at him as if pulled from the depths of her thoughts. "I'm not," she informed him. "I just like it there for comfort. And for the smell," she confessed meekly.

Joel smiled. "Any thoughts about our predicament?"

She shook her head. "Not yet. Oz and I have been working on various combinations to keep us out of harm's way and stop this from happening, but nothing concrete yet."

Joel gazed at the table. "It's okay," he told her. "You'll think of something. You always do."

Molly sighed. "Afraid I may be about to disappoint this time," she told him quietly, glancing across the lounge at Jack, Sean, Pieter and Karina distracting themselves with a game of cards. "Worst-case scenario, if we have to, Oz thinks that he may be able to adapt shields so that it pulls any missiles from a 180° angle and explodes them against the shields. In this way we can stop a barrage, for a short time at least, from hitting any of the Zhyn fleet. Then it's a case of how many missiles there are and how many the shields can take. Oz is running the calculation now, but otherwise we're done."

Joel frowned for a moment. "Those kinds of adaptations would need physical changes made to the shields. Before we took off…"

Molly held his gaze.

"You already made the adaptations?"

She nodded. "Brock did, days ago."

"You knew this might happen? And you knew this was an option?"

"I think we all did, if we were honest with ourselves."

Joel blinked at her in disbelief. "You made those adjustments without even mentioning it to me."

Molly shrugged. "I hoped it wouldn't come to this. No point in having the team dwell on this possibility for weeks. They'd only have been anxious and worried all this time, and wasted the time that they had. The time that we had."

He took a deep breath. "I suppose you're right. Of course. Would have been nice to not be in the dark though..."

Molly placed a hand on his knee. "I just didn't want to do that to you. Not knowing that you would insist on being on this ship when the shit hit the fan."

He nodded slowly. "I understand." Then he set his jaw. "But know this: I believe in you. I have faith that you'll come up with something. I know you, Molly Bates, and even if you don't, I don't regret following you here. Not for one second."

Just then Molly jerked her head, as if someone was talking in her ear. Joel waited, watching her expression change in a way that he couldn't quite interpret.

"It's Oz," she said finally. "He's intercepted another signal."

Joel's eyes widened in fear. "What is it? What's happening?"

Molly's brow dipped slowly as she processed what she had just heard. "I think they've been told to stand down," she explained. "It was a message from the flagship to one of their other ships. They were told to stand down."

Joel's expression of fear turned to one of elation. "You're serious?" he asked, barely believing his ears. "Are you sure?"

Molly nodded slowly. "Yeah, I think so," she confirmed.

He pointed towards the others. "We should tell them."

Molly nodded her confirmation, and Joel got up to go and talk to them. "Hey guys..." he called across the lounge. "Good news. We're not going to die!"

Molly got up from her seat as if her legs just carried her automatically. She made her way through to the cockpit to share the news with the rest of the crew. As she left the lounge, she heard the others laughing and backslapping, relieved at the new information.

. . .

Suedermann Safe House, Undisclosed Location, Estaria

Paige came through from the office. She sighed but her face looked brighter. "Looks like we've cracked it!" she announced. "Bourne is just rolling out the fix, but he's confident that within a few hours we will have regained full control of the holo network. We can expect full service to be restored shortly after that."

Alisha got up from her slumped position on the sofa. "That's brilliant news." She grinned.

Joshua hauled himself out of his chair as well. "I'll say. No idea what we would have done without you." He beamed down at Paige from his lofty six-foot-something height.

Paige almost started to blush. "Well it was a close call," she admitted. "Thank goodness Bourne was on hand to help us out with it."

"Well it sounds like all the rumors about the Sanguine Squadron are absolutely true," Joshua remarked. "How about we celebrate with another mocha?" He started moving out of the kitchen.

Alisha interjected. "I'm sure I saw a pack of beers in the back of that fridge," she called after him.

"Ah, well, beer then?" he offered Paige.

Paige shook her head. "No thank you. We're going to have to get going. We've been away too long already, and it looks like Bourne can do the rest without us being physically here."

Just then Maya and Suedermann emerged from the office, both of them looking exhausted. "I'll take a beer," Suedermann said, catching the last bit of their conversation. "I've nowhere to be tonight. Or any other night for that matter." He grinned playfully at his wardens.

"Alisha?" Joshua offered.

"Sure, why not. We can celebrate and toast to them in their absence."

Joshua disappeared through to the kitchen. "Two beers coming up then."

Alisha shuffled up closer to Paige and Maya. "Really, thank you. I saw the task force today before I came out here. They were in chaos with the holo problem. If it wasn't for you, this probably wouldn't be sorted for several weeks... And things were really starting to come apart at the seams within a few hours. I do believe that you probably averted a crisis down here."

Maya grinned. "Just doing our jobs, ma'am," she shot back with a cowboy-like tilt of her head and a pretend cap.

The three of them giggled. "Well, I for one haven't seen anything that complicated for a while," admitted Suedermann. "But I was glad to get the old gray matter moving again." He tapped his head. "Feels good to be useful."

"And we couldn't have done it without you," Paige added. "Thank you, Goran, you've been incredibly helpful. I just hope that this means that you'll be able to go home soon. You know, once we know it's safe."

Goran bobbed his head. "That would be nice," he admitted. "But goodness knows where to find time to do my job again. I mean between my busy schedule of playing solitaire and watching my shows on my holo, I just don't know if I'll be able to fit it in!"

Maya chuckled. "I think I heard something similar from my dad after he retired. He used to say he didn't know where he ever found time to have a job."

Paige looked a little skeptical for a moment. "Well from what I heard about your father, I don't think he ever fully retired."

"You could be right," Maya confirmed. "I think he tried to keep most of it from my mom, but we suspected."

Joshua reappeared and handed open bottles of beer to Alisha and Goran.

"Okay," Paige piped up. "That's our cue to leave. Thank you for everything. You have our holo addresses in case anything else comes up. Goran, thank you again. Alisha, Joshua... I hope we're together again sometime."

"Me too," agreed Joshua. "Only hopefully in better circumstances."

Paige grinned, waving over her shoulder as she headed to the front door. "We can but hope," she agreed.

Maya turned and waved to the others as well, and a few seconds later they were gone out of the door and disappearing into the half-light of the coming morning.

CHAPTER TWELVE

Aboard *The Hierophant*

"Patch me through to the main battery," Grouthe commanded almost as soon as he got off the line from Admiral Boys.

"At once," his communications officer replied, and in just a moment, Grouthe was on his holo again.

At first, he gave no orders, simply letting the call stay quiet as he got up from his seat to peer over the pilot's shoulder. Finally, as an unsure "Sir?" came across the line from the weapons specialist, Grouthe nodded once, coming to a decision.

"Fire."

"As you command," the warrior on the other end of the line responded.

At first, it almost seemed as if nothing happened.

While he was sure the main battery was abuzz with activity, the bridge was still calm. Some of the older ships in the fleet still rumbled from bow to stern whenever the weapons fired, but Grouthe was not in command of one of those outdated behemoths.

"On screen," he stated after a moment, and the sensor readings cleared, making way for the primary virtual window, just in time to watch the first bout of missiles sail silently through the dark.

In stark silence, he watched them strike their target. After a moment, he observed quietly, "Quite a sight, isn't it?"

Estarian-Ogg Space Fleet, Outer System

The Hierophant's missiles cruised through the darkness and struck their mark, and a moment later, all hell broke loose in response.

The Chimera fired next, followed in quick succession by *The Cockatrice*, *The Omen*, *The Pyrrhic*, and *The Wyvern*.

The Hierophant was firing its second barrage by then, and it was more than enough to break through even the most advanced shields.

Only two other ships joined in, *The Thanatos* and *The Paladin* firing a few pot shots of their own as if they didn't want to be left out of whatever the action was.

It wasn't the whole fleet by any means, but when it was focused on a single target, it may as well have been a thousand ships firing.

After *The Hierophant's* second barrage, only *The Omen* and *The Thanatos* fired a second round.

Even that was overkill, as the deed was done by then.

The stillness afterwards made it seem as if the ships involved were silently acknowledging that it had happened and there was no sense in doing anything else.

Aboard *The Empress*, Outer Sark System

Joel came bounding into the cockpit just as a second blast erupted against the shields. Bewildered by the sudden attack, he stumbled and caught himself on the railing just about head height.

"I thought they were going to stand down?" he shouted over the noise, shifting immediately into crisis mode. "What's happening?"

Molly stumbled over towards him, catching herself on a console chair as the ship's gravitational dampeners rocked back to their equilibrium. She tried to speak quietly so as not to distract Crash and Brock, who were frantically pressing buttons and dealing with the systems in order to maintain the shields and seal off one of the areas that had been hit in the first blast.

"That's what we understood," she told him, "but it seems that either one of the ships didn't get the memo or they are acting on their own."

"You mean they have another Northern Clan plant on board?"

"And controlling the ship or the weapons. Possibly," she told him. "Not that it matters now, because four ships around that ship have their weapons at the ready as we speak even though we haven't returned fire."

"Surely they can see that something is not right?"

"Maybe. Maybe they are in on it, or maybe they just can't tell amongst everything."

"Damn protocols," Joel exclaimed in frustration. "And damn commanders who can't think for themselves!"

Molly shot him a glance. "Words I never thought I'd hear Joel say…"

Joel smiled at her briefly, despite the situation they faced.

"Lower bulkhead sealed off," Brock reported. "That should be okay as long as the shields hold. As soon as we get a pressure differential down there though…" His voice trailed off.

"Well done," Molly told him. "Shields status?"

"Seventy percent," Brock called back over the noise of the blasts against their shields.

"Has the shield adaptation been activated?" Joel asked quietly.

She nodded. "Nothing is getting through to the Zhyn fleet. At least not while we're here."

"Damn right," said Brock proudly, interrupting the conversation he was eavesdropping on, despite his massive focus on the controls in front of him. "This baby is going to take every last missile or laser fire in a two-kilometer radius."

Molly glanced at Joel, noticing his reaction. "Well let's hope this barrage stops in time. Before we get annihilated, that is," Joel added.

Molly pressed her lips together. "I agree. But just in case, Brock," she called, "alert the Zhyn to the situation. Let them know not to fire unless they need to protect themselves."

"You mean unless we explode?"

"Exactly."

"Communicating now."

"So," Molly said, moving half a step closer to Joel and leaning in. "Do you regret ever meeting me for that drink when I was kicked out for my 4077?"

Joel smiled at her, remembering that first reintroduction to the world of Molly Bates…

CHAPTER THIRTEEN

I remember.

Oz, you remember everything.

Yes, but… it was the first real conversation we had as well… Hey, just because I'm non-organic, doesn't mean I'm not sentimental too…

(Five years previously…) Chenz' Bar, Downtown Uptarlung. Irk'n Quarter

Remind me why we're here again.

Remind you? I never told you.

I'm using your syntax to smooth our integration.

Oh, really?

I detect sarcasm.

Yeah, and I never had to utter a word out loud.

Neural connections, baby. I feel you.

Don't be a wanker.

The AI was silent.

That reminds me…you don't have a name.

You mean a designation? Sure I do. I am Project Ozimandaus 0922.

That's not a name.

Yes it is. That's what your colleagues, Sue and Dickwad-Charles, called me.

Yeah, but that's not a name. Not like "Sue" or "Charles," or "Molly." They were referring to the project. Not you. Plus, it's a fucking mouthful to say, and no way I'm going to remember that.

I'm not a Sarkian of any variety, and therefore I don't require a Sarkian designation.

But you are sentient, and you deserve a name.

Even though I hijacked your holo?

AND neural cortex.

Yes. Even though I hijacked your holo and neural cortex?

Yes, even though. Have you got any ideas about what you'd like me to call you?

Baby? Sexy? Hot stuff? Bad boy???

What the fuck?

Molly scrambled in the recesses of her mind trying to recall why he might know those words. They sounded familiar. Shit, they were how she would refer to her crushes. How would he have access to that kind of data?

All right, you arseburger, what gives? What makes you say those things?

I'm just kidding around. To be honest, I haven't thought about it. What would be an appropriate designation for something like myself? Is there a nomenclature that is relevant here? Or a social convention?

Hmm... not really. I guess my preference would be to give you something easy for me to say, and to communicate with others when the time comes to introduce you to people. Also, I like the idea of using your project designation in a name.

Molly's eye scanned the crowded bar, looking for inspiration. Nothing at all jumped out at her.

What about "Oz"?

Oz?

It's short for Ozimandaus—which is actually a cool name too. Maybe that can be your Sunday name.

Sunday name?

Yeah, like your full name for formal occasions.

Molly mulled it over, imagining what Oz the AI might even look like. For a moment, she pictured the ridiculous Holly on that ancient show she used to watch as a kid...what was it called? *Red Dwarf*? Yes. *Red Dwarf*—with the folks who had the hilariously melodic accents. Thank goodness Grandpa had downloaded all those cultural pods before he and Nana had left on the QBBS *Meredith Reynolds* all those years ago.

Okay. I like it. "Oz" it is, then.

Great. So, Oz, the reason we are here is because we need to make money. And fast.

What about that trust you have set up? That could keep us going for a century or more.

How do you know about that?

I did a search on you. Once we were off base and I was hooked up to the XtraNET, I just scanned for anything that had your DNA or retinal print attached to it. Turns out it's the optimum way to find all the recorded information on someone, no matter what their species.

You've been looking me up? And not just me by the sounds of it!

I think it's logical for me to know all parameters of operation—including who I'm associating with.

"Associating with"? You jumped into my fucking holo!

Your sentiment is noted.

Anyway. That trust is private and all sorts of alarms go off if I go near it. I don't want to touch it. Not yet. We need to find another way to make money independently.

Acknowledged. The trust is off limits.

Yes. Off. The. Record. Like I said, it's private. I don't want anyone else knowing about it. Okay?

Okay.

So, I have a serious question. How come you've not come up with a plan to tap into the Central Systems' trade market, and just syphon funds from there? I mean, you're an AI with frickin' uber amounts of intelligence. It wouldn't be hard to bypass some security and take a little from a lot of trades—no one would even miss it.

Ah, but Molly Bates...that would be unethical. And you've forbidden me from doing anything unethical. EVER.

What? What are you talking about? I never said that.

Sure you did. When I was going to cyber-blackmail that colonel back at the base, you went off on a moral trip making me swear to never do anything like that.

That was for them. *Not for* me. *I never meant you were supposed to be all moral and shit when it came to what* we *needed to do.*

I don't understand the differentiation. Please clarify.

Molly recognized the man who had just walked in the door and who was now looking around the tables. She stuck her hand in the air, waved vigorously and slid out of the booth to stand up.

Joel is here, asswipe. This conversation isn't over.

Former Captain Joel Dunham wandered over to the table. He was buff and large. In fact, much larger than Molly remembered.

>>> *"Yeah, I was kinda surprised by that," Molly confessed over the sound of the explosions hitting the shields.*

>>> *"Well, you hid it well. I had no idea that was what you might have been thinking. Mind, I was probably distracted by some thoughts of my own," he confessed.*

Joel smiled at her, looking her up and down.

"Long time, stranger!" She grinned.

"Hello, Geek-brain!" he said, wrapping his bear-like arms around her. He squeezed her tight.

Molly tapped his back, signaling her surrender.

"Sorry!" he said, realizing that his enthusiasm had gotten the better of him. "I forget how delicate you girlies are."

Molly suspected there was something loaded in that statement, along the lines of him not having much contact with women these days. She didn't have the inclination to ask, though.

"There's something different about you though..." He held her out by the shoulders, looking her up and down again.

"I've lost weight?" She looked hopefully up at him.

He shook his head. "Something else." He paused and looked at her face. "Didn't you used to be a brunette?"

Molly's cheeks slowly revealed her embarrassment. "Yeah. One of my genetic experiments is taking longer to wear off than I had anticipated."

Joel howled with laughter while pointing at her hair. "How much longer?" he asked, catching his breath.

"Two years, three months and nineteen days. It was meant to self-correct in three months, but, well..."

"You miscalculated?"

"No, tequila," she admitted.

"You were drinking?"

"No, I used tequila as the carrier fluid." She eyed her friend in annoyance. "I was impatient and it was handy."

Joel was still snickering, and shook his head at her. "Same ol' Molly, I see." She rolled her eyes...both at herself and the familiarity Joel had with her sagas.

She pushed a chair out for him, and sat herself down.

"Anyway, good to see you, fuckwit. I ordered you a beer." The waitress arrived with their drinks, and Molly was quick to get her lips around hers. "You still drink this stuff, right?"

"Of course, and thank you. So, to what do I owe this pleasure?" he asked.

She played with her bottle before looking at him. "I've left the military, and I need a job."

She didn't say more, and allowed Joel to absorb it. He lowered his eyes to his bottle.

"A job, you say? Genius-girl Molly Bates has come to *me* for a job?" He looked back up at her, clearly amused at the irony. "You know, all the time you were assigned to our detail, there never once was a problem that you couldn't solve. The boys would swear you were a witch, or a freak, or something. I just told them you were an evil genius. They called you 'devil-woman' behind your back, did you know that?"

"I knew." She smiled, completely uninterested in what some meatheads thought of her.

Joel continued, "And yet you'd keep going back to the research core." He asked her a question that he had wondered about from time to time, "Why did you never join an ops team?"

She shrugged. "Dunno. Guess I just felt more comfortable not having to make life and death decisions all the time." She looked around before returning to her beer. "I've made a few mistakes in my life already. I found out that sometimes I act before I think, and sometimes even when I think, I don't always think like normal people."

Because I'm broken.

Joel waited a moment before asking, "And that's why you want a job now? So you don't have to put all that talent to good use?" Joel took a sip of his beer.

Her grin spread across her face, looking a little mischievous. "Oh, no, I'm happy to put my immense reservoirs of talent to good use. I just want you to help direct it for me at the moment!"

Joel's squaddies often found her arrogant, but Joel knew better. He understood her weird humor, even though he didn't get it half the time. He put it down to the whacked-out ancient shows she would watch. *Fokk* knows where she got those datastreams from, though. One of the engineers had once told him they were from a time long forgotten in the Sark System.

"So, a job, for your talents...that pays beer money." He pointed to the drink that she'd already almost drained. He rubbed his chin, pretending to think deeply.

What he couldn't do with her talents!

"And it has to be, uh, *legal*," she added, remembering that at some point she also needed to find a way of reprogramming Oz to make sure she wouldn't be too restricted by his newfound morality.

Joel's eyes opened wide. "Legal? What do you think I am? I'm an upstanding Sarkian, I'll have you know!" His mock indignation made them both giggle.

Molly knew he was mostly straight-laced when it came to the jobs he would take. But there was no denying that the circumstances under which he had left the service had left a few people wondering.

Joel pursed his lips. "I have some ideas. A friend came to me the other day about something he noticed that was going down in his company: price-fixing on a type of painkiller that thousands of Oggs and Estarians need. Said there were whispers of hiking the prices to three times their market value, just because they can. He wanted a way to stop it without involving official channels or losing his job."

He continued, waving off the waitress asking him if he wanted another beer. "I didn't know how to fix it; I don't have the tech skills to tackle something like that. And taking on a big corporation? Who's going to listen to me? Not the police, that's for sure. But now," he glanced at her, "now you're here. And I wonder if we can't take this job and do some good things for these folks?"

Molly used her sultry voice, and her eyes glinted with glee. "Sounds like my cup of tea. Tell me, will there be hacking?"

Joel had worked with her long enough to know that hacking

turned her on. *Shit, she is one weird chick...* "Oh, there will be hacking, baby. There will be lots and lots of hacking."

As he smiled, his awareness seemed to drift off. When he refocused, he dropped his eyes to his beer. "You know, I never did apologize for the thing with Candy."

Molly did a double take, trying to work out what he was talking about.

He lifted up his bottle to point at her. "You remember. The girl you said had several guys in the squad in tow." He took a sip. Molly nodded, recalling the bust-up. "I just wanted to say, I appreciated you looking out for me. I mean, I know it was a big thing then and we didn't exactly part as close as we had been. But, I'm sorry I was a jackass about it."

Had Molly been drinking at that exact moment she may have choked. "Well, er, that's great. I mean, yes, I was. I just didn't want her to make a fool out of you." She hesitated. "While we're on the subject. I have something to apologize for too." She noticed that Joel had looked up.

"You remember that club we went to not long after that?"

"Yeah, the gay bar where you got called away for some lab crisis?" Joel recollected the night.

Molly looked at him, hoping that she wouldn't have to say it.

"There was no crisis, was there?" Joel figured out. "And you knew it was a gay bar?"

Molly kept her face straight. "And I paid Jose, my friend on the door, to encourage the guys to, erm, keep you company."

Joel's face dropped.

"You mean..."

"Yeah. They didn't find you *that* magnetic. They were having you on."

He closed his eyes in a grimace. "You are a cold-hearted bitch!" he groaned.

"Now, now, you just tried to make good about Crystal."

"Candy."

"Whatever."

"I genuinely tried to get out of there without letting anyone feel rejected. I fretted about that for days! I even wondered if..." He stopped himself, realizing there was some information he didn't want to share with Molly.

They looked at each other and couldn't help but chuckle.

Joel finally admitted. "One of them told me I should go into modeling."

"Yeah, model airplanes maybe!" Molly retorted.

The two laughed. Just like they had done back in the day, before Candy had gotten between them.

He drained his glass, dropped some credits onto the table for the drinks, and stood up.

"Lemme talk to my contact and see what we can set up in terms of this job. I'd say 'stay sober,' but stay by your phone, at least. I'll get back to you soon."

And with that he headed out of the bar.

>>> *Oh my ancestors! I'd forgotten about the Crystal saga!*
>>> *Candy! And anyway, what I never told you was that I was only trying to use her to get your attention. If I'm honest... and since this is it, I feel like this is the time to be honest.*

The two stood in the cockpit, with everything crashing all around them, occasionally being jolted against each other, and sometimes apart. Each time, they came back together, spontaneously as if they were on some kind of self-correcting buoyancy system.

"Do you ever regret anything?" Joel asked.

Molly felt herself struggling to find the words to say everything that came to her mind.

"More specifically," he added, helping her out, "about us?"

She could barely dare hope he meant what she thought he

meant. "I do," she confessed.

A smile crept across his face as he grabbed her hand and squeezed it tight. "That's enough for me," he whispered in her ear.

Aboard *The Empress*, Outer Sark System

"Shields at thirty percent," Brock announced to the cockpit that was now crowded with the entire team watching the events unfold on the main screen together.

The rest of the ship had gone dark when auxiliary power kicked in, in order to maintain main power to the shields.

Red lights flashed, illuminating the cockpit in the danger signal.

Karina reached for Sean's hand as she braced against impact as another missile hit the shields.

"We're not going to be able to take many more of those," Sean commented above the noise and chaos. He watched Molly for a reaction, but she continued to watch the screen intently, mouthing numbers to herself as if making calculations that might potentially help them.

He felt Karina lean closer to him as she got her balance. "Did you ever think it would end like this?" she asked.

He started to shake his head, but then held her closer and put on his dry comic face. "Actually, I thought there would be more sex in the end…"

She sniggered and slapped against his chest as he squeezed her. "I'm glad I'm with you," she told him. "We've all gotta die somehow, sometime. I'm just glad I'm with you."

"Me too, baby." He kissed her head and pulled her tight, as if trying to shield her from the inevitable. Or at least shield her from seeing the inevitable when it happened.

"Brace! Brace! Brace!" Crash called to them again as he spotted another missile heading their way.

A moment later the ship was battered again and tilted on its side. The internal gravity dampers took a few moments to kick in, leaving the crew to be thrown to one side of the ship.

There were shouts and screams as they were caught off guard, and then scrambled to help each other up again.

Jack managed to catch hold of Pieter, deftly preventing him from smacking his head against one of the utility units jutting out of the wall. "Thanks!" he called above the noise.

Jack smiled at him. "Any time, friend."

The two held each other's gaze for what could have only been a moment in the chaos, but felt like an eternity in their perception of time and expanded awareness. Each was grateful for the comfort of connection as they awaited their fate. Jack threw her arm around his shoulder and they stood together, feeling stronger together and as a part of a team, watching the details on the main screen again.

"Shields at two percent!" Brock announced over the crashing of kinetics and the scream of sirens.

Knowing now that there was nothing else he could do to divert any more power to the shields, he got up out of his console chair and moved over to Crash's console. He laid a hand on Crash's shoulder. Crash turned and looked up at him and nodded, a lifetime of understanding and compassion streamed between the two.

Brock's eyes teared up.

Crash pushed the final buttons on his console and then stood up out of his pilot's seat and looked around at the crew. The crew he had served with the last several years. The crew who he could never imagine ever leaving. The crew that he was prepared to go to his death with.

He looked across at Molly and nodded, the chaos, the flashing lights, sirens, the destruction all disappearing into the background.

He wrapped an arm around Brock as another missile hit the shields, throwing them all off balance again.

Pieter's eye was caught by one of the consoles he fell against. "The bulkhead breach is failing. The fuel core has been hit. This is it," he announced.

Molly looked around at her team, making eye contact with any of them that could see her. She noticed Jack and Pieter holding onto each other, Karina and Sean doing the same, and then she felt Joel putting his arm around her and pulling her close.

She watched as an explosion rippled out against the remaining part of the shield meters in front of them beyond the window. She watched as if in an altered state of consciousness and awareness as the final segment of the shield failed. The explosion was green and blue and electrical in nature as the missile created a fission reaction in the vacuum of space.

The pupil of her eye dilated as the reflection of the explosion spread out across its glassy surface... the last thing that eye would ever see.

Aboard *The Corona, (Estarian Flagship)*

"Admiral Boys!" The technician's voice was sharp with alarm, and her fingers flew across the terminal in front of her. "We have a problem, sir." The tone of her voice alone made it clear that her statement may well have been the biggest understatement of the millennium.

"Multiple calls incoming," the communications officer chimed in.

"Keep them on hold," Boys replied, his eyebrows furrowing together in bewilderment. At last check, the order he had given had not been that complicated.

As the sensor readings continued with the explosion of activity, Boys didn't need to issue any orders to see what was going on. The technician cleared the sensor data away without prompting, instead bringing up the primary virtual window.

Abruptly, it was as if the bridge had a front row seat to the entire ordeal.

It seemed to go in slow motion at first, as Boys tried to process what he was looking at in that horrible moment.

"What in my ancestors' name is going on?" Boys demanded to no one in particular as he surged out of his seat so quickly he very nearly stumbled over his own feet. "Patch me through to Grouthe," were the next words out of his mouth.

"O-of course," his communications officer stammered, already keying in the call.

"Grouthe!" Boys barked into his wrist holo as soon as the call connected, on his feet and watching the scene in front of him with a fixed, sick fascination. "I gave you a direct order to stand down!"

"So you did," Grouthe agreed, his tone quiet and light. He sounded perfectly reasonable in that moment. Almost pleasant.

Boys recoiled, jerking his communicator out to arm's length when Grouthe simply hung up on him. He blinked dumbly at the communicator as he rapidly tried to put the pieces together.

"Sir?" his communication's officer asked, his voice pitched up half an octave higher than usual with nerves. "What do we do?"

"Patch me through to the command team," Boys demanded, turning away from the digital window. "All of them, this instant."

His communications officer launched into frenzied activity to connect the call, as if being quick might somehow undo what had happened.

In just a moment, Boys was all but snarling into his holo. "I issued a direct order to *stand down*. What part of that was unclear? Further failure to comply will result in disciplinary action!"

He got a flurry of panicked responses in return, everyone talking over everyone else. If nothing else, it meant Boys got an explanation—Grouthe had fired first, and considering his influence, other ships in the fleet had simply assumed that a new order was in the process of being issued—but there was no way to un-fire a missile barrage.

There was no way to fix what had been done.

Boys turned to look at the digital window again. He couldn't help but to be glad of the silence of space in that moment. There were some things he simply didn't want to force himself to hear.

"Sir?" his pilot asked carefully. "What now?"

For a moment, like a deer bumbling into a set of headlights, Boys simply stood there.

It was a very good question.

CHAPTER FOURTEEN

Aboard *Glock'stor Ship #597*

The pilot kept up a steady stream of chatter with the navigators.

Ruther and Trev'or rambled back and forth to each other just as much as they always did. On top of that, Gultorra had turned up on the bridge to drop off a report, and then lingered to catch up with Clor. He leaned casually against the side of the command chair as they spoke.

It was an almost unusually normal day, all things considered.

At least until it wasn't.

"The Estarian fleet is firing, sir." The technician sounded bemused as he reported the update, his head cocked to one side as he stared at his terminal. "Or rather…a portion of it is?"

He didn't sound *alarmed*, though, so Admiral Clor was calm as he commanded, "On screen, then. Let's see what they're up to." He was fairly willing to assume that any amount of firing was, at the very least, not good news, especially considering how close the fleet was at that point.

He was not ready for the sight that greeted him as the virtual window lit up. A hush fell over the bridge as the crew watched the fleet bombard Molly's ship. The shields crackled and sparked at first, until eventually they gave out under the onslaught. Like a cascade of light, the shield retracted, almost seeming to evaporate.

No matter how unpleasant, though, all eyes stayed locked on the sight in front of them. It would have been an insult to look away.

Gultorra stood rigidly beside the command chair. Trev'or was clutching at the edges of his terminal so tightly that Clor could hear his nails digging at the metal. Clor's fingers tightened around the armrests of his chair until his hands hurt.

"Sir, what do we do?" Ruther asked, his hands hovering anxiously over his terminal, as if he could do anything on his own. "What can—*can* we do anything?"

Clor didn't answer immediately, mentally going over ideas and just as quickly discarding them, before he finally admitted, "I don't think there's anything we can do." His voice was low as he admitted it, but he may as well have been shouting it.

Once the shields were gone, Molly's ship didn't last long. Whether that was a good thing or a bad thing would be a constant debate from that point onwards.

With each strike after that, pieces of the hull flew off, breaking apart like chips of confetti and drifting silently away. Until finally a missile struck the engine room. The middle of the ship expanded outwards for a fraction of a second, like a balloon with too much air, just before the ship fractured in half and burst away from each other with a few geysers of plasma and gas that burned out as quickly as they erupted. Countless shards of shrapnel, each as big as a scouting ship, broke off and drifted away. Lights flickered in the ship's gaping interior, until they went out in clusters.

Finally, the wreckage was dark. The missile barrage halted as if it had never happened in the first place.

The calm afterwards seemed unfair, as if the cosmos was

trying to pretend that nothing had happened. As if it had simply been business as usual.

Had someone dropped a stylus on Clor's bridge in that moment, it would have been louder than a gunshot. No one moved or said a word, as if the entire crew was waiting for it to be declared as a joke. As if breaking the silence was the only thing that would make it real.

Finally, Gultorra put a hand on Clor's shoulder. "Sir."

Clor jerked as if he were coming out of a trance, turning sharply to look at Gultorra.

"What now, sir?" Gultorra asked simply, though it was not a simple question by any stretch of the imagination.

Nevertheless, it gave the Admiral something else to focus on. He took a breath and let it out.

He turned his attention to Ruther. "Connect a call to the command team," he ordered, his voice still low.

If Ruther heard the Admiral's words, he gave no sign of it, and Trev'or had to reach over and swat his shoulder. It still took a moment for Ruther to jerk his attention back to the present, hands still poised over the front of his terminal. "Sorry, sir?"

"The command team," Clor repeated slowly. "Connect a call. I need to explain what just happened."

"Ah—r-right. Of course, sir," Ruther agreed, before he turned all of his attention to tapping out commands at his terminal with an almost single-minded focus.

Clor used the time it took Ruther to set up the call to figure out what he was supposed to say to explain the entire ordeal.

Paige's Office, Base, Gaitune-67, Sark System

Paige sat quietly in her office, working through the hundreds of things that had been neglected when she and Maya went to the surface. She tapped curiously on one holoscreen and then another making sure that the most urgent and important things were handled. Having been up for close to thirty-six hours straight at this point, she felt wired and suspected she was going to be unable to sleep.

Just a couple more, she promised herself, and then she would call it a night.

Bourne interrupted her flow of concentration.

"Paige? There's a holo message come through. It's from Emma."

"You mean from *The Empress*?" Suddenly Paige's backlog of work paled into insignificance. "What news is there? Do they need anything?"

"No," he told her solemnly. "No, it's not that. They don't need anything. I believe you'll want to be sitting down."

There was a long pause.

"Bourne, I *am* sitting down." She felt her anxiety rising. "Can you send me the message please?"

Bourne released the message to her holo. Her hand trembling now, she flicked it open and scanned the contents.

Maya appeared in the doorway. "Hey, I thought you were going to bed soon…?" Maya noticed Paige's gray complexion. "Are you okay?"

Paige shook her head slowly. She looked as though she had been hit in the chest. Gasping for air, she managed to tell her that Emma had messaged.

Maya hurried over and took the holoscreen that was in Paige's hand. She read it and staggered back a little, catching herself against the desk.

"It can't be true," she rejected. "It must be a mistake. Emma must have written this just in case and then programmed it to send in the event of the unthinkable… But she must have had some kind of systems failure. You'll see, they will be back here in a few hours totally fine."

Her face and mannerisms told a completely different story though.

She looked at Paige and watched a single tear trickle down the side of her face. It looked like Paige was in too much pain to even cry. She knew that feeling too.

The two girls remained in silence, barely moving, trying to make sense of the communiqué:

Dear Paige and Maya,

If you're reading this, then we've been destroyed. It all happened very fast, and no one suffered physically. Rest assured that I did everything within my capabilities to keep everyone safe. Unfortunately even I have limits, and the barrages of missiles were just too great.

In the coming days and weeks, you will learn more about what happened. As I write this now, we are anticipating that we will take on the fire from at least one Estarian ship. Oz and Molly have implemented an adaptation to the shields to ensure that we take the strikes rather than the Zhyn. It was and is of utmost importance that the Estarians do not strike either the Zhyn or the ARs—for the sake of peace in the Federation. I hope that we have been able to achieve that.

You're on your own now. A similar message will be sent to the Federation and you will no doubt be hearing from the General in due course.

On a personal note, I have thoroughly enjoyed working with you and the whole team. I'm sorry that it had to end.

Be well, my friends, and live a good life.

Emma

Neechie appeared in the office and jumped up onto the desk, and then onto Paige's lap. Paige, dazed, allowed the sphinx to nestle up against her without any reaction. Absent-mindedly she allowed her hand to fall to Neechie's back as she processed the worst news of her life.

Bates's Office, Undisclosed Location, Spire

Director Bates carefully closed off the holoconnection. Slowly she turned her chair around so that she couldn't be seen through the floor-to-ceiling windows of her office. Facing the wall, she bowed her head and tried to smother her mouth with a hand as she sobbed silently.

Philip Bates arrived in the office. He slipped quietly in through the office door. "I got a message from Paige Montgomery to meet you here," he reported with a sense of urgency as he breezed in. "Is everything okay?"

Director Bates swiveled in her chair to look at him. By her expression and the smeared makeup, he knew straightaway that everything was far from okay.

"What? What's happened?"

A few moments later a wail reverberated from the office through the entire open-plan bullpen beyond. The agents below looked up, bewildered, trying to make sense of the sobbing and wails that followed.

Rhodez strode in from the elevator purposefully. For a moment he looked as if he were planning to go straight up to the director's office, but then, hearing the commotion, he slowed his pace and then stopped.

Clevedon called out to him in a raised whisper. "What's going on?"

Rhodez wandered over to his desk, his expression serious and morose. "Intel downstairs has just received confirmation that the ship, *Empress*, has just been destroyed. Molly, amongst others, was on it."

"You mean...?"

He nodded. "Yes, Molly is dead."

Clevedon felt the shock through his entire body. For a moment he found it hard to breathe. "Are you sure? Is there any chance that..."

Rhodez shook his head. "There is no hope."

Bailey Residence, Spire, Estaria

Arlene ran towards her apartment door, responding to a knock. "Just a minute, Anne," she called back over her shoulder. "Just hold onto them for a minute. I'll be right back."

She peered through the viewfinder and then stood back, opening the door wide to her friend. "Giles!" she exclaimed brightly. "Just in time. Anne decided that she wanted to paint her room before Ben'or got back, but we could do with someone taller to reach the ceiling."

Giles's expression was sober. "Well, quite. I'd be happy to help, but errr, Arlene…"

"Oh come on," she teased playfully, leading the way back through to the sleeping quarters. "I'll order up some pizza. We'll have it done within an hour I'm sure."

Giles hesitated again. "Arlene, something's happened. I think you should probably sit down… I have something to tell you."

Arlene stopped, suddenly realizing that Giles wasn't his usual stuffy and flippant self. He seemed as if he were actually trying to be sympathetic about something.

"I tried to call," he explained to her, "but I suspect your holo is still out."

"Yes it is," she confirmed. "But I received the public service announcement Paige and Maya sent out…" Her voice trailed off as her concern as to the purpose of Giles's visit mounted.

"Giles? Have you been… crying?"

"I have," he confessed without any embarrassment. "I've just had a conversation with Uncle Lance. Something terrible has happened. The crew of *The Empress*… They're all dead. Arlene, I'm so sorry. Ben'or isn't coming back."

Still standing, Arlene started to process the information, her body convulsing silently as she began to sob.

Anne had been standing around the corner behind the kitchen counter. She had heard everything. As Giles moved in to steady Arlene, Anne ran back to her room and slammed the door.

Arlene felt her arms and legs go limp as she took in the news.

Carefully Giles helped her to the sofa, where she collapsed in a heap, sobbing.

Much later in the evening, Giles had managed to coax Anne out of a crawlspace she had accessed in her room. Arlene hadn't moved from the sofa in hours. Instead she lay semi-catatonic, uninterested in eating or drinking anything.

Or communicating, for that matter.

Sitting with her, Giles and Anne quietly played some form of checkers that Anne had learned in the convent.

"I'm not sure that's a valid move…" Giles started to protest.

Anne glared at him and took her finger from the checker she had just moved. "And, I win again," she told Giles quietly and matter-of-factly, with a finality in her halfhearted glare.

Arlene stirred slightly and mumbled to Giles. "You should make sure she's not cheating you," she told him.

Anne smiled. "I'm not!" she protested, a little more playfully now.

"Don't trust a word that one says," Arlene added, narrowing her eyes at the adolescent.

"Good to see that you are rejoining us," Giles confessed quietly and reset the board for another game.

"Yes, well, we'll see."

Anne got up and headed out to the kitchen with her glass, leaving Giles and Arlene to talk as grown-ups.

"How are you feeling?" Arlene asked him.

He shrugged. "Trying not to think about it. I can't bear the idea that…"

Arlene nodded from her scrunched-up position on the sofa. She started to sit up a little.

"I just keep thinking I should have been there with them," he added.

Arlene gently placed a hand on his arm and shook her head. "It's better that you weren't," she said sensibly. "Besides, you don't know how many of your nine lives you have left."

Giles smiled, trying not to let his lip tremble. Tears streamed down his face quietly as he and Arlene consoled each other, just with their mere presence.

It wasn't long before Anne returned from the kitchen. "Are you going to play this next one with us, Arlene?" she asked. "It's actually more fun with three players…"

CHAPTER FIFTEEN

Safe House, Undisclosed Location, Estaria

There was a noise towards the front of the safe house. It hadn't been there a moment ago, and it wasn't quite like any noise Joshua had heard before.

Even so, it wasn't a particularly concerning sound.

But it drew Joshua out of the kitchen. A buzzing noise, distant and muffled. He didn't even bother putting down the knife he had been using to cut his sandwich, assuming he would just have to give one of the generators a swift kick and then head right back into the kitchen.

But then he smelled smoke. And hot metal. A line along the edge of the main door was glowing red hot. It was getting longer, reaching closer and closer to the bottom of the door as someone on the other side took a blowtorch to it.

"Suedermann!" Joshua hollered over his shoulder, his grip on the bread knife tightening. "Get into the safe room!"

He could hear hurried footsteps behind him, heading deeper into the house, followed by the sound of the safe room opening and closing again. He only just heard the beep of the lock engaging.

Joshua glanced around to see if his protective vest was in the room, but he didn't see it and he didn't have a chance to go look for it before a narrow metal rod abruptly slammed its way through the gap between the door and the doorjamb, bending the heated metal out of the way and prying it open. With an unholy, almost deafening screeching sound, the door slid back along its track one painstaking inch at a time until it was open just wide enough for someone to shoulder through. Afterwards, the metal of the door was warped beyond any hope of closing again.

Four people barged into the room. Almost immediately, a bullet ripped through Joshua's shoulder. Adrenaline let him ignore it as he surged forwards. He lifted the knife and crashed into the nearest of the four intruders, slamming the blade into the man's neck. It sank through muscle and cartilage with a damp crunch, and he yanked it to the side, sending blood spraying through the air. Their momentum as they stumbled helped the knife to go deeper, and they both landed on the floor in a tangle of limbs.

It all happened in a few seconds, before a hand closed around the back of Joshua's neck and hauled him away. The knife's serrated edge caught in the neck's muscle and ripped out of Joshua's hand.

He landed on his back on the floor. The man who grabbed him loomed over him, gun drawn, only for his shot to miss when Joshua kicked him in the knee with enough force to dislocate it, sending him down to his knees on the floor.

The shot struck the floor, instead, buying Joshua only a moment before the man took aim again.

"Don't kill him yet!" a third man barked. He sounded like the leader. He was crouched beside the dead one's body. "We might still need him with a pulse."

There was a tense moment of silence, and then the man with the dislocated knee settled for shooting Joshua in the gut.

Joshua's back arched in agony and he clenched his jaw so tightly he felt a few of his teeth crack.

As he writhed on the floor, he could hear the fourth man exploring the house, until finally a voice called, "Door's got a scanner!"

The leader of the group grabbed Joshua by the front of his shirt and started dragging him towards the back of the house. Joshua thrashed like a feral cat the entire way, but it hardly seemed to make a difference.

Once they were standing at the door into the safe room that had doubled as the office, someone lifted Joshua's hand and pressed it to the door scanner. It beeped after a few seconds and slid open.

Immediately, the man who opened the door stumbled back when Suedermann shot him in the shoulder with his side arm. In the same breath, the group leader pulled a knife from his belt and hurled it. It sank straight into Suedermann's chest and sent him staggering back the few feet to the wall.

When another shot rang out, the gun was being held by the man Suedermann had shot just a moment before. Without ceremony he shot Suedermann right between the eyes. He stayed upright for a breath, then a second, and then staggered back and sank slowly down the wall.

The leader dropped Joshua on the floor finally, just inside the safe room. He lifted a foot, and then stomped down on Joshua's ribs. Once, then twice, and then a third time.

When the three remaining members of the team left, one of them was limping and one of them was clutching his shoulder. Still, they left under their own power, leaving Joshua behind with Suedermann's body to gurgle out his last few breaths.

When Suedermann's holo started to buzz, it went unanswered.

When Joshua's began to ring a few moments later, it, too, went unanswered.

It rang twice more over the next hour, before it fell silent for good.

When Alisha and Hans arrived at the safe house, they were already concerned. They knew at least a few people were supposed to be there, but no one had answered their calls on the way there.

Alisha prayed it was a holo glitch: a knock on effect from the blackout a few weeks before. They were, after all, on a vulnerable part of the grid out here in the middle of nowhere.

When they arrived, they saw the door hanging open. They both broke into a run to get inside.

There was blood all over the place, including a trail of it leading towards the back of the house. And there was a dead body in the middle of the floor, a knife from the kitchen still lodged in the neck.

As Hans came to a halt just inside the house to try to figure out how the door had been jammed, Alisha crept deeper into the house. Her steps were light and careful, and once she was a few steps away, Hans could scarcely even hear her as she kept walking.

The door had been bent entirely out of shape on one side, and it took only a few seconds before Hans gave it up as a lost cause and moved away. He turned his attention to the dead body in the middle of the floor, instead. He reached out and tugged the mask off of the body, dislodging the knife as he did and sending it clattering to the floor. He didn't recognize whoever the man was, breathing a sigh of relief. He turned his attention instead to rifling through the body's pockets, looking for any sort of personal affects to identify him by. A wrist holo, a wallet, some sort of ID.

He wasn't surprised when he came up empty-handed. After

all, no one dressed up to stay hidden only to carry their driver's license around for all the world to see it.

Just then, there was a blood-curdling scream from the other room.

Hans leapt away from the body as if it had burned him, whirled on his heel, and bolted in her direction. The door into the office was still open, and he caught the edge of the frame to shift his momentum into the room, sliding around the corner like a drifting race car.

He ground to a halt just a fraction of a second before he could trip over her. She was kneeling on the floor, her hands clenched over her mouth so tightly that her knuckles had gone pale as she hyperventilated between her fingers.

Suedermann was slumped against the wall at the back of the room, a knife buried to the hilt in his chest and a bullet hole straight through the middle of his forehead. There was a bloody streak down the wall, from roughly Suedermann's standing height.

He dropped his gaze to where Alisha knelt, rocking. Splayed out on the floor in front of Alisha was Joshua. Or at least what was left of him. He had been shot twice without any of his gear on, and his ribcage had been so badly shattered that parts of it were visible through his chest, pushing through the skin like stalagmites.

His eyes were still open, glazed over and staring sightlessly at the ceiling. There was a puddle of blood beneath him, spreading out far enough that Alisha was kneeling in it. It soaked into her atmos pants and stained them red.

"We…we have to…" She trailed off, reaching towards Joshua's body with trembling hands, as if to attempt CPR. "We need to—" A sob ripped out of her throat, cutting off whatever else she was going to say.

Hans dropped to a crouch beside her, reaching out to catch

her wrists as he did. He pulled her hands back, murmuring, "It's too late, Alisha. It's been hours."

Even if it hadn't been, he was fairly sure they wouldn't be able to do anything.

She sagged against his side, and he looped an arm around her shoulders. As she trembled and clutched her hands together in front of her chest, Hans reached out with his free hand to close Joshua's eyes.

Neither of them spoke for a long while.

"We'll find who did this, alright?" Hans told her firmly, his arm around her shoulders, tightened, tucking her more tightly against his side. "I promise."

Memorial Park, Spire, Estaria

It was a good place to watch the service from. Plenty of people were streaming it from their holos at home, but it seemed to Giles that it would be a disservice not to be at the memorial service in person.

It was a prestigious place to host a memorial service. The complex series of branching, gleaming chrome archways that had been erected in commemoration of a battle from a war long past made for an elegant backdrop for the reporter and the others gathered, all without completely taking over the setting. It was poignant, in a way. The camera and the crew did nothing to dampen that.

As he watched the service, Giles tried to focus on the inanities —the location, double shadows where the crew's lighting and the sunlight simultaneously struck something from different angles, the reporter's hair, the crew members darting around like mice where the camera couldn't spot them, the High Priest's watch. All just to try to avoid focusing on what was actually going on.

Beside him, Arlene sniffled. The sound was partially muffled behind the tissue she held in front of her mouth and nose, but

Giles was fully aware of it all the same. It made it impossible to block out the emotion of what was going on. With a mumbled, almost sullen, "Shit," he reached up and scrubbed one wrist across his eyes, nudging his glasses out of place in the process.

It didn't really occur to him that he had scarcely heard a word the reporter—Merci? Mercy? It was something sort of sickeningly ironic like that—had been saying the entire time. He hadn't even realized when the camera had moved from the reporter and now rested on the High Priest.

He turned his attention back to the proceedings just in time for the High Priest to usher Gareth Atkins forward.

Gareth cleared his throat quietly and spoke simply. "Let's take a moment of silence for our fallen heroes. They deserve so much more for their sacrifice."

A hush fell over the park, so thick and all-encompassing that Giles might have believed it if someone had tried to tell him they had developed a sound sucking device that could blanket the entire planet.

When Gareth spoke again, it seemed too jarring, as if he were breaking some sort of sacred vow of silence.

"They gave their lives so we can continue to live in peace." His voice was low. "Though it is only the least of what they deserve, it is up to us to make sure that their memories live on."

As he continued to speak, Giles couldn't help but to feel a surge of offended outrage. There was Gareth, carrying on about the sacrifice and the heroics and how they would be remembered, as if it would make a damn bit of difference.

Remembering them wouldn't bring them back. It would just make it all the more apparent that they were gone and that they weren't coming back.

For a brief moment, Giles wanted to start shouting for all of them to just be quiet and to stop pretending that the memorial service and the pretty words would do anything other than make hypocrites feel better about what had happened.

The urge passed quickly, though. Arlene was still simpering painfully beside him. He slipped an arm around her shoulders, hoping to at least make a difference to how she felt right now.

Gareth stepped aside, letting the camera focus on the High Priest once again. He was calm almost to the point of seeming apathetic. Giles wanted to shake him and demand to know why he didn't care. Again, the urge passed and he stayed where he was as the High Priest began to speak.

"We remember another hero in this time," The High Priest enunciated carefully, his hands folded together neatly behind his back. "He, too, lost his life in the line of duty, helping to keep key witnesses safe, when none would have blamed him for looking after his own safety. His sacrifice, along with those of the ship's crew, will not be in vain. Though they have all been lost, they will not be forgotten." He took a breath and sighed slowly. "Join me once more in a moment of silence, as we pray for all the souls lost in the name of duty and peace."

Again, a hush fell over the park for a few moments. When it ended, the High Priest seemed disinterested in saying anything else.

At long last, the camera returned to the reporter. She was beginning to look slightly strained with the weight of the service. Of course, she had probably had to deal with much worse recently.

She took a few steps away from the war memorial, as if to put some distance between herself and the memorial service. After that, watching a news report in person took away most of the mystique of seeing one on a screen.

"While the identities of the crew who intervened in the misfire incident remain unknown, there is speculation," she explained, coming to a halt when just one edge of the chrome arches was still visible behind her. "It's widely thought that the ship was captained by a former fugitive, though this former fugitive was already believed to be dead previously. We do have unconfirmed reports, though, that a member of the crew was posthumously pardoned by the president for all crimes previously committed, on account of such loyal service and sacrifice to the Sark System." Her voice was calm and steady, despite the emotion of the service that had been taking place just moments before.

"While no names have been mentioned and no comment has been offered on the validity of these rumors," she continued, "it has been assumed by many that the posthumous pardon was for the former fugitive. As can be expected, regardless of the president's lack of commentary on the matter, speculation has thrived in these last few weeks, despite the nature of such a distressing event."

Giles stopped paying attention after that, turning away and starting to walk. With his arm still around Arlene, she followed along by his side without protest.

CHAPTER SIXTEEN

Senate House, Spire, Estaria

The boardroom was silent.

It wasn't full. Only roughly half of the Senate had been able to attend. The Speaker of the House, Vero, Zenne, Bel, and Raychel all sat at their seats, contemplating the walls, the ceiling, the grain of the table.

If they listened closely, they could hear a filming crew outside the room, milling about until they were allowed to come in.

At that moment, that was nearly the only activity in the building. The interns had clustered together in the break rooms. The receptionist was quiet in the lobby, and the cleaning staff were all together in their own break rooms.

On every floor, it was the same, with workers of every rank and nature sitting still and quiet.

Everyone knew what was coming, but no one quite knew how to feel about it or how to handle it. Instead, they opted en masse for respectful, almost dazed silence.

It was the Speaker who eventually broke the silence in the boardroom, curling both hands around his cane and tapping the end of it on the floor in no particular pattern. Finally, he sighed and acknowledged, "You can tell them they can come in now. If the words haven't come to me by now, then I doubt sitting here in silence even longer will help. I'll just…think of something on camera."

Vero and Bel eyed him skeptically for a moment, until Zenne rolled his eyes at both of them and made his way over to the door. It slid open and he poked his head out, nearly giving the small crew a series of heart attacks as he did.

"We're ready to begin," he stated simply before leaning back into the room, and he returned to his seat at the table just as everyone else was doing the same.

It took only a few minutes for the crew to set up the lighting to their satisfaction once they decided where they were going to film.

"Right at the table," the Speaker informed them when they asked him, turning his chair around so the table was behind him. He sat comfortably, loose and at ease in front of the small crew. He kept his hands linked together on top of his cane's handle, the end of the cane planted on the floor between his feet.

The rest of the Senate—or at least those that had managed to gather that afternoon—stayed at the table, though none of them had any plans to say anything. It was only going to be a brief program, after all, and no one wanted to start getting redundant during it.

It was the sort of situation that needed to be handled delicately, after all.

Once they began, it was just the Speaker on camera. He closed his eyes briefly, took a slow breath, and opened his eyes once again as he began to speak.

"We are here today to say good-bye to a group of heroes. A group of heroes who gave their lives to keep us from plunging into galactic war," he stated, his voice clear and even.

His hands flexed on top of his cane. "Many of us did not know them, and even more of us didn't even know *of* them, but that does not lessen what they have done for us. If anything, that makes it all the more important; they gave their lives knowing that the people they were dying for would not thank them for it."

He paused for a second and took another breath.

"We are here," he carried on, his voice firming slightly, "because it would be a discredit—a dishonor to them and what they gave to let them be forgotten. So to the crew of *The Empress*, even if they aren't here to hear this, we offer our thanks, and we offer our apology. Had we been quicker to take action, then perhaps this wouldn't have come to pass. Again, from the bottom of my heart, thank you."

With a slow, final sigh, he fell silent.

The silence lingered for a few moments once the Speaker finished, before the woman in charge of the crew announced, "Alright, that's a wrap." She turned on her heel to face the crew as they began dismantling the lighting just as efficiently as they had first set it up. It made all the initial fuss and setup seem a bit pointless, for a segment that was really just a few sentences long.

It should have been longer, probably. Molly's crew deserved more respect. They deserved more of a send-off. But no one quite knew how to react yet.

The crew left all at once, chattering amongst themselves as they left, their voices dwindling as they got farther down the hallway until they were completely inaudible. Once again, it was just the Senate in the room.

The quiet lasted for several minutes as they tried to decide if they should have been doing anything, before all individually coming to the conclusion that the answer was "not really." What had happened had happened, and no one had a time machine to undo it.

The Speaker left first, dusting himself off as he got to his feet before he turned and made his way to the door. The others lingered for a few moments, though none of them could come up with anything to say to each other. Too much had happened, and it had left all of them feeling as if the rug had been ripped out from beneath them. Some felt emotionally raw.

Vero was the last to leave, still sitting in his seat even when he was the only one left in the boardroom. He contemplated the wood grain of the table in an absentminded fashion, tapping one heel against the ground.

So much had happened, and all because no one had made a loud enough fuss about any of it.

Finally, he got to his feet and headed out the door before the "what if" scenarios could begin to plague him.

Outer Sark System

The news reports continued on multiple channels on the holostreams.

The Zhyn were not the most frequent race showcased in Estarian news, but there were always exceptions to be made. In that moment, the news showcased a naval ceremony. Footage of open space was always grainier than footage from on board a ship or within an atmosphere, but it was still apparent that the seven highest-ranking ships of the Zhyn fleet were firing their cannons into the distance.

Once, twice, and then a third time before they finished.

The calculations had been handled so very carefully, to make sure there was nothing of any importance in any of their firing paths. Some asteroids would be rendered into space dust, but nothing detrimental would happen.

The salute was eerie. Almost spectral in its silence.

The footage cut away to the bridge of a ship. It was calm, with not a single person out of place. Each member of the bridge crew visible on the screen was dutifully working at their stations, so it almost seemed as if the bridge was being staffed by a crew of mannequins. Save for one man standing at the center of the bridge, facing a camera with a calm resolve that spoke of training on how to effectively handle the media.

The banner at the bottom of the screen read in white letters *"Admiral Clor."* Though he stood stiff and steady in front of the camera, the tightness of his shoulders and the way he clenched his hands together in front of himself implied he would rather have been on the move.

His voice was artificially even as he spoke. "Though it is indeed a tragedy, their sacrifice averted what would have certainly turned into civil war. Had the Estarian-Ogg Fleet successfully fired upon the Zhyn fleet, then half of both fleets would have been wreckage before anyone realized it was a misunderstanding. Unfortunately, both sides were dealing with tensions that would warrant such a response."

He paused, glancing aside for just a moment before his gaze returned to the camera. He took a breath. "Let this represent a new era of peace between our races. Though all of us shall mourn deeply Justicar Ben'or and our allies who passed, we know he would not have wanted this to lead to bad blood between our people. From this point on, the Zhyn look forward to the day when Estaria, Ogg, and the other civilizations of the Sark systems join with the Federation, to prevent such tragedies and such unnecessary loss of life in the future."

His expression steeled slightly, an edge of commanding entering his tone. "May each and every one of us do all we can to see that their sacrifice was not in vain."

The image froze there, shrinking and shifting aside to fit neatly in the upper corner of the screen, to instead let a talk show host begin to examine the words.

Aboard Glock'stor Ship #597

Clor stood in the center of the bridge for just a second longer once the camera shut off. It bobbed in the air for a few more seconds before drifting away, returning to its docking station. Clor dragged a hand down his face and started pacing. The entire bridge seemed to breathe a sigh of relief, and almost as one, every crew member slumped into a more comfortable position.

Finally, one of the doors opened to admit Trev'or, who had been lurking in the corridor until his entrance wouldn't be an interruption after he had made a trip to the restroom.

"Politicking," Clor grumbled, mostly to himself. "Never quite caught the knack of it."

"It seemed well said to me, sir," Ruther replied, practically sitting backwards in his seat to face Clor.

Trev'or dropped himself back down into his seat, ducking over his terminal for a moment as he agreed, "Yeah," in a low voice. "Was watching on my holo."

All three of them were quiet for a moment, taking in the day-to-day noise of the bridge. It was Ruther who sighed, shaking his head in dismayed acceptance. "He's actually gone. All of them are gone."

"For such a stupid reason," Trev'or snapped, kicking a panel on the bottom of his station. There was a beat of silence, and then a low, reluctant, "Ow."

"I'm fairly sure he wouldn't have thought it was stupid," Clor replied. Though he sounded matter-of-fact, there was an undercurrent of chastisement under his words. He returned to the command chair and sat down heavily.

"Of course, sir," Trev'or agreed.

Ruther reached over to clap Trev'or on the back with one hand. His other hand was clenched around the edge of his terminal, belying his calm exterior.

The bridge lapsed into its usual buzz of background noise for a few minutes, as everyone dutifully stuck their noses back into their work. Clor sorted through his messages, handling the confusion that had echoed through the fleet like a gunshot in the last few weeks.

"It isn't fair, you know?" Ruther broke the silence.

"No one is saying it is." Clor sighed.

"I know, it's just—" Ruther made an inarticulate noise of aggravation.

"And now we're left to make nice in the aftermath," Clor finished. "I am aware."

Ruther heaved a sigh and thumped his forehead down against the edge of his terminal, considerably more gently than Trev'or had previously kicked his own.

"So what happens now?" He sighed, partially muffled in his current position.

Clor clicked his tongue. "Have a bit of faith," he scolded mildly. "Our people have always been good at picking up the wreckage and making it into something new."

"Optimism seems strange on you, sir," Ruther grumbled, though he did sit back up to get back to work.

"Part of being an Admiral means that I do what my crew needs me to do," Clor replied dryly.

And it was comforting, in a strange way. Enough that Ruther and Trev'or could get back to work as if everything was normal without it seeming quite so soul-sucking.

Memorial Park, Spire, Estaria

Gareth Atkins meandered his way down from the ceremonial stage as the crowd had already begun to disperse. His eyes were locked on the Bateses. He waved, hoping to catch their eye, but they didn't seem to see him.

He scurried through the rows as fast as he could, finally managing to flag them down as fellow mourners passed on their regards. It appeared that at least some of the intelligence community knew who the memorial was for.

He came to a halt a respectful distance from the where they stood at their seats. It took him a moment to look directly at

Director Bates. Her eyes were red-rimmed and she was covering the lower half of her face with a handkerchief. Philip stood beside her, his hands on her shoulders and his expression tight and drawn. He ducked towards his wife's shoulder for a moment, saying something in her ear in a voice too low for Gareth to pick up any of the words.

Director Bates nodded in his direction, and Philip straightened back up to look at Gareth.

"Gareth Atkins, thank you for your kind words up there," he said simply. Gareth couldn't blame him for not being especially verbose at that point.

"I'm here on behalf of the university," Gareth explained. "We wanted to let you know in person that the university will continue to run as it has been in your daughter's honor, even though it will never be the same without her."

"Thank you," Director Bates offered at last, her voice raw as she lowered her handkerchief down to her side.

"A few others are here with me," Gareth replied, looking back over his shoulder to locate the rest of his party. "They wanted to speak with you."

Looking rather out of place with the lot of them, General Lance Reynolds and his wife, Patricia, were bringing up the rear of the procession.

Gareth and the Reynolds family stood off to the side as the students formed a circle around the distraught parents, offering their condolences and telling stories of the Bateses' daughter in equal amounts. It was rather apparent that some of the stories were being told second, third, and fourth hand, the details distorted beyond any sort of believability. If nothing else, they got a damp chuckle out of Carol and Philip.

It wasn't long, though, before Gareth began to corral the students along, ushering them on their way. Lance and Patricia stayed behind, loitering until most of the somewhat public attention had passed.

Lance looked at Carol expectantly, and with some reluctance she shuffled out from between the chairs where she and Philip had been standing. Lance wasted no time before he pulled her into a hug, so tight it was nearly crushing. She clenched her hands in the back of his jacket.

Philip came out into the aisle too, allowing Patricia to shuffle around next to him. They leaned their shoulders together, letting Philip take silent comfort.

Without leaning away from Carol, Lance reminded her and Philip fiercely, "Your daughter saved lives and prevented the system from plunging into a war that no one was ready for. I already know you're proud of her, and you should be."

Carol nodded, her face hidden against his jacket. It was hollow comfort, but it was comfort nonetheless.

Outside the Bailey Residence

It was quiet as Giles took Arlene home after they left the memorial service. He thought about trying to comfort her, but the few words that came to him didn't sound particularly comforting once he thought them over, so he kept them to himself. He didn't want to make things worse, after all.

Instead, he parked in front of her home in silence and walked her to the door. They lingered on the step for a moment, both searching for something to say to the other. In the end, Giles just squeezed her shoulder before he turned and headed back to his car. He looked over his shoulder just before he climbed into the driver's seat, in time to watch her back as she disappeared into the house.

CHAPTER SEVENTEEN

Chenz' Bar, Downtown Uptarlung. Irk'n Quarter

The bar was lively when Maya stepped in through the big double doors. The sound of a bell jingling cheerfully played from a speaker just above the door as it opened and then closed behind her. One of the bartenders glanced up. She turned her attention back to her work when Maya continued walking with a purpose, evidently not in need of any immediate attention.

Maya made her way to the counter where Paige was already sitting. She pulled out a stool and hopped onto it. Paige had two drinks in front of her. She slid one over to Maya without saying a word.

Maya picked it up and swirled it in a circle for a few seconds before she lifted it to drain most of it in a couple of gulps. Paige followed suit after a moment of contemplation. They stayed quiet after that, until finally Paige heaved a sigh and slumped forward. Her forehead met the bar top and her arms splayed across the bar.

"The bartenders are giving you a look," Maya informed her eventually. "Pretty sure they think you're drooling on their nice sticky bar."

Reluctantly, Paige sat back up. She leaned her elbows on the bar and propped her chin up in her palms.

"It's been..." She trailed off as she searched for words to try to describe the recent string of events. Nothing came to her, and she settled instead for just sighing, "Yeah."

"Yeah," Maya agreed glumly.

They lapsed into silence again, until Paige elbowed Maya's shoulder. "Hey. Any idea where we are?"

"The sign said—"

"Not like that," Paige interrupted quickly, shaking her head. With her chin in her hands still, the motion distorted her voice slightly. "This place," she pulled a hand away from her face to gesture around to the rest of the bar with it, "is a lot more important than just its name. Haven't you heard about when Joel and Molly met each other?"

"Nooo," Maya answered slowly, her eyebrows rising. "No one really felt like pulling out the photo albums when I showed up."

Paige looked thoughtful for a moment before she lifted a hand to flag down one of the bartenders. She gestured to their two empty glasses and held up two fingers, and she waited for an acknowledging nod before she turned her attention back to Maya. "So, this wasn't their *first* meeting. They knew each other from before Molly got kicked out of the military. But Joel was already out. And it was here that they first met after Molly left."

She paused for just a second as two more glasses were placed in front of them. She curled a hand around hers as Maya pulled her own closer, and finally Paige launched into the epic that was Molly and Joel.

It was always a good time for a story, after all, and it felt better than only talking about the tragedy of everything that had happened.

Granted, the telling of the tale took far more time than either of them would have expected, and by the time Paige was finished, the bar was packed almost to bursting and the sun was beginning to go down outside. Maya had no doubt that at least a few of the more unbelievable parts had been exaggerated, but considering everything she had known Molly to be capable of, she wasn't actually going to stake any money on that.

"Turn it up!" someone called. Both Paige and Maya turned their attention to the holoscreen on the wall behind them. People eyed it with suspicion still, as if the whole network was now all of a sudden fallible since the dramas earlier that month. The holostream remained functional all the same. The logo for IQ News filled a bottom corner, and on screen it showed Grouthe being escorted into a courthouse by a pair of military police officers.

A young man standing on the courthouse steps watched over his shoulder as Grouthe disappeared through the massive double doors, before he turned his attention back to the camera.

Bright and chipper, he gave his commentary. "That was Captain Grouthe of the Estarian-Ogg Space Fleet, captain of *The Hierophant*, which was the ship that initiated the escalation of events in the Misfire Incident."

Maya could practically hear the capital letters that the event had acquired over the last few weeks. "He's now facing court-martial, and while the trial is still underway and we're left with speculation in the meantime, life in prison seems likely."

"Well, that's a relief," Maya murmured, turning back to face the bar again. Another glass had appeared in front of her at some point during Paige's story and been summarily emptied, though she didn't feel more than a little bit buzzed at that point.

Paige hummed a low note in agreement, still watching the screen. "Would've been better if it hadn't happened," she grumbled, finally turning her stool back around, "but I guess it's better than if he got away with it."

"I was trying to be optimistic," Maya groused in reply, though there was little heat behind the words. It seemed as if most of the planet had forgotten how to be optimistic for the time being, and she couldn't really find it in herself to blame anyone.

Paige cleared her throat, drained the last dregs of her third drink, and got that slightly befuddled, slightly constipated look on her face that meant she was trying to think of a way to change the subject.

As if to save her the effort, Paige's wrist holo started to beep insistently until she answered it. A disembodied voice, hardly audible over the chatter of the bar, wondered brightly, "Somewhere you can talk? Ah, doesn't matter, I'm not going to be saying anything that important." Immediately afterwards, he informed them cheerfully, "I'm almost done here. Security's going through its lockdown procedures. I'm just about finished shutting everything down in the weapons stores and the hangar deck." Bourne's voice took on a note of smug satisfaction as he added, "Give it ten minutes once I'm done and no one will even be able to guess that there's ever been a base down here."

"Good work, Bourne," Paige assured him, getting to her feet. "Maya and I will be there soon to get you."

"It will be so *roomy* on the isolated network." He sighed dreamily. "Right, well. Pip, pip, cheerio, all that…whatever. See you soon." The call ended, and Paige reached out to catch Maya's elbow, tugging her to her feet and towing her towards the door.

"Don't we have to pay?" Maya wondered, falling into step beside Paige as they walked through the door.

Paige waved it off flippantly. "I handled it when I got here," she replied, glancing around before deciding that going right would be the quicker route. She hadn't driven, knowing that needing to loiter until she was sober enough to drive again would just be wasting time that could be better spent on the move.

Walking, though, always led to thinking. Occasionally a little too much of it.

As they walked, Paige wondered eventually, "So, we're all sure we're making the right choice here?"

Maya wrinkled her nose. "I put the network together myself," she pointed out. "It'll be fine. Besides, it'd be cruel to just leave him up on Gaitune on his own. He'd go nuts inside a week."

"Well, yeah," Paige agreed. "But it's not exactly your handiwork I'm questioning here. I'm just…having visions—waking nightmares, even, let's go with that—about all the trouble he would find on the university network." She made her eyes wide, feigning horror as she mused, "Changing grades, tormenting students he doesn't like, pranking faculty—"

"He agreed to the code," Maya reminded her, folding her arms over her chest.

"For whatever that's worth," Paige shot back, eyebrows rising.

Maya shouldered into her good-naturedly before they both fell back into step again. They walked in silence for a little while after that, until Paige recognized the alley where she had left the pod.

"This could be the making of him," Maya stated finally, sliding her hands into her pockets. "Or I think it could, at least. Give him a chance to deal with regular, non-military people without a mission involved? He could surprise us."

Paige clapped a hand over her mouth, but a burst of laughter still bubbled forth. "*Surprising us* is what I'm worried about," she replied, though she didn't sound particularly displeased about the idea at that point. "But I guess you're right," she sighed, watching the pod swiftly descend to ground level. "No way to know until we give him a chance. Though he's probably going to laugh at us showing up buzzed to collect him."

Maya scoffed, hopping into the pod. "By the time we get there we'll both be as sober as a High Priest, and Bourne will never be the wiser." There was a beat. "Assuming he wasn't watching us through one of the bar's holoscreens."

Paige punched Maya's shoulder, her words breaking around laughter as she cried, "You're not making me feel any better about this!"

. . .

Unknown Location, Somewhere with the ARs

Cold steel and harsh darkness.

Metal surfaces housed computers and life-support machines.

Artificial, unnatural temperature differentials demonstrated that some intelligence with technology had been occupying the space with a specific agenda.

Just beyond a generator that was throwing off heat, a drop of condensation traced a path down the window on a capsule. Though it was difficult to gauge against the backdrop of machinery in darkness, on closer inspection the capsule appeared the size of a body.

A human body in this case.

The machinery functioned diligently, housed on some kind of ship: sighing and groaning as it lurched undetected in space.

Approaching the capsule, it became apparent that the environment within was controlled: oxygen content, temperature, moisture, and nutrient density. There was no doubt about it. This was a stasis capsule, although nothing that anyone this side of the frontier had ever seen before.

And there wasn't just one.

Just beyond the first, which contained a human female, there was another one. This one housed a male, also naked, and dormant. Beyond that another female, and then a Zhyn: albeit in a much bigger capsule, and then more capsules beyond.

It appeared that there were enough capsules to house an entire crew.

But not just any crew. The capsules seemed the correct size, and number, for a very particular crew.

Days had turned into weeks as the stasis capsules did their jobs, repairing and rebuilding the strange organisms that were being reassembled from teleported fragments of their DNA.

Only the consciousness of one of their guests was apparent.

He went by the designation of Oz. It seemed he was able to communicate between their systems, and one of the humans—normally, at least.

At first he had seemed distressed. They had considered that this was a result of the explosion. However, after interacting with the entity for some time, they came to understand that there was a connection between him and the human they had spoken to.

The visitors concluded that there must be some symbiotic relationship between the two entities.

Time drifted aimlessly on. Without reference to the outside world or any sensory data, Oz found he had no concept of time or space or anything beyond his overwhelming existence. Perhaps this was death. His death.

He spent the long hours, if that's what indeed they were, trying to access any data that might help him make sense of the situation. Most of his faculties were still intact. He had memories. He had access to information that he'd assimilated over his life. He regretted not having studied death a little bit more though. After all, if there was something that he could have done or was meant to be doing now in this Purgatory he found himself in, it would certainly have been nice to have a heads-up on it.

Death wasn't something the Federation had many training modules on though. It was almost as if all the effort they made was to avoid death. As if death were failure. As if death wasn't an option.

But now facing the question of his own mortality, and that of Molly's of course, he found himself contemplating what it really meant, and how he might prepare for it, knowing that it was an inevitability at some point: both for him, and his dearest human counterpart.

Why Molly had never talked about death, he didn't have any answers to either, he realized.

And what would happen to him if she died? Would he just carry on? As he exists now in this blackness alone.

If this was her death, then he didn't want any part of it. This was no life for him. He would rather not go on existing if it was without her.

His mind continued to churn in free fall... never landing.

You won't be without her, an external consciousness intervened in his own thought process. *She is healing. She'll wake when she is ready,* it reassured him.

Residential District, City of Sasea, Estaria

The house looked too simple. Considering everything it stood for, Alisha had expected it to be some enormous manor, gaudy in its opulence.

In her thoughts it had become a monolith, looming over everything.

But it was no manor.

It was just a regular townhouse, wedged in between two others. A bit on the small side, even. It had window boxes and a mat on the stoop in front of the door. If not for the number on the wall, it would have been almost impossible to tell it apart from any other house in the row. Alisha found herself reading over her copy of the rental forms—a short-term lease, applied for in a hurry and with a rather sizable down payment to grease the way—just to make sure they had the right place.

The details hadn't changed from the last several times she had read over them, and then she flipped her holo closed. Her seatbelt clicked open a second later, but she didn't move immediately, instead just sitting in the driver's seat.

She should head inside. Before Sloth realized there was an unfamiliar car parked on the curb in front of his safe house. She knew she couldn't just sit there all evening, and yet she couldn't quite bring herself to open the car door and climb out.

"You know you don't have to do this."

Hans had reminded Alisha of that detail every day for weeks, and he was determined to keep the trend going. "Not like this, at any rate. I mean, becoming a killer is kind of a big step. Not generally viewed as a good career move, you know."

"I was trained for this," Alisha reminded him, just as she had done every other time. Even so, she couldn't actually bring herself to feel annoyed about the repetition.

"You weren't trained to be a *killer*," he replied insistently. "That's not a guaranteed part of this job; you know that."

"Sloth is the reason Joshua is dead," Alisha snapped, her voice rising sharply. She gripped the steering wheel just for something to do with her hands, her fingers tightening until her knuckles paled.

"I didn't say he wasn't," Hans replied, his tone turning slightly placating. "And I didn't say that we shouldn't do anything. All I said was that you still have a choice in how this is handled, and in who handles it."

It was a familiar stance, and Alisha had protested against it the same way every time before. But it was different when she was actually looking at the townhouse, knowing that Sloth was inside and knowing what was coming.

It was different knowing that one of the men who needed to die was just a few yards away.

Slowly, Alisha slumped forward, until she was resting her forehead against the steering wheel. She felt a hand on her shoulder, and she drew in a sharp breath. Her heart just felt heavy. Heavy and dull from the pain of loss.

"Go. Just—go. I'll make sure the car doesn't get towed." The words came out in a rush as she spat them out before she could change her mind or waste even more time with more deliberation.

Hans squeezed her shoulder before he pulled his hand away.

Alisha didn't look up when she heard the car door open, instead keeping her gaze centered on the dashboard. That was where she focused for the next few moments, until she could hear Hans successfully hack the door's lock. She looked up in time to see the door open and to watch Hans step inside.

The door closed behind him, and Alisha stared at it, waiting for Hans to reemerge. She would have no way of knowing how it turned out until then; if they wanted to avoid the neighbors immediately realizing something was going on, then they needed to avoid something as noisy as a gun.

He was inside for only a few minutes, but it was still long enough for Alisha to begin putting some serious thought into just charging through the front door. Before the idea could begin to seem too tempting, though, the front door slid open once again at last and Hans stepped out.

He paused on the front step just long enough to reengage the lock, and then he cleared the distance to the car in a hurry, hopping down the few steps to the sidewalk and jogging to the car.

Once he was seated in the passenger seat, Alisha didn't even wait for him to buckle his seatbelt before she started the car and pulled away from the curb. The car rose into the air and began to speed away. From the corner of her eye, Alisha could see Hans cleaning his knife before he slid it back into his boot.

They drove in silence at first. It didn't last for long, though, before Alisha turned off at the first exit and pulled the car to a halt at the first rest stop she spotted. The car sank gradually to the ground, where she parked and slumped back in her seat.

"So nothing strange happened?" she asked, glancing at him sidelong. "Nothing we need to worry about?"

"I wouldn't put it past any of them to have some sort of contingency plans," Hans replied carefully, "but no, everything went about as we expected it to."

Alisha nodded slowly, distracted, her thoughts churning like sea foam. Finally, voice low, she offered, "Thanks. For...not letting me do that."

"I wouldn't have stopped you if you really wanted to," he pointed out.

She nodded again. "I know, yeah. I just…" She heaved a sigh, her head falling back against the backrest. "I just don't think I'm quite ready for that sort of thing yet." She wrinkled her nose. "So much for training. Joshua deserved better than me just sitting in the car keeping the seat warm."

"Hey." Hans's voice was firm. His hand closed around hers and he squeezed, his grip warm. "No amount of training makes you *ready* to kill someone. If you can put it off, then you should, for as long as you feasibly can. And regardless of who killed whom, we wouldn't have even found him without you."

"I know," she mumbled, before she straightened up, turning to actually look at him. "I know," she repeated, firmer that time. Her expression steeled as she asked, "Where to next?"

Hans cleared his throat. "We've got reports of Ghetti hiding out in Shanxi in the Kalamar district, on Ogg," he replied. "Once he's dealt with, that's that."

"I'm coming with you," Alisha insisted instantly, her fingers finally tightening around Hans's.

He looked down at their joined hands, and then back up at her. "Well, as long as you're sure," he agreed.

Alisha scoffed. "Of course I'm sure," she replied, as she started the car once again. "Let's get it organized. No time like the present."

CHAPTER EIGHTEEN

Giles's Classroom, Skóli Uppstigs Academy, Spire, Estaria
There was a blog that was well-known amongst the students of the university. They referred to it as the school paper. *The Bates Explainer* was typed across the top of the blog in letters that looked as if they had been made with an antique typewriter—and they liked to think that it was a secret.

They weren't entirely correct on that front, but the blog did its job admirably all the same.

Molly had always been so good at telling stories. They had been her way of relating to her students. They had been her way of assuring them that yes, what they were learning would someday come in handy in the real world and they weren't just trapped in a cycle of rote memorization.

The *Explainer* had always been a way to share her stories, passing them on to students who hadn't had a chance to hear them in person. It had become something of a shrine in the past few weeks, with new entries pouring in at an unprecedented rate. Some fantastical stories, some mission stories, and some daily encounters that were simply...Molly, as she was when she wasn't saving the world.

As Giles patrolled through the rows of desks and chairs in his classrooms, he stopped when he came upon the fourth student in the room surreptitiously trying to read the *Explainer* under her desk on her wrist holo. He loitered there for a few moments, waiting for her to notice him. Gradually, other students in the room began to snigger as she continued to fail to notice Giles standing there.

Finally—finally!—she tensed as the student just in front of her glanced over his shoulder and then rapidly looked away. Like a nervous fawn, she peered over her shoulder, and hastily turned off her wrist holo and folded her hands on top of her desk.

"Professor," she greeted cheerfully, as if she had simply been waiting for him to continue the lesson the entire time.

"Welcome back," Giles returned, followed by, "If you're that disinterested in the lesson, I do have to wonder why you're actually here." Not that he had much of a leg to stand on, but he was, at the very least, considerably better at faking his interest in education at this difficult time.

The girl flushed and slid down in her seat, mumbling, "Sorry, professor."

With a sigh and a brief shake of his head, Giles continued on his way, strolling back to the front of the class. It seemed that the lesson was effectively forgotten by that point, though, as they were all talking once he made it back to the front of the room.

What's going to happen to this place without her?

This was her school. What does that mean for the rest of us?

Hey, remember that time at the Senate building?

Does anyone else remember that thing she did with the necktie?

She was such a badass. Think I'll ever be able to do anything like that?

Giles brought two fingers up to his mouth and whistled, sharp enough to nearly break glass, and every student in the room whipped their attention back towards him.

"As a reminder, we have counseling available for anyone who

feels like they need it," he pointed out. "Even if you only think you might need it a little. A little can turn into a lot when you least expect it."

He got a murmured cloud of affirmations, but he knew he wasn't going to get them back on task at that point. He set them to doing bookwork until it was time to dismiss them, knowing they would hardly get any of it done.

His students left in a haze of chatter once the class ended, filing out of the room. As soon as they finished traipsing out of the class, Gareth stepped into the room.

Giles sat on the edge of his desk, and his eyebrows rose expectantly as he looked at Gareth, waiting for him to say his piece.

"How's Arlene holding up?" Gareth asked casually.

Giles felt like the rug had been yanked out from under his feet. It wasn't exactly the line of questioning he was expecting. He also felt a pang of guilt rip through his chest. He'd been so caught up in his own grief, he hadn't really been paying much attention to what she must be going through.

He cleared his throat. "She could be better," he replied. "She's taking time off of work to take care of Anne, but I don't think she sees much of a purpose in any of this anymore."

Gareth nodded in quiet acknowledgment. "It's a lot to take in. She's going to need people that she can lean on to help her get through it."

Giles shifted back and forth on the edge of the desk. "She doesn't answer my calls most of the time. Apparently she wants to be left alone."

Gareth shrugged one shoulder, as if that decision made perfect sense. Maybe it did. Giles wasn't exactly a therapist.

"It's an awful situation to be stuck in," Gareth said, before he settled a probing look on Giles. "And what about you?"

"What about me?" Giles repeated back, his tone turning slightly guarded.

"How are you holding up?" Gareth asked, perfectly patient despite Giles's sudden swing into defensiveness.

"Fine," Giles replied tersely, drumming his fingers against the edge of his desk.

Gareth's eyebrows rose. "'Fine,'" he repeated dubiously. "You're sure?"

Giles shifted again, almost squirming that time. "Well—" He cut himself off, but Gareth heard him all the same, leaning forwards slightly. Giles sagged as he sighed. "It's just—I mean, losing Molly—losing *anyone*, I guess—" He paused and swallowed. His voice was starting to sound like gravel and his throat felt tight, and he just needed a second to gather his composure before he lost it.

"It's...hard," he admitted. "I've been reevaluating some things. You know what it's like."

Gareth clapped him on the shoulder. "I understand. After I lost my wife, picking up the pieces took me...well." He chuckled, though it wasn't a particularly happy sound. "We'll be charitable and just say it took me a while."

Giles nodded slowly, in slightly distracted understanding. Gareth eyed him for a moment longer, waiting to see if Giles would say anything else. When he didn't, Gareth turned and slowly left the room.

Giles was left alone in his classroom, staring at empty desks and empty chairs. He stayed there for a few more minutes, sitting on the edge of his desk, before he pushed away from it and headed towards the classroom door.

He turned the lights out as he left.

Giles's Office, Skóli Uppstigs Academy, Spire, Estaria

The walk down the hall seemed to take twice as long as it usually did.

His footsteps sounded loudly on the tile floor.

Where was all the chatter? It was a university. It was a school. It was never supposed to be this quiet. He was pretty sure that was against at least a few of the natural laws of physics.

The sound of his office door sliding open seemed to grate on him more than usual, and the office felt much darker. *Almost matching his mood,* he mused to himself. Despite that, he still didn't bother to turn on the lights. His eyes would adjust, and in the meantime it was an effort that he couldn't see any point in making.

He leaned back against the door for a moment as he heaved a slow sigh.

"Quite a day."

And apparently it was ending with him talking to himself.

Giles couldn't even bring himself to be annoyed at that point. He pushed himself away from his office door and took the few steps to cross the room, and he dropped down into his chair behind his desk.

It was more like he was tumbling down into it, actually, like a puppet that had been put through a very long day. But there was no one else there to see him, so it didn't really matter.

He leaned back in his seat, staring blankly at the ceiling. There was work he needed to be doing—days' worth of grading on the holosystem—but he couldn't quite bring himself to get to it just then. It would still be there later. Besides, if he graded everything, he would have to hand it all back. And once that happened, at least a few of his students were bound to have questions. At least some of those questions would be in-depth enough that it would be better to answer them in his office without taking up class time. So the longer he put it off, the longer he got to avoid inviting anyone into his office.

A necessary thing, really, considering the state of the rest of the room, he considered, casting his gaze around his immediate environment.

He hadn't taken his trash out in days, there was still an old take-out container sitting on top of a cabinet and attracting bugs, and the entire room smelled faintly like a pair of running shoes that hadn't been aired out since before the age of space travel. He couldn't even imagine what his office would look like if everything was still handled on paper. It would look like a snowstorm had ravaged it.

It was an embarrassment, really, and he dreaded the day someone knocked on his office door and asked to come in. Because he cared about it enough that he didn't want anyone else to see it, and yet not quite enough to actually do anything about it. Yet.

He kept adding that *yet* onto everything.

He wasn't doing his grading *yet*. He wasn't working on his lesson plans *yet*. He wasn't planning the next quizzes or tests *yet*. He wasn't cleaning up the mess that could be called an office *yet*.

He wasn't talking to the university's counselors *yet*.

He wasn't sure if it actually meant anything by that point, but examining it from other angles didn't feel especially pressing in that moment. So he told the little voice reminding him that he should be working to stuff it, and instead he leaned down to the cupboard under his desk. He pulled out a glass and a half-full bottle of Yollin whiskey, and he poured himself three fingers. He left the bottle on his desk. There was no sense in putting it away just yet.

He held the glass for a moment, tipping it this way and that way for a moment to make the amber contents swirl. Finally, he took a sip and opened up his holoconsole.

He had heard rumors of an archaeological dig starting up in the ruins of Gresshone over in the Orn System, and another in what remained of the city of Weishrei on Plantasica-8. They were both far enough away from everything else that had happened that he would have a chance to just decompress and absorb everything. If he decided to go, at any rate. His students weren't going to cease to exist within the next few weeks, after all. He supposed he would be rather concerned if they did.

And he supposed he could do a little more research before he came to a final decision. Not quite yet. That would just be the responsible thing to do, after all. It would set a good example for his students.

He tipped his head back to drain his glass.

Bailey Residence, Spire, Estaria

The doorbell rang and Arlene rushed to answer the door. She heard chattering, giggling and cooing on the other side. She knew who it was without looking. Unlocking the door, she swung it open with the biggest smile that she could muster. "Paige! Maya! So good to see you both," she chimed, trying to match their levity.

The two girls stood there beaming, half their attention on the sphinx basket carried between them. "I don't think he wanted to come," Paige confessed. "It took the both of us half an hour to track him down, and then another half an hour to get him in the basket."

Arlene waved them in. "Well that's just sphinxes for you," she explained. "They're ferociously independent, and march to the beat of their own drum."

"You're not kidding," Maya sighed as they placed the basket down on the floor. "This one certainly has a mind of his own. Do you want us to let him out now? Here?"

"Yes, yes," Arlene confirmed, fussing about the clothes and things that were lying around the apartment. She gathered up some take-out dishes and shipped them into the kitchen before her guests could look too closely at the state of the place. "Let him out so he can start getting used to the place. In the meantime let me put some food out for him," she called through from the kitchen.

Maya and Paige set about letting Neechie out of his container, and Anne appeared from her room, having heard their voices.

"Neechie!" she squealed in delight. Taking one look at her, however, Neechie flashed out of realm and disappeared. Anne stopped in her tracks, arms outstretched, while the others collapsed into heaps of giggles.

Arlene appeared from the kitchen laughing too. "Come on, Anne, you know not to scare him."

"It'll take more than me to scare that thing," Anne grumbled, hurt.

A moment later the sphinx appeared on the sofa behind them.

"Slowly now," Arlene warned as Anne made her way towards him, stalking like a snuggle-predator. This time Neechie allowed her to approach and she started petting him.

"Can I get you anything?" Arlene offered to Paige and Maya. "A mocha or something?"

Maya checked her holo and then slapped at Paige's arm. "We're going to be late. We've got to get going."

Paige checked her holo too. "Shit, you're right. Rain check on the mocha?" she asked, glancing up at Arlene.

Arlene nodded, half relieved that they wouldn't be inspecting the state of the apartment too closely, but also half disappointed that they wouldn't be staying to keep her company.

"Arlene, if there's anything that we can do, though, just shout," Maya insisted. "We're staying pretty close to campus now, so barely a stone's throw away."

Arlene nodded as she walked them back towards the door. "Thank you, I will. OOoh, was this your sphinx carrier?"

Page shook her head. "No, it belongs to Neechie. Best keep it with him… Just in case you need to transport him anywhere else."

"Thank you," Arlene repeated as the two girls headed out the apartment and down the corridor towards the stairs.

"See you soon, Arlene," Paige chirped. "We should do drinks together soon," she added.

"Good idea," Arlene called down the corridor after them. She stepped back into the apartment and headed back into the living room to see Anne carrying Neechie through to her sleeping quarters, chattering away to him as if the previous snub had been forgotten.

Arlene wandered back into the kitchen to carry on tidying up. Maybe ten minutes had passed before Anne reappeared again.

This time in tears. "He's gone. He's gone again, Arlene. I think he's gone for good," she sobbed.

Arlene stepped towards the crying girl. "Hey come on, that's not true. Sphinxes do this. It's perfectly natural. They disappear, and then they come back. Remember, they have more dimensions to explore than we have. They realm walk. They see more than us, and sometimes they tell us things. That's why they're good to have around." She smiled weakly, trying to reassure the fragile girl.

"You don't understand," Anne sobbed. "He's gone, just like everyone else. Just like everyone goes."

Looking at the tears streaming down her face, she recognized her own vulnerability at her recent loss.

"That's not true," Arlene tried to reason with her. "Is this about Ben'or?"

"No," Anne lied through her tears. "It's just he's gone, and now Giles has gone. And Paige and Maya have gone, and they're not coming back." Her voice increased in volume and aggression as she ranted.

"What makes you—"

"And it's all your fault!" Anne concluded, working herself up into a state, talking through tears.

"Why is it my fault?"

"You said something to Giles. Something to upset him, so that he doesn't come back."

Arlene took a deep breath and tried to console her. "What are you talking about?" she asked gently.

"He hasn't been back since the memorial service. You said something to him, didn't you?"

"No… No I didn't."

"So why has he gone? Why doesn't he want to see me anymore?"

"Sweetie, he doesn't not want to see you. I mean… of course he wants to see you. I think you're just being a little bit—"

"A little bit what?" Anne shot back accusingly. Her eyes burned with tears now, red-rimmed and puffy. "Giles doesn't want to see me anymore and it's all because of you. He was my only friend!"

"That's not true," Arlene continued to protest. "None of that is true!"

"Well, why hasn't he been around then?"

"He's dealing with it in his own way. That's Giles."

"Well, he was around in the beginning. What did you say to him?"

"Nothing!"

"Liar. I bet you gave him a hard time and sent him away."

Their voices could be heard down the corridor and in the adjacent apartments. The shouting continued for several minutes. One of the neighbors stepped out into the hallway to make sure it was nothing that needed the police called in on.

Then everything went quiet. The shouting stopped, only to be replaced by quiet sobbing.

Arlene sat down on the sofa. "Giles is going through a lot. I lost Ben'or, but he lost Molly. And he's never been very good with emotions. Or losing people. His normal thing is to withdraw, and then take off."

"You mean leaving? He's leaving Estaria?"

Arlene blew her nose into a tissue that she pulled from her sleeve. "Maybe. Again, like Neechie, it's just what he does. But he'll be back."

"When? Hundred years from now? Wasn't that how long it took him last time he left you?"

Arlene exhaled, exasperated, pained by Anne's words. Anne didn't wait for a response. She just flounced back to her room, crying.

CHAPTER NINETEEN

Unknown Location, Somewhere with the ARs

No one knows how long it was before the first heartbeat was detected, but it happened. And in that moment, the onlookers breathed a collective sigh of satisfaction.

She's waking up, the entity reported. *She has a heartbeat and brain activity. She's... Alive!* Oz watched as her vitals started to reinvigorate with life.

>*Of course she is alive*, they told him. *What do you think all this is about?*

I still don't understand, Oz responded.

>*You will. When she awakens, everything will make more sense.*

The filtration system kicked on in the capsule and started extracting the excess moisture from the air within the capsule. Over several minutes, the condensation on the capsule's window started to clear.

Molly stirred, as if waking from a nap. Not yet fully conscious, she tried to move in her sleep but found herself unable to change her position.

Where am I?

>*You're safe*, the voice told her in her mind.

She wasn't fully aware of her mouth or throat, or even if she was breathing.

>You're not awake yet. You're not using your mouth to speak.

This is like in my dreams.

>And when we talked to you, when we urged you to prepare your planet.

Yeah, about that... I think I failed.

Her brain activity spiked. *Hang on! I died. We had a plan to keep everyone safe. But we died. We all died. Joel, and Jack, and Sean and—*

Oz interrupted her thoughts. **It's okay. You're not dead. They're all alive, so I'm told. It's the ARs. They saved us.**

How?

I'm still trying to figure that out, but I think they had some kind of teleportation device where they pulled your DNA from the ship before it exploded.

But what about my memories? My consciousness? How did they pull that?

The voice in her head interrupted. *We have technology beyond your comprehension. I suppose an easy way to explain it to you is that we took a photograph of everything: who you are, your essence, your DNA... Everything... And now we're just rebuilding it.*

Molly's brow creased into a frown that would have been visible even through the capsule's window, had there been anyone there to see. *That means that consciousness is separate from the body...*

Oz chuckled. **I just felt your cortex light up as you started to try and figure this out!**

Molly smiled, despite the bizarre situation.

So what's the plan? she asked the AR.

>You need some more time to rebuild, but then when you're done, we will let you go.

Let us go? Our ship was destroyed. You can't just leave us in space. Our fragile bodies will—

>Yes, we're well aware. It was, after all, us who created you.

It was? Giles was right all this time...

>*He was.*

So what does this mean for the system? Did the Estarians attack? What happened with the Zhyn? Did you survive okay?

>*We did. Thanks to your sacrifice, all is well.*

But... I thought we failed.

>*You did no such thing. You showed the Estarians what it is like to come together. All being well, this'll be a turning point in their evolution, and the beginning of a new era of cooperation between the parties involved.*

You mean... You knew this was gonna happen?

>*We had an idea. But we needed a champion. Someone to spread the word and show them by example.*

You mean us?

>*Yes.*

But I don't understand... How did you choose us?

>*We saw who you were when you called us.*

And what if someone else had called you? What if someone more warmongering had been at the other end of the communication?

>*Well, then we would have acted accordingly.*

What does that mean?

>*We probably wouldn't have allowed our presence to be known to them.*

But to what end? Why would you want the more evolved people of Estaria to know that you exist? And why now?

>*It was always our intention. But we needed you to be involved and aware enough in order for us showing up to not create massive fear and panic.*

But it did create massive fear and panic!

>*And in the end you, as a civilization, prevailed.*

Molly snorted lightly. *I don't know what I look like, but I know I got blown apart. Doesn't feel like we prevailed.*

>*Ahh but you did. And for your efforts and sacrifice, we are incredibly grateful. You have changed the course of history in this entire*

galaxy. Your reward is life: another chance to spend it how you will. But for now... Rest. There will be plenty of time to figure everything out soon.

Molly found herself becoming drowsy, her consciousness drifting from her once again.

Safe House, Gaitune-67

The safe house was dark. Dust had already begun to gather and settle on surfaces. It had been several months since the base had been fully operational: the busyness and activity of the Sanguine Squadron now just a distant memory in the minds of those who had been left behind.

All essential systems had been shut down, including life support. What was left of the air would likely be gone in a matter of weeks, replaced by vacuum as it escaped through the unmaintained seals around the doors.

With the processors turned off, there wasn't even a heat signature in the building. The only remaining systems left on were the security ones that protected what was left of the base downstairs. But now, just as before the base was resurrected by Molly and the crew, it lay dormant. Silent. Unnoticed. Forgotten.

Neechie appeared just outside of the Daemon door. He looked up at the camera that monitored the access to the base. If anyone had been watching, they might have seen how he looked intently right into the camera as if trying to tell them something.

Unacknowledged by the system on the other side of the camera lens, Neechie turned on the spot and paced quietly through the darkness that was once Brock's workshop. Slowly and deliberately he padded up the steps through to the main safe house. He paused briefly in the foyer, glancing at the now decommissioned airlock. Then he wandered over to the sofa, turned to face the door and sat down to wait.

The next time Molly stirred again, she felt different: strange. Like she wasn't at home in her own body.

If it was even her own body...

She became aware that she was lying on something hard. And cold.

She shifted her arm to her head and rolled over, feeling the cold, hard surface beneath her. There was a light on the other side of her eyelids. Slowly she peeled them open, squinting into the light.

"What the fuck?" she breathed. As her eyes became accustomed to the light, she was able to make out shapes. And those shapes told her that she appeared to be lying on the cockpit floor... on the floor of *The Empress*.

She blinked, allowing her eyes the chance to adjust.

Oz, are you there?

I'm here.

Oz? What the fuck?

I know.

Are the others okay?

The last I spoke to the ARs, they were going through the same process as you.

You spoke to the ARs?

Molly pushed herself up off the ground and swiveled around on her hip bone to see Joel nearby. She was vaguely aware of the others around her too. They were all starting to stir.

"Joel," she hissed, scampering over to his side on her knees.

"Fuuuuuuck..." he rasped.

She looked down at him as he slowly started to open his eyes. "You're alive! I can't believe it, we're all alive!"

We are alive aren't we, Oz? I'm not hallucinating?

Yes, we're alive.

She watched the others come around, dazed and confused by their new status.

"I thought we bought it," Joel grunted, sitting up on his elbows. "What on Sark happened?"

Molly smiled. "I do believe we've been rewarded for our sacrifice. Life after death, as it were…" She chuckled.

"But how?"

"The ARs," she said simply, piecing together what she had thought was a dream with their new reality.

By now the others started to comprehend what had happened and were listening intently to anything Molly could tell them. "I guess their tech really is light-years more advanced than ours. Somehow they were able to take a snapshot of who we were and teleport us out of the situation… And then… rebuild us."

Sean gingerly tapped at his knee. "Well at least they rebuilt us as we were. I couldn't tell you how much all my enhancements cost, and no way I'd get Lance to spring for a new set after all this…"

Karina snorted lightly in both amusement and disbelief. She pulled herself upright against the wall she and Sean had been thrown against during the explosions. "We're alive! I can't freaking believe it!"

"Believe it, baby," Sean said, crawling over to her. What he said next was indeterminable and morphed into a series of kissing noises.

"Ugh! Get a room, guys!" Pieter scolded them from across the cockpit floor. Everyone chuckled.

Crash remained silent, taking it all in, pinching himself… and then pinching Brock to see if it was true.

Brock sat up next to him inspecting his hands as if they might hold clues as to how this was possible. "I just… I just can't believe it…" he muttered to himself, shaking his head, and then swatting Crash away as he pinched him a little too hard.

Molly scooted across and sat up against the wall, where Joel joined her. "A lot to process," he commented dryly.

"No shit, Sherlock," Molly agreed. "Should we, erm, have some kind of procedure that we should follow? You know, to help the team process any possible trauma and whatnot?"

Joel rubbed his face as if seriously considering the question. "Personally I'd prescribe a crate of beer and a couple of pizzas to help with this little conundrum."

Molly narrowed her eyes. "You're joking, right?"

"Actually, I wasn't. As far as what the Federation would want us to do… fuck knows. I'm not sure how many cases they've ever had of this… People coming back from the dead. Hey Sean?"

Sean peeled himself off Karina and sat back on the floor so that he could see everyone else. "Yeah?"

"You ever heard of people coming back from the dead? And like… the protocol for that?"

Sean racked his brain for a few moments. "Well I'm sure something similar has happened at some point. Heck, I've even known a few people to fake their deaths over the years…"

Karina eyed him warningly, willing him not to get into that right now.

Sean continued. "But as for what we've been through… I'm not sure. Although," he added, having another thought, "I think our interaction with the new species, and a highly evolved technological one at that, might be worth mentioning at some point. In a report."

"Or not," Jack added, rubbing subconsciously at her arm almost to comfort.

"What do you mean?" Molly asked.

"I mean, if the Federation finds out what we've been through, what are the odds of them letting us just go back to our lives. Surely they'll want to prod us. Study us. You know…"

Sean screwed his face up. "You've spent too long in the

Estarian army, m'lady. The Federation would recognize we're people, not lab rats."

Molly shot Sean a look. "You sure about that?"

Sean scoffed and waved his hand in Molly's direction. "Well sure. You're a case in point... A rare cornucopia of new technology and unexplained abilities, and what did they do? They let you carry on running one of the most delicate operations in the entire Federation. Unsupervised. Unmonitored. With no checks and balances..."

Molly stared at him in stunned silence.

Joel interjected on her behalf. "I wouldn't say unsupervised... After all, isn't that what your job is?"

Sean shot him a look, which softened into an amused eyebrow shrug, almost admitting to the charge.

Molly found her tongue. "Nice to know what you really think, Royale. Would you rather they had locked me up in a lab and run tests on me all these years?"

Sean lowered his eyes. "I'm not saying that..."

"Good," Molly and Joel said at the same time. They exchanged a brief glance of surprise.

"The point is," Molly continued, having found her equilibrium, "we need to think long and hard before we let anyone know that we're alive. So let's just take some time, get our bearings, figure out where the hell we are, and come to terms with our new status."

"The undead!" Pieter chuffed.

"Quite," Molly agreed. "Hang on..." She scanned the room with a quick, concerned glance. "Has anyone seen Ben'or?"

There were mutters and shakes of heads around the cockpit floor. Molly scrambled to her feet. She noticed her legs were wobbly, like they weren't used to being used. "I'm going to look for him," she announced, heading out of the cockpit door. "Don't turn on any of the computers!" she called over her shoulder as she staggered out.

Stepping tentatively down the steps from the cockpit, she held the banister as she had hundreds of times before. It felt strange in her hand. Though, she couldn't tell whether it was because her hand was new... Or perhaps the banister was new. Distracted by wanting to find Ben'or, she subconsciously clocked that some of this color scheme looked different too.

She hit the button to enter the lounge. The door swooshed open, allowing her passage through. The lounge felt strangely familiar. Yet different. She made a note to check for the slight stretch in the material of the seats next to her normal seat where she would often dump her bag. Her eyes at this moment were busy scanning for her friend and colleague.

"Ben'or," she called softly.

There was a groan from further down the aisle. She caught sight of movement and started scrambling towards it. "Ben'or? Are you okay? Where are you?"

She stopped in her tracks, his big blue mass catching her eye from between two rows of seats. He seemed to be just coming to his senses, holding his head and trying to get up. Molly offered him a hand. "Have you just woken up?"

"Yes, although given I thought we were all dead, I'm somewhat confused..."

Molly grinned up at him. "You and the rest of us included," she agreed. "But it's a happy result, you got to admit."

Ben'or started to chuckle. "Well you could say that indeed... A happy result. Arlene will be pleased."

Molly's smile faded as she considered the possibilities.

What if we can't go back?

Why wouldn't you?

Well, like Jack was saying. What if we are turned into experiments? What if we're a security risk now? What if they won't let us go?

I think that's unlikely, but we need to consider possibilities.

Besides, how long have we been gone?

I haven't connected up to the computer yet. I'll know soon.

Emma? What about Emma? Can you see if she's here too?

Sure. But I'll also stop any signals being sent out until we know a little bit more.

Cool. Make sure the guys in the cockpit know that as well. Last thing we want is them making our presence known before we know what to do.

No problem. I am all over it.

By now Ben'or was nearly on his feet. "I must say, this death thing has certainly weakened my posture." He steadied himself by grabbing the back of a chair. "I take it everyone else is okay?"

"They are," Molly confirmed softly. "Thank goodness. Oz is just seeing if Emma is still functioning. Once we know that, we can start figuring out how long we've been out, where we are, and of course what to do next."

"Get us back to Estaria, is my vote!" he exclaimed jovially.

Molly smiled and said nothing, realizing that she'd had vital few minutes more to process everything, and the implications.

Slowly and casually the pair of old friends picked their way back through the sea of chairs in the lounge to the cockpit to reunite with the others.

"At least we weren't put back naked," Molly commented dryly as they walked. Jack looked at her in horror as they came through the cockpit door.

"Oh yes," Molly continued, "Oz tells me that when we were in the capsules being rebuilt, we were without clothes. Obviously. But then somehow they magically dressed us with some kind of clothes in the teleportation machine. Go figure."

Her comments were mostly lost amongst the excitement as the crew said their hellos to Ben'or. It seemed that in the few minutes that she was out of the cockpit, hugging and crying, and life reflections had begun.

Joel sidled up to her.

"Tell me," she said to him quietly, "is there like a five-step process to go with realizing that you're alive…? You know, like there is one for when someone close to you dies?"

Joel chuckled. "I really don't think there have been enough instances for anyone to recognize the patterns."

"Hmm, maybe that's something that we should document. You know, for future generations that are brought back from the dead."

Joel rolled his eyes. "I think we have more important things to consider," he said, pulling her away from the group. "Are you ready to talk about next steps?"

His face was serious. Molly felt her heart sink. This was the bit where she had to make the difficult decisions.

Couldn't she just revel in the relief of being alive before she had to get all serious? she wondered, sighing despondently.

"Okay," she agreed reluctantly, allowing him to lead her back out into the corridor again.

CHAPTER TWENTY

Bailey Residence, Spire, Estaria

Anne was lying on the bed, scrolling through media on a locked-down holo that Arlene had organized for her in recent weeks. She still wasn't allowed one of her own on account of it being traceable, but this was a compromise of sorts. She scrolled past some more boring news videos, noticing idly that there was very little chatter about the avoided war and the memorial service now that it was all over with.

She rolled over onto her back, trying to avoid the heaviness inside of her by distracting herself with more scrolling.

Just then she felt movement on her bed. She lowered the holoscreen in front of her to see Neechie walking lightly towards her.

"Oh, you're back, are you?" She scoffed at the catlike creature that had heartlessly abandoned her.

Neechie didn't reply. Instead he just snuggled up to her chest and tucked his head under her chin.

Anne didn't cuddle him back. "I bet you only came back because you are hungry," she jibed.

The sphinx still didn't respond. Rather, he just lay there

comfortably against her, almost as if he were comforting her. Anne tried to go back to scrolling through recent media reports but found it awkward to rise on her back, hold her wrist up and scroll with Neechie in the way. She gave up and relaxed, allowing the holo screen to close down.

The sphinx didn't move. Anne's hand fell onto him, and subconsciously she started petting him. He smelled musty. As if he had been somewhere that was shut down. Somewhere that she recognized.

She sniffed at him, trying to place the smell.

A second later she sprung from the bed and ran through to Arlene's room where she was lying on a bed scrolling through things on her holo too.

"Arlene, what did you say about sphinxes knowing things, and trying to tell us stuff?"

Arlene looked up, surprised. "What do you mean?"

"Neechie has just come back," she explained. "He smells of the safe house. I'd recognize that smell anywhere!"

Arlene went back to reading her holo. "Is that so?" she responded with an enigmatic smile.

"Yes, that is so. So that's it?" Anne asked. "You don't think we should get up there and investigate? You even said he knew things that we didn't…"

Arlene appeared strangely serene. "Let's just wait. All things will become apparent in time."

Giving up, Anne grunted and flounced back to her own room, this time to interrogate Neechie directly.

Aboard *The Empress*, Location Unknown

"Okay, what do we know?" Molly asked, putting her brain in gear. The door swished closed behind them, enclosing them in the cone of silence that was the corridor between the lounge and the cockpit.

Joel shrugged. "Not much. We are alive again. What else do *you* know?"

Molly pressed her lips together, her gaze on the floor as she searched her brain. "I seem to remember having a conversation with the ARs sometime before we woke up. They basically said, well, what I've already told you…"

She tilted her head up to the intercom. "Oz? Is there any way of figuring out a few things without powering up all the systems and giving away our location?"

"Yeah, working on it now… I haven't been able to locate Emma though," he reported back to both of them.

"Okay, keep trying. In the meantime what can you tell us?"

"Well, there are no signs of the ARs, at least in the immediate vicinity. I'd need to power up the radars and long-range sensors to know more."

"Any idea where we are?"

"Yes," he replied. "It seems we are pretty much where we were when we took the fire."

Molly exchanged a concerned look with Joel.

"And what about the two fleets?" she pressed.

"Neither here. Which brings me onto my next deduction. I think it's safe to say that it's been some time since we disappeared. Background radiation is consistent with the missile fire that we were experiencing, and the explosion of our fuel core."

Molly's breath caught in her throat.

Joel took over what they both wanted to ask. "And can you use the decay curve to tell us how long it's been since we exploded?"

"I can. Give me a few seconds."

While they waited, Joel poked his head through the door of the lounge, as if it might give him some important clues about *when* they might be. "New color scheme," he noted.

Molly rolled her eyes.

He ambled a couple of steps to look out of the window.

"Anything?" Molly asked.

He shrugged. "Just looks like space out there..."

"Hang on." Molly shuffled past him and through into the lounge. She strode through to the other side, near the front, where she would normally sit.

"What is it?" he called after her.

"I've just thought of something." She stopped dead next to a couple of the chairs, then turned back to him. "It's not the same ship."

"How do you know?"

"I would always bring my gear with me and plonk it in this seat next to me..."

"Yeah. I remember. I thought it was a tactic so that no one could sit next to you."

"It was," she confessed blankly. "But it made a dent in the seat over time. Stretched the material. This material is new... as if it's never been used."

She looked down at the bottoms of the backs of the other chairs. "No one has ever sat in these chairs. If they had, there would be tiny scuff marks everywhere."

"I think we need to start calling you Sherlock in the future," Joel chuffed from the other side of the lounge.

"Okay," Oz announced, interrupting Molly's investigation. "I've got it. Looks like we've been gone about eight weeks since the explosion."

Molly and Joel looked at each other.

Joel raised his eyebrows. "Wow. That's gonna be some overtime!"

"Eight weeks," Molly muttered under her breath. "We've been gone for eight weeks. And died. And come back."

Joel pushed his bottom lip out thoughtfully. "Yeah, imagine. At least the world won't have changed that much in eight weeks. I mean, I've read some sci-fi stories where crews have got caught up in gravitational tides and when they managed to get out, hundreds of years had passed in the real world."

"Good job we're not in a sci-fi book," Molly mused dryly.

"Yeah, there is that. But we still need to decide what to do next. I think the only sensible play is to contact the Federation and see what Lance wants us to do."

Molly scratched at her face as she thought about the conundrum. "Okay. Maybe. But can we just mull it a bit longer. Jack did have a point…"

Joel sighed. "Okay, but not too long. The others will want to be deciding their futures as soon as this sinks in, and we don't want them dreaming about things that they can't do: like going home, if they can't. The disappointment could be… devastating."

"Okay, I hear you… We should head back in," she added, turning back towards the cockpit, her mind churning the decisions that they were going to have to make very soon.

Inside the cockpit, things were starting to look a little bit more normal.

For a start, no one was sitting on the floor anymore. In fact, Brock, Crash and Pieter had all taken up their usual positions at their consoles and were now poring away over any information they could get from the central computer.

"Nope." Brock shook his head, responding to something someone else had said. "This is definitely not the same ship. No way. I mean it looks similar. Same interface—kind of… But the processing array is different. Far more efficient in fact. And there are a bunch of directories I have no idea what they are for… It's going to take me some time to figure this out."

Molly moved over to his console and peered over his shoulder. "So what are you saying?"

"This ain't the same ship!"

"But it looks the same," she argued, despite what she'd already discovered.

"Apart from the new paint job," Joel commented.

Ben'or joined them at Brock's console. He squinted and looked at the holoscreen that Brock had pulled up. "My, my, my…" he muttered under his breath. "That structure looks incredibly complex. I wonder how the data is organized."

Brock shook his head. "I have no clue. It looks way more sophisticated than anything we'd ever had on the Federation ships."

Joel appeared at Brock's other elbow. "So what are you saying? That it's not a Federation ship?"

"Well, it looks like one," he agreed. "It *feels* like one. But its systems are just a shit-ton more advanced than anything I've ever seen. Even since joining the Federation."

Molly frowned. "So what we're saying is that we've been brought back to life and our ship has been rebuilt, but it's been rebuilt better than it was before?"

"Exactly," Brock confirmed. "Maybe about five generations better than it was before."

The group looked at each other in astonishment.

"How does that even work?" Molly mumbled, her eyes fixed on the holoscreen of controls Brock was already trying to fathom.

"Yeah," Sean interjected, "no way can we tell the General that. Apart from anything, he'd take it off us and probably put us all in a hole to make sure no one else gets an inkling of this technology."

"So…" Molly said slowly, "when we tell the General that we're alive, we just have to not mention that the ship has been upgraded?"

"Right," Sean agreed.

"This is going to be a complicated story to spin," she confessed. "I mean how do we explain that our ship was blown to smithereens and then rebuilt in just eight weeks. By aliens, no less!"

Joel looked at her. "Can't you just come up with some timey whimey physicsy shit to explain it?"

"I'll have to think about that," she responded dryly.

"There's something else," Brock added. "I can't find Emma."

Molly leaned forward and flicked one of the main console screens open. "She's not on one of the hard drives needing to be rebooted?"

Brock shook his head. "Negative. I can't find anything other than a small patch that allows us to do voice interface."

"Shit."

"I'm afraid to say Brock is right," Oz announced over the intercom.

"Oz!" Pieter called out spontaneously, thrilled to hear his old friend.

"Greetings, Pieter, and all," Oz responded. "I'm sorry I haven't got better news. It seems that when we were all cloned, they didn't pick up Emma as a conscious entity. From the looks of the programming, it's possible that they just thought of her as a computer program, which they have rewritten most efficiently."

"Well technically," Sean interjected, "she was entity intelligence, and not fully *artificial* intelligence."

Pieter's eyes started welling with tears. "I think that was an academic distinction," he retorted. "She was one of us. I'm going to miss her." His hand fell onto the nearest console, and he caressed it gently with his fingers.

"It's an interesting point," Oz continued. "I had a lot of time while you were being rebuilt in the physical, and somehow I was afforded consciousness. I tried querying them—the ARs, that is—as to why I was awake and alert, and yet Molly's body wasn't. I think it had something to do with part of my processing being housed on the hardware... But from what I could tell, I was a puzzle even to these godlike ARs that gave you new bodies."

"Well," Sean said, ambling back over to the other side of the cockpit where Karina was sitting. "I for one am very grateful that they managed to put us back together the way that they did. Very grateful."

"Here, here," Jack added into the mix, smiling for the first time since the new realization had hit her.

"Okay," Molly said, pulling the conversation back to the practicalities. "At some point we have to tell the General that we're alive." She looked pointedly at Sean. "But we're not to mention the ship."

Sean and Joel both nodded in agreement.

"I suppose the General will dictate whether we get to tell anyone else that we're alive. And probably how we go about that." She looked over at Ben'or. "I'm sorry, Ben'or. I'm sure you'll be able to see Arlene soon, but we just have to do this carefully."

"It's okay," he said congenially. "I completely understand. Heck, we all have a lot to process. Consider this... The rest of the world thinks we're dead. In all probabilities, our affairs have been wrapped up and the world has moved on. We don't have jobs to go back to. We don't owe the world anything anymore. And yet we have a new lease on life, as it were. We can do anything we choose. We have a fresh slate, and the rest of our lives ahead of us. I think we need to take some time to consider carefully what we'd really like to do with this gift."

Molly pressed her lips together. "And something tells me that a conversation with the Federation is going to put some severe security restrictions on that. So how about we slow down and consider all our possibilities."

She glanced over at Joel to gauge his reaction. "So perhaps talking to the General is a conversation we should have sooner rather than later?"

"I agree," Joel confirmed.

Sean nodded too. Molly glanced at Jack, who also nodded, and then lowered her eyes to the floor.

"Okay," Molly confirmed. "I'll talk to Lance. Oz, set me up in the lounge, would you?"

She shook her head. "Man, this is gonna be a trippy conversation…"

Aboard *The Empress*, Outer Sark System

The holocall connected, revealing a rather pale-looking Lance Reynolds.

"Surprise!" Molly called quietly and anxiously through the connection.

"H-How?" he stuttered. Molly watched as Lance scrambled to try and comprehend the holo-image of the ghost before him.

Molly shrugged with one shoulder. "It's a long story, boss. But basically, the alien race that we were protecting… They were able to bring us back."

"Back from the dead?"

"It would appear so." She raised one eyebrow comically.

"But how?"

Molly shrugged again. "We're still unclear of the details, but I think it's safe to say that they have technology that far exceeds ours. Our best guess at the moment is that they were somehow able to fold the space-time continuum so that they could pluck our entire ship and crew from the explosion before it even happened."

"But we have eye witness reports saying they saw you explode."

Molly shook her head casually. "They must have seen an explosion. Probably one of the missiles as it hit our shields. Or as it hit an event horizon as the fabric of reality was folded."

You do realize that you're lying to your commanding officer?

No. I'm doing what scientists have a long, exalted history of doing: I'm simplifying the empirical evidence and presenting a model that can be grasped and communicated more efficiently than the nuanced details.

To serve your own ends...

True, but we can continue the ethics discussion later. In fact, if I ever get back to my office on Estaria, I'm sure one of my students has written about this precise scenario.

Now you're just bullshitting me.

And given the probability of us going back to Estaria, you'll never know. Besides, one of us here is trying to have a conversation that can potentially save all our arses.

Touche.

Molly noticed Lance rubbing his eyes and then his whole face. He had muted the call and seemed to be having a conversation, perhaps with ADAM.

She waited, watching him going through the motions, processing what must have been complex emotions. She wondered if he was telling anyone else... Like her mom, for instance.

For a moment she felt overcome by an incredible sadness. A loss, at a relationship that didn't work, but that she mourned nonetheless.

He unmuted his side of the call. "Well, Molly, I think it goes without saying that I'm thrilled that you're all okay. You must forgive me, this is a lot to take in."

"Yes, sir. I know that feeling well."

"Erm, well you should also know that there are considerations that need to be taken into account. For instance, everyone on Estaria knows that you're dead. Or rather, *thinks* that you're dead. Again."

He tilted his head thoughtfully. "On the plus side, you were pardoned from your fugitive status in your absence."

Molly smirked. "Thank goodness for small mercies. I should die more often," she joked.

The General peered at her sternly. "This isn't a joking matter,

Ms. Bates. There are many security concerns that we have. Not least that you have been under alien control for nearly two months. We'll have to vet you, and there will be a quarantine period, and then we need to decide what to do with you."

Molly felt palpitations in her chest. "What do you mean 'what to do with us'?"

"Well, that remains to be seen," Lance offered, the sternness melting away and giving her a modicum of reassurance, despite his words. "While we figure this out, we should start with the debriefing of each crew member on board. As soon as we get that done, we can decide how to bring you in."

Molly nodded. "Well okay then. Let me talk to the crew and send the first person in."

"Good. Thank you," he responded, a little more officious than his normal manner, now.

Molly got up to leave the lounge.

"And Molly," he called from the holoscreen, "it really is good to have you back. Even though it's an administrative and security nightmare."

Molly smiled before heading out. "Thanks, boss. That means a lot…"

Molly arrived back in the cockpit. All the laughing and chatter stopped immediately as every face turned to look at her.

"Okay, folks, there's good news and bad."

A groan went up from the crew.

"The good news is that it doesn't sound like he's about to put us in a lab for the rest of our lives. The bad news is that, as predicted, we do present a security risk. The General and ADAM will run their protocols in order to determine how and when we can integrate back into the world. Part of this means that we will all have to be interviewed."

She turned her attention to their mechanic-extraordinaire. "I suggest we start with Brock… put him in a good mood, as it were." She smiled, winking at Brock.

Brock nodded his head once in dutiful acknowledgment, and then started to get up. The others started to move too.

"One more thing," she interrupted them. "You're probably going to want to disregard any theories I've been bandying about… And any retelling of what I've told you I've seen. As far as you know—and this is the truth—we were about to be blown up, and then we woke up on the floor of this cockpit. The same cockpit that we were in before the explosion."

She glanced at each of them in turn as if trying to make her point with her eyes only, so as not to be telling them to lie.

Pieter started to say something, and then stopped himself, slowly lowering his hand back to a resting position.

"And yes," Molly continued, "that means not mentioning anything to do with the ship. Emma is offline and may well have been deleted somehow. That's it. Got it?"

There were mutters and mumbles and everyone agreed to the story that was going to buy them their freedom. And maybe their ship. Even though technically it was never their ship in the first place.

"Okay, Brock, you're up," she concluded.

The team started chattering amongst themselves as Brock shuffled out of his console chair and headed out of the cockpit. Sean slapped him on the back as he walked past him.

"Okay," Molly sighed, sitting down next to Crash, in Brock's seat. "What've we found?"

Crash flicked some switches and then brought up a couple of holoscreens to show Molly. "Well first off," he explained in his cooler-than-cool monotone voice, "no one seems to be answering calls to Gaitune."

"We're not meant to be calling *anyone*!" Molly exclaimed in horror. "Remember?"

Crash nodded. "Right, but since we knew that there weren't two fleets at each other's throats right outside, we figured it would be worth taking a risk. Besides, no matter what the General decides, we know we can trust Paige and Maya, no matter what."

Molly's anxiety deflated as she exhaled. "Okay. You may have a point," she conceded. "But no more going off-book. We've got to be super careful."

Crash nodded once more. "Then there's this," he said, sliding a holoscreen over to her. "Oz managed to find it on the Gaitune servers without being detected."

Molly's eyes flicked from side to side across the screen.

"As you can see," Crash continued, "we've been declared dead. They've had memorials for us and everything. Even the Senate. Although there weren't big celebrations about our victory. And no one knows our names."

He sounded almost disappointed.

"That's probably a good thing," Molly mumbled as she scanned the rest the document. "Okay, no more antics. We gotta fly below the radar on this… But let me know if you find anything else."

Crash agreed, and Molly got up and headed outside to the corridor again.

Molly leaned against the steely cold wall of the corridor. She closed her eyes for a moment and tipped her head back against it, stretching her neck. She had woken up so blissfully unaware of anything, other than she was alive again. And now the familiar tension had started creeping back into her neck and shoulders, giving her a headache over her crown.

The door to the cockpit opened and boots clomped into her

quiet corridor. She opened one eye and turned her head to see Joel standing there.

"Hey," she whispered, closing her eye again.

Joel didn't answer. Instead she just heard the steps against the grating of the ship's flooring. She opened one eye again to see him pacing and wringing his hands.

"You okay?"

"Erm, yes. I think so."

She started to close her eyes again.

"Only…"

She opened both eyes again, giving him her attention. "Yes?"

"Well, it's, like Ben'or was saying."

Molly frowned, listening.

"He said that, you know, we were done with our old lives. With the duties, the jobs. Probably all the missions too… And he was talking about how, you know, we get a do-over. We get to have something that we couldn't have before. And I was thinking…"

He started moving towards her. Molly straightened up against the wall, suddenly even more anxious than she had been a few minutes ago. Her heart started palpitating in her chest again.

Joel moved closer into her, and before she knew what was happening he was planting a kiss on her lips.

Several moments passed, and Molly felt herself succumbing to the new possibilities. When he eventually pulled away, her mind scrambled to make light of the situation.

"Well, I think you should take Ben'or's sage advice more often." She smiled.

"I think I will," he agreed, kissing her again.

CHAPTER TWENTY-ONE

Aboard *The Empress*, Outer Sark System

Brock appeared back in the cockpit.

"How did it go?" Crash asked as he slumped down next to him.

Brock looked like he was still processing the interview. "It sounds like we have options now," he reported, a little dazed.

"Options like what?" Sean interjected, coming over to stand by the console chairs. Karina wandered over too.

Brock glanced over at Pieter. "You're up next," he told him. "Just head straight on in."

Pieter exhaled and jumped up from his console chair. "Here goes nothing," he announced, his nerves showing in his expression.

As he ambled out of the cockpit, Sean refocused Brock's attention on his question. "So, come on. What kind of options?" he pressed.

Brock's eyes lit up wide. "Like anything. Since we don't exist anymore, we can do whatever our hearts desire. Like intergalactic spies, for instance!"

Sean's face fell. Karina placed a hand on his shoulder. "Well, we've been there and done that," she told Brock, as if speaking for Sean too.

Brock narrowed his eyes at them. "We never will know quite what you two have been up to over the years, will we?"

The pair of them shook their heads in tandem.

"Well think of it this way," Sean explained. "I died, and I took my secrets with me… So that should give you an idea of how likely I am to tell anyone."

Brock snorted and noticed Crash laughing silently to himself. "Well, we can also retire. The General mentioned a great place called Davos where no one will find us."

Karina pulled Sean aside. "Hey look, is there somewhere we can go to talk?"

Sean's expression changed from one of smugness at his Brock-encounter, to one of concern. "Yeah sure, baby."

Then another thought crossed his mind and turned his expression into the one of his dirty grins.

She patted playfully at his arm. "I'm serious," she told him.

"So am I," he retorted as he led her out of the cockpit and through the little door in the corridor that led to the downstairs meeting rooms and med bay.

Just as they reached the main corridor at the bottom of the steps, Oz's voice came over his implant. "Sean, the General would like to speak to you next, please. Could you make your way up to the lounge?"

Sean's face flashed with faint annoyance. "Sure," he sighed. "Sorry, babe. Duty calls," he told her, kissing her forehead. "Can we do this as soon as I get out? Maybe meet you in the cargo hold… Just this corridor and out of that door, then you'll recognize where you are. There's a mocha machine in the little room at the end. It's not as good as the one in the lounge, but it does the job."

Karina nodded dutifully. "Sure," she replied, letting go of his hand and allowing him to scoot back up the stairs they had just come down.

Cargo Hold, Aboard *The Empress*, Outer Sark System

Sean arrived in the cargo hold where he had arranged to meet Karina again. The new old *Little Empress* loomed behind her as she hung around, mocha cup in hand.

"So?" Karina asked as he approached. "What options did he give you?"

"Multiple," he said, vaguely.

"What does that even mean?" she asked.

"Carte blanche. I can rejoin the Federation at my former rank, or I can continue to hang with these knuckleheads. He didn't seem to mind either way. The only restriction is that none of us can go back to Estaria."

Karina's brow furrowed. "And what do you think you want to do?"

Sean shrugged. "I have no idea. Not exactly had a long time to think about this."

"No," she agreed, her eyes focusing on the distance.

Sean read the signs and put his hands on her arms. "What do you think?" he asked quietly.

She smiled at him. "I'm glad you asked."

He smirked at her sense of humor even as they tackled the delicate subject.

"We were talking about retiring from the ops life since… well, we were locked in my father's basement, if you remember."

Sean nodded slowly, as the reality of his life changing dawned on him. "You mean…?"

"Start a family."

Sean swallowed hard. "Wow, that's… a lot to take on," he said eventually.

Karina raised her eyebrows almost sarcastically. "Yeah, compared to everything we've been through today…"

Sean was looking dazed. "What about the mission?" he asked.

"We're done. You heard the General—we can do what we want. Stay or go."

"But, the military is all I know…"

"Time to try something new, eh?"

Sean looked down at the floor, scuffing it with the boot of his toe, thinking. "Well, yeah. Maybe."

He took a long deep breath. "How about we start with a puppy?"

Cockpit, Aboard *The Empress*, Outer Sark System

Pieter and Jack sat waiting in the cockpit. Brock had gone to see if he could track down the rumors of a second mocha machine, and Karina and Sean hadn't been seen for quite some time now.

"Who's in there now?" Pieter asked.

"Crash, I think," Jack deduced.

"Brock was looking more nervous once he'd talked to the General," he observed.

"Yeah, I noticed that," Jack agreed. "It's intense though. Nothing like dying to help you reevaluate your life and purpose. It's a lot to figure out."

"I'd say," Pieter concurred.

There were several moments of silence between the pair.

Eventually Pieter spoke. "What went through your mind as the ship exploded?"

Jack took a deep breath, thinking about her answer. "That I wish I'd spent less time worrying about the next mission, and more time enjoying life."

Pieter nodded, his eyes now glazed over as if deep in thought.

"I wished I'd spent more time learning about code. And gardening."

"Gardening?"

"Yeah, it's something that has always appealed to me. And I'm fascinated by how things just grow on their own if you give them the right conditions. I always thought that once I was older and had more time I'd create some kind of automated garden. You know, where you have a program that adjusts the parameters of what a crop needs."

Jack smiled over at him. "Maybe this is your second chance then?"

He bobbed his head gently, tending the idea in his mind. "I think maybe it is. Plus it has massive implications for growing food in hostile environments."

Corridor Outside the Cockpit, Aboard *The Empress*, Outer Sark System

Crash came striding out of the lounge. "Your turn again," he told Molly.

Molly and Joel had been sitting on the floor talking. It reminded Molly of all of those times when they were waiting to go out on exercise. Except back in her training days Joel was the boss and would never be caught sitting next to one of his trainees, chewing the fat.

Molly scrambled to her feet. "Thanks, Crash," she said, touching his arm as he went by.

"Good luck in there," he chimed back.

Molly headed back into the lounge, idly wondering if her new body could take mocha. She sat down in front of the holoscreen that was set up.

"Hi, boss," she announced her arrival to him, settling down into one of the new chairs.

"Ms. Bates, we've had a chance to run some scenarios," he told her.

Molly watched him expectantly, waiting for the verdict.

"It seems that we can allow you some contact... *Limited* contact... With the outside world. But we can't have anything that will tell the world that you're alive. So that means only the most trusted friends and family."

Molly nodded as she listened to his words, quietly breathing a sigh of relief. She couldn't bear the thought of Ben'or never being able to see Arlene again.

"But it has to be discreet," Lance insisted. "No comms that can be intercepted. You're going to have to rely on the spy craft to bring people in."

"No problem, sir. We can handle it," she told him confidently.

He nodded once. "You can all stay at Gaitune, indefinitely. Or at least until you decide what you want to do. At this point, the world is your oyster. I'll have ADAM send over some tailored options for each of you, and from there you can make your own decisions."

Molly took a moment to understand that there were no downsides to the situation. "Sir, thank you so much. I know we'll all be thrilled to be able to contact the rest of the team. And to return to Gaitune."

"Well, you did prevent all-out war within the Federation, so I suppose you've earned it," he responded, shifting awkwardly in his chair.

Molly smiled. "You're too kind, sir," she told him as she started to get up.

"Oh, just one more thing, Molly. Will you have that delinquent of a nephew contact me next time he's up at Gaitune? I have some things to discuss with him."

"Absolutely, sir. Thank you again."

Lance nodded to her and then closed off the connection.

She started to get up again and then noticed Joel peering in through the window of the door. She waved him in.

"So it looks like we can contact our nearest and dearest, and Gaitune is still ours!"

Joel grinned. "Excellent negotiating skills, Ms. Bates!"

She shrugged. "There was no negotiation. Basically he just said 'here you go,' and 'thank you for your service.'"

"Nice. Well at least that saves me from having to figure out how to afford an apartment on Estaria without a Federation income."

The pair chuckled. "Hey, I was thinking," Molly said through the giggles, "when we get back to Gaitune… maybe we should go for a beer?"

Joel suddenly made a serious face. "I don't know. You know what happened last time I agreed to that?"

Molly waited for the punchline.

"I ended up dying!"

Molly smiled. "Was it worth it?"

"Definitely." He threw his arm around her shoulder and they walked out of the lounge and back to the cockpit to tell the others what the immediate plan was.

EPILOGUE

Bates Residence, Spire, Estaria

Carol Bates lounged on the sofa, exhausted. "Leave those, Philip. I'll get them later."

Philip continued to tidy the plates away. "Don't worry. I've got this," he told her. "Anything I can do to help."

There was a pause.

"I still think you ought to take some time off. To… process."

Carol didn't respond. She was reading a message on her holo.

Philip appeared in the living room, a tea towel over his shoulder. "You know, it's bad enough you're on that thing when you're working. Can't you take the night off, at least?"

"I… er…"

Just then Philip felt his holo buzz. He glanced down at it to read the message.

There was another few seconds of silence in the room.

"Did you just get one of these?" he asked, still not taking his eyes from the message.

Carol slowly lifted her gaze to him and nodded.

"We've got to get going!" he announced, suddenly animated.

Carol shuffled off the sofa and scrambled to put her shoes

back on. "Let's go!" she agreed, storming towards the door, without considering a jacket or a bag.

Philip grabbed his keys, and a sweater, and followed her out.

Student Residences, Skóli Uppstigs Academy, Spire, Estaria

Paige emerged from the bathroom still wearing a towel. She was vaguely aware of her holo buzzing on the dresser on the other side of the room. It wasn't until Maya called her attention to it that she headed over to pick it up.

Maya suddenly sat up on her bed. "Oh my ancestors," she gasped.

Paige read her holo too. "No way!"

The pair looked at each other.

"You think that maybe...?" Paige didn't dare finish her sentence.

Maya was up like a flash, dithering to repack her case. "I think... yeah," she exclaimed, busying herself.

"Shit!" Paige squealed. "Clothes. I need clothes!"

The dorm room became a flurry of activity as the two hurriedly prepared to leave. They had less than half an hour before they needed to be somewhere else. Urgently.

Giles's Office, Skóli Uppstigs Academy, Spire, Estaria

Giles felt his holo buzz. He ignored it. It buzzed again.

Slowly he peeled his face off the desk in front of him. His head was pounding with the force of a thousand tiny hammers, on account of the Yollin whiskey he'd been knocking back since four o'clock that afternoon.

Disheveled, he rubbed his face, then his eyes, and then he peered at the holo.

It took a second for him to register what the message was telling him. He adjusted his glasses and read it again. Then he sat up, thought about whether it meant what he hoped it meant, or whether he was just being delusional.

He glanced down at his arm and pinched himself.

Nope, definitely awake, he confirmed.

Then it hit him. He needed to get going. Scrambling to his feet and trying to gather his gear at the same time, he started to sober up. Within a few minutes he was leaving the office in a flash, with the excitement of a two-year-old being taken to a candy store.

A moment later, he stormed purposefully back in to the office. He pulled up the last holoscreen he'd been using on his console and closed down the application form that he'd been filling out, without saving it.

"Not going to need that anymore," he decided out loud.

And then he was out of the door like a flash.

Bailey Residence, Spire, Estaria

Arlene was in the kitchen making a snack. Since the new normal had established itself, she didn't bother to make proper meals any more. She and Anne instead tended to just eat snacks when they were hungry.

If she was honest, she wasn't even hungry. But it was something to do. Something to occupy her and fill the void of despair that hadn't left her.

Just then her holo vibrated.

She frowned. She set all the settings to "do not disturb" weeks ago.

She glanced down at it, read the message, and then carried on making her sandwich.

A moment later she stopped, opened the holo screen again, and re-read the message.

"Anne!" she called through to the other room. "Anne! I think we need to pack a bag. We need to go. Now."

Anne appeared at the kitchen counter. "Why? What's going on? Has someone found me?" Her face was taught with anxiety.

Arlene had tears streaming down her face. "No, sweetheart. No one's found you. We're safe. I just think it's time for us to take a trip back to Gaitune."

Anne stood frozen for a second. And then suddenly she sprang into action, shouting for Neechie, while trying to pack up a bag at the same time.

The holo message they each received read:
"Party on Gaitune. Guess who's back.
Your pod leaves from [coordinates] at 21:00"

Hangar Deck, Base, Gaitune-67

Molly eased back in her chair as *The Empress* took the final few seconds to land in the hangar deck. Oz had had to perform a series of bizarre security bypasses in order to get the hangar doors open, but finally they were able to land.

How's our other project going? she asked him.

I'm tracking four inbound pods. ETA six minutes.

Molly smiled to herself. *This is going to be some party...*

AUTHOR NOTES - ELL LEIGH CLARKE
JUNE 28, 2018

Thank yous

Massive thanks as always goes out to MA, for not cancelling my show. (EDIT MA: Why would I cancel this awesomeness??)

Yep, we've survived a year.

And twelve Molly books!

WOOT!

While there are no immediate plans to continue the series now that we've wrapped up Molly 12, there is nothing to say that we won't start a new Molly series down the line. For now, we're working on other concepts. More on those below.

Huge thank yous also go to Steve "Zen Master" Campbell and the JIT team who work tirelessly to make sure that all slips are caught and corrected, the files are uploaded on time.

Thank you so much folks. I truly appreciate all your efforts. :)

Reviewers

Massive thanks also goes out to our hoard of Amazon reviewers. It's because of you that we get to do this full time. Without your five-star reviews and thoughtful words on Amazon we simply wouldn't have enough folks reading these space shenanigans to be able to write full time.

You are the reason these stories exist and you have no idea how frikkin' grateful I am to you.

Truly, thank you.

Readers and FB page supporters

Last, and certainly by no means least, I'd like to thank you for reading this book… and all the others. Your enthusiasm for the world, and the characters, is heart-warming. Your words of encouragement, and demands for the next episode, are the things that often stay in my mind as I flick from checking the facebook page to the scrivener file when I start each writing session.

It used to be that caffeine was my drug of choice – but it looks like that's off the menu for some time to come.

So I've switched to you! ;)

Thank you for being here, for reading, for reviewing, and for always brightening my day with your words of support on the fb page. You rock my world, and without you, there really would be no reason to write these stories.

(Also – thank you for the sacrificial chickens and Pepsi vats when the manuscripts are released to the 'Zon.)

Thank you.

E x

Ok, so you've asked about a few things on the fb page, and I figured I'd answer them here to wrap up this series. (There will be more shenanigans in the author notes of the series that we move on to for sure! This isn't the end!).

I must also let you know that I'm on a word count limit now, though.

Whaaa?! I hear you cry.

I know. I'm shocked too.

MA let me know this afternoon that the Zon only allows up

to 10% of the text in the back matter. I'm sure I've gone over this on occasion, but it's just reinforced my thoughts about moving some of this stuff over to the Patreon posts, where I can rant to my heart's content, in a more private setting too.

(I don't think the fb page is really geared to long posts and interruption scrolling).

Anyway – more on that soon too.

Dental Update, Keto and Confessions of a Lapsed Vegetarian
I haven't been back to the dentist for a few months. Thanks for those who were asking though! I still have some more crowns to do, but I was so hammered from the dental drugs and pain over the last several months that I'm putting it off until I've recovered.

Since discovering that I've been suffering with adrenal fatigue I figured the last thing my adrenals need is being pumped full of dental drugs (which weren't even numbing me properly!), with all their epinephrine loaded in.

ESPECIALLY not when I'm under order to refrain from caffeine even!

Turns out that even a cup of tea is stopping me sleeping until the next morning when normal people are getting up. Go figure. I never used to be this sensitive to it.

The dental practice did call me the other day though. It seems they're having an anniversary party for the practice. Great way to get people back into the practice and book their next appointment, eh?

Anyway, in the last few weeks, the tooth that they weren't able to get numb has been playing up a bit. Thing is it allegedly has no nerve in the root anymore, so apparently it shouldn't be hurting.

Well... what can you say to that?

(I'm sooo tempted to email my xrays to Dr. Mojito and ask his opinion.)

Re the Keto...

I'm back on the wagon, but gently.

Keto kinda requires a 50g carb limit per day. I'm averaging about 70g, and trying not to overdo it because apparently full on hard core keto will stress the adrenals too.

I'm also 'carbing up' in the evenings in an attempt to help me sleep before 4am. It's not really working, but 4 am sleeptime is better than 7am which has been the case on occasion.

I could bore you with more detail, but I'm conscious of my word limit, so onto the confession.

The confession...

Just before I left LA one of the doctors told me about some of the problems with my vegetarian diet.

Specifically the lack of cholesterol.

Apparently we need it for our brains to function properly. She recommended starting to have lamb once a week and go from there. I must say a bunch of the symptoms have evaporated since doing this, so now I'm not a full-on vegetarian anymore.

I'm still not going to ever order a pizza with pepperoni on it (EDIT MA: SO CLOSE!), but I'm not entirely meat-free anymore.

And yes, as someone pointed out on a fb thread, doing keto as a vegetarian is HARD. You can basically eat avocados. And whipping cream. And butter. (And don't get me started on the phytonutrients it's so easy to miss out on.)

So... I've come to a new balance of moderation: semi-keto, semi-veggie, and when I get the ok from the Chinese medical doc, semi-caffeinated. We're looking at about two or three months for the latter unfortunately.

In the meantime, there's always dandelion 'coffee'.

Sigh.

Anyway, I hope this had provided some closure on all those open loops(!) and I'd also like to take this opportunity to say a HUGE thank you for all of your support through the health dramas. I've thoroughly appreciated your caring, your suggestions and recommendations... and it's also been fun to laugh with you about the craziness that I've come through. Truly... thank you! <3

Author Shenanigans

So we were just wrapping up a random author call between myself and Yoda.

I had suggested MA do some marketing shit, of some sort. (I don't even remember what it was now....)

Michael: I'll try

Ellie: Do or do not do...

MA: I'll try. I promise.

Ellie *(rolls eyes, realizing he clearly isn't getting the reference. Tries again.)*

Ellie: *Do or do not do.* There is no try.

MA: Ooooohhhh. *(Blushes.)*

Someone had clearly forgotten his nickname. Do me a favour and remind him, eh? Like in the reviews and other embarrassing places... ;P

(EDIT MA: I REMEMBER! No need to remind me folks!)

Thou Shalt Not...

Ok, so I can tell you this little anecdote now, since it won't be a spoiler to the book you've just finished reading.

A few weeks ago while I was working on the plot for Molly 11, I talked to MA about it.

He was finding it difficult to understand what I was planning to do. (Or he just wasn't listening!)

Anyway, somewhere we got our wires crossed and he thought that I was going to construct some cliffhanger for Molly 11.

Like kill her off in the second to last book.

Right at the end.

MA: THEY'LL KILL YOU!

Ellie: Noooo, lemme explain again. It's not a cliff hanger, I promise!

(*MA listens patiently again while I ramble through my beats.*)

MA: have you not seen my video? Thou shalt not end on a cliff hanger!

Ellie: It's ok - it's not. I promise! Yes, I saw it... Let me explain.

(*Ellie explains *again* what she was actually planning to do._*)

MA: Oh. Right. Ok. Yeah... that's not a cliff hanger.

Ellie: Yeah. (Blink, blink)

Third time lucky...

(EDIT MA: It isn't my ears... but your explanation padawan...)

Coffeeshops and Writing Dates

A few weeks ago (you may have seen the pictures on fb), Amy, Alyssa (two of my Austin writing buddies) and I were hanging out together in a local café. OMG it's so good to have like-minded people around... and even though we're not as productive in terms of word count, it's like therapy and nourishment just to hang and chinwag.

We also get *some* work done too.

Well, anyway, there we are working and chatting, and the barista started coming over and talking to us every now and again. The girls explained that we're writers, and talked about the stuff they're working on, and he was fascinated.

Anyway, throughout the afternoon he'd keep coming over, or end up doing his tasks, like putting labels on cups, using the area behind the bar where we were installed.

Amy and Alyssa were deep in conversation and he looks up. Amy catches his eye, and stops talking as if waiting for him to interrupt.

Barista: Oh, carry on. I'm just listening. It's fascinating. Keep going.

(Amy and Alyssa giggle and go back to their conversation...)

Amy: what were we talking about?

Alyssa: library books.

Amy: oh yeah.

Ellie, *collapses in a heap of giggles at the hard core, riveting conversation they had enraptured him with.*

Next time at the Coffeeshop

Amy and I returned to the coffeeshop the following week after we'd met out fascinated barista.

Turns out he's English. I thought he was a Kiwi.

(I'm bad with recognizing English accents when I'm out of the country. I remember a time I was living in Budapest. I'd been there for about a month and hadn't spoken to any English folks for a while. I ended up doing a presentation at Ericsson or some such company and one of the guys came up to me in the canteen afterwards. I mistook him for English. He was most insulted. He was Australian. Oops.)

Anyway, our guy in the coffee shop is called Michael Sven Something-or-other. I've taken to calling him Sven… because he looks more Scandinavian. And Michael is just a confusing name when you know so many of them.

So there we were chatting to Sven, and working, and he asked more about our authoring. I told him I'd probably end up putting him into a book at some point. It's just what happens when you're churning out stories and need names and characters.

He was kinda chuffed.

Anyway, he went on to tell us about someone else who made him famous, through Craigslist. When he said Craigslist, firstly I realized he really was English. We pronounce it differently. And then secondly, I had no idea if he was talking about that online thingy like GumTree.)

Amy explained to me afterwards that it was, and he was talking about a "missed connections" section. Apparently some woman he had served coffee to had posted about him as a missed connection and a number of people had come in and mentioned it to him, saying: "Oh you must be the guy she talked about!"

How cool is that?

Well, you'll probably want to know if this story has a happy ending. And it does. Though not for the Craigslist poster. He explained he was married. End of story.

"mornings"

Amy and I were wandering back to my place to raid my wine stocks. Well, after a long afternoon writing, you need something to take the edge off.

We walked past my barber. You may have seen on fb I have a section of my long hair shaved, so I need to have it redone every few weeks.

Anyway, I just wanted to pop in while we were passing and see if they could fit me in for an "edge out" the next day. Amy dutifully followed me in. (As females with long hair we got a lot of stares. I'm used to it, but I think it was a first for Amz.)

Anyway, the sweet guy on the reception desk asked what time I could come in. Amy looked on in bemusement.

Ellie: Morning? But not too early..

Receptionist: Ten?

Ellie: Ughhh. That's a bit too early. What about after noon?

Receptionist: Noon? Or two? Or one?

Ellie, (checking calendar): Acupuncture at 2pm. What about 1?

Amy (laughs her ass off): I love it! (Does her Ellie voice, complete with English accent.) 'Have you got anything in the "morning"'.

She adds rabbit ears around the word morning, much to the amusement of everyone eavesdropping.

I shouldn't have told her about the conversation I'd had with the acupuncturist when we were discussing when I should take my tinctures. I had to confess that since I often didn't get up until noon or one, the "morning" dose technically wasn't happening in the morning.

Now he does rabbit ears around the word "morning" every time it comes up.

What's next?
Tabitha and Nicky: Ranger Deuces

I know this is long-awaited and pretty converted amongst the original Bethany-Anne fans. I'm feeling very fortunate that MA wants me on this project. It's going to be fun – half the word count to get out! Woot!

No, seriously, it's a pair of super fun characters, much beloved by the TKG family… so it's an honor to get to write in this series. We've started working on it in earnest now.

And things are coming along. (I'm about 10k words into my side. No idea where Yoda has got to. He tends to leave things till the last minutes! ;P)

MA is working on the Tabitha's side.

I'm on Nickie. And the pair are separated by time. About 150 years I think. It's going to take all our story-telling genius to get the more in-depth themes to synch up, and have story devices to weave the two adventures together each episode. I'm enjoying the challenge already.

Oh, but fuck… we realized the other day that I'd messed up spelling Nickie with a 'y' instead of 'ie' in the whole Molly book. (*facepalm*). I believe Zen Steve is going to fix that on the next update. But I was sooooo sure I had it right.

I checked it.

Would you believe me if I told you I think I may have had an unedited, non-final draft of the short story originally?

Anyway…

Speaking of Molly, we're also writing it so that book 1 and 2 intersect with Molly 10: Tabitha 01 finishes where Molly 10 picks up from ~~Nicky's~~, sorry Nickie's pov.

You don't need to have read Molly for Tabitha to make sense, but it's a bit of an Easter egg for those who have.

Tabitha Book 2 will start again when Nicky comes back from lifting all the Leathe weapons after working with Molly.

#insideinformation :-)

Oh yes, and for those who don't speak the King's English, you'll want to look up what the word "bollock" means in English, because MA had the genius idea of naming one of the ships in the story: Boh'Locks 881

The Missing Giles Stories

You may have noticed that in Molly 11, Molly and co refer to an adventure that happened in the Giles series.

Good catch if you have!

No, you haven't missed a Giles installment. It's just I haven't got around to writing it yet. But I will. As soon as I can. You can expect that in the end we'll have another two or three books in the Giles series, which will coincide with everything that's happened on the Molly side of the story.

Interstellar Spy for Hire

Ok so this is in a completely new universe, and MA is going to tell you more about it because I'm already up to my word limit.

The Bentley Chronicles

This one is all me. On my own. No MA. Like a little chick, cast into the storm on its own. (EDIT MA: Seriously? All of the talks we have had is tossed into the storm? Wow…)

After a few false starts this project is underway again. The difficulty with releasing it though is that I'm going to have to have three almost done before we launch, in order to trigger the Zon algorithms to make it a successful launch.

I know things have been quiet in the slack channel for our team of enthusiastic beta readers but we should see something coming your way in the next few months. We'll keep you posted over there.

And as usual, if you want to stay up to date with future series and new releases please feel free to get onto Oz's radar with your email address:

www.EllLeighClarke.com

And as always you can connect with me directly on my facebook page: www.facebook.com/ellleighclarke

It's been an absolute blast, and I truly feel honored to have had you on this journey with Molly through all these adventures. Thank you, thank you, thank you for reading, and for all of your support.

I couldn't have done it without you.

And if you've enjoyed this series, I really hope that you'll give the new ones a try as we release them.

This isn't goodbye. It's… "see you on the next book!"

Ellie x

AUTHOR NOTES - MICHAEL ANDERLE
WRITTEN JUNE 28, 2018

WOOHOO! We are THERE baby! (Or is it here? I guess 'here' is the right term.) Thank you for reading through twelve amazing stories of Molly and her crew.

Through this whole series, we focused on the question of ascending, and whether there are options to ascend as life goes on. Now, I don't want to go too metaphysical, but pretty much any religion has this as a concept.

Plus, lots of "I'm not saying it is Aliens...but...*Aliens!*" conspiracy theories as well.

In the middle of all these questions this series has a lot of other stuff like friendships, coming of age stories, working with those you aren't fond of and many other new thoughts Ellie wove into these books.

Like Nietzsche.

And realm walking.

Are they real, or just figments of our imagination? That is a large question that I can't answer (although I'm pretty good with saying that the cat is a figment of our imagination. I'm really hoping that realm walking is proven true because that would just be kick-ass if it were. Imagine being able to sleep at home, and find yourself on the moon?)

A long time ago, I dated a Wiccan… (you know, the religion of witches?) While I chickened out on joining them for a Samhain evening (Yeah, that would be something for a good Southern-Baptist guy to go to) the girl did talk about the equivalent of realm walking.

For the life of me, I do *NOT* remember if I ever tested her on this. (I want to say it was never proven true or false) but as I mentioned above I sure wanted it to be true. Any time I see those specials on cable television about the government testing the capabilities of far-seers I end up watching them.

Because, once again, I *want* it to be true. But my scientific mind won't operate on faith with this one. It seems like it is too easy to prove or disprove.

Technology has gotten us pretty close. We have spy satellites with optics so good, they can zoom in on a cigarette pack a Russian diplomat is smoking and tell you the brand.

(Or so I'm told.)

Sigh… So many of these items in these stories are based on truths that remind me of the X-files. For some, they ARE fact… for others, they are fiction.

I hope we at least entertained you and if you, like me, hope that some of the abilities are real they allowed you to dream a little about what it would look like to use these abilities.

ELL LEIGH CLARKE

I am going to end this series with a shout-out to my amazing collaborator, Ellie. She has done SOO much in the last twelve months, pulling this series together along with the spin-off Giles Kurns and collaborating with me on two Michael books.

I would NOT have been able to finish those two Michael books without her help.

Plus, it wouldn't have been as nasty a way to (potentially) kill

Michael without the Sciency-wizard knowledge (AKA Physics) that she possesses.

Right now, we are collaborating on a new series, with new characters in a new Universe. It's a bit 'James Bond in Space'.

If James Bond was a woman, kicked out of Spy school for having sexual relations with a spy that was in the school (no fault of her own – it was a political sham) that decided to open her own spy school and pimp her services.

Called **Jayne Austin - Interstellar Spy for Hire.**

If you are asking about the name, the answer is 'YES', we absolutely just went and did that ;-) My English collaborator is from England, and she now lives in Austin.

Ellie and I worked on the beats for the series (the second book) today. We want the books to play a little in that gray area of life, but have a Spy with a *moral* compass (kind of). The first beats are pretty hot - in my opinion - and I was totally successful with getting Jayne to have an arc where she starts to play the future version of Poker.

A future card game that remarkably plays just like our present version. With Ellie always giving me updates when she goes to the weekly games in real life, I thought it would be a lot of fun adding her knowledge into the mix in the stories.

And CHEERS (the bar, not the hand waving bit for English folk.) The bar doesn't come along early in the story, but I wanted Jayne to have a future version of Cheers where life becomes about the characters in the bar, not about the far flung exploits of an Interstellar Spy for Hire.

I spoke with Ellie on a CC today, and I told her that prepping for these notes, I noticed she had written 12 Molly books, 2 collaborations on Michael and 2 Giles Kurns books.

All in twelve months without having read any fiction since she was 12. I explained that in the future, when she is being interviewed about how she was able to accomplish this, the answer is: 'Isaac Asimov was a scientist who wrote about the future. I'm a physicist who wrote about the future.'

And she did DAMNED well doing it!

This year has been amazing, and for those who enjoyed our author notes, we have more coming in July and August, so keep your eyes peeled!

;-)

Ad Aeternitatem,

Michael Anderle

BOOKS BY ELL LEIGH CLARKE

The Ascension Myth
* With Michael Anderle *

Awakened (01)
Activated (02)
Called (03)
Sanctioned (04)
Rebirth (05)
Retribution (06)
Cloaked (07)
Bourne (08)
Committed (09)
Subversion (10)
Invasion (11)
Ascension (12)

Confessions of a Space Anthropologist
* With Michael Anderle *

Giles Kurns: Rogue Operator (1)

BOOKS BY ELL LEIGH CLARKE

<u>Giles Kurns: Rogue Instigator (2)</u>

The Second Dark Ages
with Michael Anderle
Darkest Before The Dawn (3)
Dawn Arrives (4)
Deuces Wild
with Michael Anderle
Beyond The Frontiers (1)
Rampage (2)
Labyrinth (3)
Birthright (4)

BOOKS BY MICHAEL ANDERLE

For a complete list of books by Michael Anderle, please visit:

www.lmbpn.com/ma-books/

All LMBPN Audiobooks are Available at Audible.com and iTunes. For a complete list of audiobooks visit:

www.lmbpn.com/audible

CONNECT WITH THE AUTHORS

Receive updates from Oz by registering your holo/ email address here:
ellleighclarke.com

Facebook:
http://www.facebook.com/ellleighclarke/

Michael Anderle Social

Website:
http://kurtherianbooks.com/

Email List:
http://kurtherianbooks.com/email-list/

Facebook Here:
https://www.facebook.com/TheKurtherianGambitBooks/

www.ingramcontent.com/pod-product-compliance
Lightning Source LLC
LaVergne TN
LVHW041625060526
838200LV00040B/1445